To my home, the hills, the trees, the sparkling granite.
To my family, my festival family, my fellow daydreamers.

And especially to Wendy.

Rune of Aberdeen

Andrew Youngson

Published in 2024 by Andrew Youngson

Publishing services provided by Lumphanan Press
www.lumphananpress.co.uk

© Andrew Youngson 2024

Cover image: 'Crow', Samuel Jessurun de Mesquita,
c. 1910. Rijksmusuem. Creative Commons CC0.

Pictish symbol chapter headers from: Noble, Gordon & Goldberg,
Martin & Hamilton, William. (2018). 'The development of the Pictish
Symbol system: Inscribing identity beyond the edges of Empire'.
Antiquity. 92. 1329-1348. Creative Commons CC BY 4.0

Andrew Youngson has asserted his moral right to be
identified as the author of this work.

Contents

Part One: The Pirate and the King / 8

Part Two: Jock o' Northfield Place / 32

Part Three: The Maiden Stone / 67

Part Four: The Dreaming Prophetess Fedelm / 94

A midnight dram between stories / 138

Part Five: The Bard of Kampala / 156

Part Six: Jack o' Bennachie / 191

Part Seven: The Wizard of Skene / 240

Part Eight: The Kelpie / 281

Epilogue: The Battle of Bennachie / 313

Acknowledgements / 321

A wife's ae sin wi' ae e'e
Sall fin' the kyey o' Bennachie
Hidden aneath a juniper tree

(A woman's only son, with one eye,
Shall find the key of Bennachie
Hidden beneath a juniper tree)

From 'The Tale of Jock o' Bennachie'
By Thomas the Rhymer

Part One
The Pirate and the King

V.

Duthie couldn't believe his eye.

He watched with rising confusion as the woman bent to the cobbles, inspected a small mound of dog poop, selected the largest turd between forefinger and thumb and dropped it into a white paper bag. Her gleeful expression was outlined in the streetlight.

Duthie shifted in the passenger seat, craning his neck up and down Don Street. He was still adjusting to the world in one dimension, half of everything hidden behind an eyepatch, but as far as he could tell nobody else was watching.

The cone of yellow streetlight hit an empty patch of ground.

"Where the hell–?" he muttered.

He spotted the swinging paper bag first, then the woman's cropped silver hair – the two connected by an almost invisible form, her dark clothing melding into the gloom. The woman crept cartoon-like to the front door of a terraced house, placed the bag on the front step then fished in her back pocket. Duthie squinted, only recognised his Zippo lighter when flame flickered from its top. The woman crouched and lit the bag then, in a few smooth motions, knocked twice on the door and jogged towards the car. Before Duthie could do or say anything, she had wrenched open the driver-side door and climbed in.

She chuckled and slapped his thigh.

"Morgan, what's going on?" Duthie said, laughing in disbelief. This night just couldn't get any weirder.

"Waitwaitwait, just watch!" the woman whispered, eyes glued to the smouldering bag.

The door of the terraced house opened ajar, then suddenly swung wide. A short figure emerged, struck an alarmed pose and stamped repeatedly on the smoking bag. The stench must have reached the man's nose quickly as he inspected his slipper's sole and bellowed in disgust. He leaned out into the street, soiled foot elevated. The streetlight illuminated his face. It was Professor Alasdair Seaton.

"Oh my God," Duthie lurched and slid down as far as the seat belt allowed. A niggle of pain sparked behind his eyepatch.

Morgan wheezed with delight and clapped her hands. She turned the ignition and flipped the Volvo's headlamps full beam. Peeking over the dashboard, Duthie could see the starkly-lit form of the Professor, berobed and hopping towards the car.

"Go!" Duthie shouted as the car screeched into motion and rumbled over the cobbles past the Professor.

As they rounded the corner out of sight, Morgan wound down the window and crowed:

"Long live the king!"

THE PIRATE AND THE KING

I.

A crow *skrawked* outside the dorm window at the precise moment Duthie and *Whatshisname* climaxed. Not that either heard the bird, their synchronised pleasure deafening them to any outside noises.

"Jesus," *Whatshisname* panted. "How did you manage that?"

"It's a gift," Duthie said. "I have excellent timing."

Whatshisname didn't respond, still hunched over Duthie and basking in the glow. The summer heat mingled with Duthie's own, he loved the dreamy sensation. A bead of sweat on *Whatshisname's* forehead caught his attention, he smudged it away. *Whatshisname* kissed Duthie's fingers. Duthie retracted at the intimate gesture.

"Okay, that's enough," he said, nudging *Whatshisname* to the end of the bed. "Pass that towel?"

The sun was dipping below the third-floor window, flaring its farewell between the grey buildings opposite. *Magic hour.* Somehow even these concrete halls of residence looked whimsical in it. The trees that hemmed the campus waved in admiration.

Duthie tracked a splinter of light back to the room where it landed on *Whatshisname's* chest. A few inches above lay a smirk.

"You know, I've never been with a *ginger* before," the guy said.

Duthie sighed. He'd heard the Aberdonian pronunciation – *singer*, rather than *injure* – each of his twenty-one years.

"You should be honoured," he said with a shrug. "I hear you never forget your first."

"After that, I'll never look at one of you the same way again." He made an exploding motion against his temple.

Duthie chucked the sodden towel at *Whatshisname's* face.

Skrawk! Dunk. Dunk.

The crow pecked at the window pane.

"Jesus!" Duthie said, nearly toppling over as he put on his underpants. "That gave me a *fleg*. Friend of yours?"

"Is it trying to get in?"

The crow twisted its head, left, right, left again, then seemed to fix on Duthie.

Dunk. Dunk. Dunk! It pecked. Not an order, just a request.

"Get out of here. Skraaaaa!" *Whatshisname* shouted from the bed.

The crow jerked its head, then pecked once more.

Duthie reached for the window handle. He was drawn forward by the bird's beady gaze, deaf to *Whatshisname's* calls to 'not let that thing in'. Duthie was transfixed by the strange sight.

The towel, thrown by *Whatshisname,* broke the spell with a *fump!* as it collided with the pane. The crow made a cry of indignation and flapped away in the direction of the trees. Duthie followed its ragged flight as it swooped below the canopy and into the darkness.

"Weird," he muttered. He pulled a pack of Marlboro Reds out of his jeans pocket. Inside were not cigarettes, but the makings of them – papers, filters and a pouch of tobacco, which he combined then placed the rollie on the moist underside of his lip. In another pocket he found a lighter. His trusty Zippo was small, scratched and dull, but it worked like a dream. He opened the window wide. Behind him, *Whatshisname* squealed.

"'S fine," Duthie said from the edge of his mouth, "'s flown away."

The smells of nature, humid and rich, mixed with the smoky plumes. It made Duthie's head spin. "God, it's hot," he said.

"So, how come I've never seen you before?" asked *Whatshisname*.

"Just visiting," Duthie said, putting on his shirt. He left the top three buttons undone, the better to gape and offer an occasional glimpse of nipple – in particular the pierced one that *Whatshisname* had so enjoyed nibbling only moments ago.

"Oh cool. I thought there was something different-looking about you. Where do you come from?"

"Northfield Place," Duthie said with a dry tone. This was also a question he had grown tired of hearing over the years. *'Where do you come from?'* Something in Duthie's features fascinated people. An otherness, an exoticness, that inspired them to ask blunt questions.

"Oh, right," *Whatshisname* said quietly, embarrassment in his tone. "Why you staying in halls if you just live a few miles away?"

"Do crows normally do that?" Duthie said, peering at the trees through the dusky light. "Peck at windows to get in?"

"Not sure. You studying? I'm just finishing up my PhD actually. Nice to see someone else at Hillhead, been so empty the past few weeks. I'm guessing you've not long arrived if I haven't seen you on the app until today? Not that I've been checking it that much. Busy with my thesis–"

"What the–" Duthie breathed. A small form was coming out of the woods from the precise spot that the crow had disappeared into. It was as if a piece of the shadow was crawling free. Duthie threw on his shorts and flip-flops.

"Are we going somewhere?" said a still-naked *Whatshisname*.

The dark form below was waiting at the edges of the trees.

"What's it about?" Duthie said, looking for his keys and phone.

"What?"

"Your thesis," he said, finding them and heading for the bedroom door.

"Maths," *Whatshisname* said, confusion on his face. "How about you? You didn't say what you were studying. Or your name."

The front door slammed, the echo ringing up and down the concrete stairway, mixing with the *slip-slaps* of Duthie's feet.

The night was hot. Where was this weather coming from? Not a drop of rain for days, and yet this moist warmth…

Duthie strode towards the trees. He couldn't see the shadowy form but intuited where it should be. He reached the spot and glanced back to check the sightline from the bedroom window. The ghost of *Whatshisname's* face briefly appeared then was gone.

Duthie turned back to the woods, but there was nothing there. Only the occasional chirp of wee birds broke the silence.

A small black shape detached from the shadows, approached Duthie's leg and brushed against it.

Meow.

Duthie huffed in relief. The cat was pitch black, a moving silhouette with amber eyes that glinted in the moonlight. Duthie tried to stroke its back but it concaved at his touch. It slinked into the woods, looked back at Duthie then padded onwards. Duthie followed, one step, two steps, three steps, giving his eyes time to adjust to the darkness. He lost the cat. Then found it. Then saw a foot, two of them, in trainers, below trousers, and a grey top, a face, and silver hair.

His breath caught and he stumbled back out to the grass. His heartbeat thumped in his chest.

"*Christ*...didn't spot you there," he called to the person. He or she didn't respond, just looked at him. No, they looked *through* him.

"You alright there?" Duthie asked, filling the silence. The cat wound around the person's feet, then flashed Duthie an amber wink and disappeared into the woods. The silver person turned and followed. In seconds, both were gone.

Duthie waited for long breaths, heart still hammering. His patience was rewarded with a voice. It came from deep within the trees.

It said: *Skrawk!*

II.

'A seat of learning.'

What does that even mean? A place to sit and discover new things? A seat that is constructed from knowledge itself?

The more Duthie unpicked the phrase he'd read on the 'Welcome to the University of Aberdeen' pamphlet, the less sense it made. His mind often did this, spooled outwards from a word, a lyric, a riff of music, until all sense was lost. If he ever stopped to notice this practice he might realise it brought him comfort, an ability to escape from thought. Say, for instance, the ability to quit replaying the previous night's mysterious events, to halt looping images of black cat and silent silver-haired person. To stop wondering why he couldn't bring himself to follow them into the dark forest. Whatever. This internship wasn't going to be about following strangers into woods.

A seat of learning. He rotated the chant in his head the whole fifteen-minute walk from Hillhead Student Village to King's College campus. It was only when his feet hit cobbles at the beginning of Don Street that his focus returned to the here and now. The street narrowed and houses seemed Dickensian and quaint. It was as if Duthie had stepped over an invisible threshold into Old Aberdeen, through a hidden veil into Briga*deen*. In a few more steps he was on campus, following the high street past a mishmash of stately granite houses, harling-pocked modern buildings and centuries-old stone walls.

And then there it was: the seat of learning. It was just like the pamphlet: a stone crown on top of the chapel, and below that spread the famous lawns, cloisters and ivy-clad walls of the quadrangle. With summer sun beating down, and sky clear but for the most ornamental of clouds, King's College looked even better than the pictures.

Duthie traced the map to the Cromwell Tower, sparking a half-smoked rollie as he mouthed the description.

A stunning tower-house popular among Scottish lairds since the thirteenth century, housing lecture and seminar rooms, topped by a small rooftop observatory and an anemometer that measures wind-force.

He blew a puff of smoke towards the anemometer, willing the smoke to take with it the nervousness that had tightened his chest these past few weeks. Inside the Cromwell Tower, a portal led to a spiral staircase. With nobody in sight to ask for help it took Duthie a while to find his destination, but in time he discovered a mezzanine level at the top of the tower. On a door at the end of a corridor was the name he was looking for:

Professor Alasdair Seaton. Celtic Studies.

Duthie knocked. Waited. Knocked again. Waited some more.

He briefly considered leaving, but then felt a surge of willpower. He needed this internship.

"Screw this," he said and turned the handle. It obliged noisily.

"Hello?" He peeked in then entered the corner office. It looked exactly as he imagined. Books. Lots of them. Shelves, bundles, stacks and piles. Nothing like what he was used to at art school, with its airy studios, the earthy scent of clay and the tang of paint. No, this was a place of dust and paper, of stale coffee and musk. But something, or rather *someone*, was missing.

There was a scuff of feet from outside a stained-glass window. Duthie spotted a pair of legs, the crease of tweed trousers on the window sill – a window sill that was five storeys high.

Duthie rushed to the window and shouted: "Professor? Professor Seaton?"

"Jesus H Christ!" bellowed a voice from above. A man, short, stocky and clinging to the side of the building looked down at Duthie with wild eyes. "You nearly killed me, boy!"

"Here!" Duthie hollered, jutting his hand out.

The professor sneered, as if it was a rubber chicken. "I don't need help, you idiot! Shift back and I'll let myself back in."

Duthie retreated as the Professor grasped the open pane of glass and swung himself into the office, not altogether expertly but impressively nonetheless for, what, sixty years of age, sixty-five? With a thump he was in, cheeks rosy and eyebrows knitted – and then suddenly unknitted, raised comically. Dark patches of sweat were under each armpit. He jerked a thumb behind him. "Bloody aerial. Always needs a waggle."

Duthie nodded, dumbstruck. He glanced around the room but saw no television, radio or anything that would require an aerial. He opened his mouth, framed a question but decided not to express it.

"Ahhh," breathed the Professor, settling behind his desk. He smiled and steepled his fingers, the very picture of calm, as if he hadn't just been dangling outside a fifth-floor window.

"Now," he said. "Yes?"

"Yes?" Duthie said, heart rate still trying to level out.

"Yes," the Professor squinted.

"Umm."

"Yes!"

"Sorry I don't underst–"

"Yeeeees?" the Professor scooped his voice and waved an open palm towards the seat opposite. "How can I help you?"

"Oh," Duthie said, sitting down.

"Are you okay, lad? You seem flustered?"

"No I'm fine. Fine. It was just, you know…" he pointed out the window then widened his eyes.

The Professor's expression remained fixed in a pleasant smile.

"…but anyway, yes. I'm, um, my name's Duthie. I'm your summer intern. Here, at the department."

"Summer intern," the Professor parroted, mulling the word over as if tasting a foreign liquor. "Mmm."

"The new intern scholarship? I applied in the spring when I was finishing at Gray's."

"Gray's," the Professor closed his eyes, exploring his enjoyment further.

"School of Art?"

"Mmm hmm."

"Uh…an internship for an arts student to work with the Celtic Studies department over the summer? I was accepted last month and was told to report to you today to begin the internship." He fished out the acceptance letter and waved it before the Professor's closed lids. "My degree show at Gray's was in sculpture. Carving. I sent pictures in with my application? I was inspired by the Picts. The symbols on the ancient stones."

"Picts. Yup, yup," the Professor nodded. "Uh huh."

"The Placement Office paired me up with you, so... Look, should I come back another time or something?" Duthie said, a kernel of annoyance rising in his voice.

"Laddie," the Professor said, his eyes finally open. His expression was sliding into a shape of mild concern, the way you might look at a kid lost in a supermarket. "It was nice of you to drop by, but I think you've perhaps come to the wrong–"

"It was a new scholarship fund. The...Dr Mary Seaton scholarship."

The Professor froze, and then for the second time in this odd conversation, his face suddenly re-formed, this time into a serious, business-like shape. To complete the look, he began repositioning books and ruffling sheets of paper. "Ah yes well. Yes, good. Well, as you can see, I'm quite busy at the moment so if you wouldn't mind coming back another time, as you say. We can discuss the possibility of this 'summer internship'."

"Possibility?" Duthie said. "But I've already moved into halls."

The Professor's eyes didn't leave the desk. "Tomorrow morning. Ten sharp. Yes that will be fine. See you then....uh..."

"Duthie," said Duthie then rose out of the seat as motioned to by the Professor. Before leaving the room, he looked back and opened his mouth to speak, but he felt dumbfounded.

The Professor continued to fuss with the books on his desk, now with more urgency as if he'd lost something.

III.

If this was food, Duthie wasn't sure he ever wanted to eat again. The macaroni cheese was somehow both over- and under-cooked, bathed in sauce yet under-flavoured, and the paper plate it was puddled on was soaked through. He considered returning the pale slop to the canteen but the almost-cute server guy kept looking over. Evidently Duthie was the only Hillhead resident who had shown up for dinner at the food hall. So, whatever; slop was fine. After all, meals were free for his three-week stay and cash wasn't something he was rich in at the moment. He lifted a grey forkful to 'cheers' the server, then shovelled it into his mouth and suppressed a shiver.

All in all, it was the fitting end to a shitty day. All Duthie had achieved was a sweaty walk to campus, an unsuccessful attempt to access the library and, of course, a bizarre first meeting with his internship adviser. Maybe not even his adviser? First contact with Professor Seaton had placed a question mark over the whole thing.

He opened his phone and considered who to share his woes with. Kenny was on that Work America thing all summer, posting crap on social media every two seconds. S-Boy was still in the honeymoon period with his new boyfriend and Duthie had absolutely no interest in third-wheeling. And Dana? Well, she'd turned out to be a bit of a bitch these past few months, incredibly up herself since finishing top of the class at Gray's. As if 'Subversive Nail Art' is worthy of First Class honours.

He headed for the hookup app instead. Sure enough, the only person in a two-mile radius was *Whatshisname*. Not a good idea.

Maybe everything would all be sorted tomorrow, the Professor would properly remember the internship and everything would be fine. He *really* needed this internship. It was his ticket out of town. The alternative was too horrifying. To return home, tail between his legs...

The sound of a slamming door echoed in Duthie's mind. *Home.* His pulse thumped at the memory. He tried to stop the train of thought in its tracks.

Seat of learning, seat of learning, seat of learning...

"Fuck this," he said with a grunt. He marched up to the canteen counter and slapped the tray down. A bloated piece of penne flopped in front of the eager server. "I think you overcooked this a bit, mate. By about a year."

An hour later, Duthie was leaving *Whatshisname's* dorm in the direction of his own. Post-coital calm hummed through his body.

It was dusky again and the student village looked all the better for it, its concrete edges softened in the half light. He walked across a stretch of grass, its fresh scent carried upwards on the humid air. Surely it would rain soon? This was Aberdeen, not Abu Dhabi.

The headlights of a large vehicle caught his attention. He watched as the van swung into the turning circle and stopped outside the main reception building. A young woman hopped out, opened the rear double doors and pulled out an armful of wooden poles with pointed ends. They must have been five or six feet long, and difficult to manoeuvre at that. A roll of material unfurled from one of the poles, a large rectangle of yellow, red and black stripes. She swore and twisted the pole to retract the flag. She didn't seem to notice Duthie watching at all. Brows knitted in concentration, she heaved the poles into the reception building. *Proof of life*, Duthie mused then continued on his way across the otherwise empty grounds.

Esslemont House, he had been told by S-boy who studied at Aberdeen Uni for a term, was categorically the shabbiest of Hillhead's halls. True, its walls were the crumbliest and its windows the mossiest, but Duthie liked it fine. He'd never stayed in halls – his parents warning him against any 'unnecessary' debt – so the experience was interesting. Sure, as far as he could tell he was practically alone in the entire block with nobody to talk to, but that was okay too. He entered Flat 3, a ground floor apartment that looked out on the trees that fringed the north west perimeter of the student village. The rooms, six in all, were arranged three-a-side along a central corridor. At the top of the corridor were two toilet stalls. These were flanked by a shower room to the left and a kitchen to the right. No living room. No en-suite rooms. No problem.

He'd had the choice of any one of the dorm rooms but had chosen the first on the left. In any case, the whole flat was Duthie's to roam. He could do what he wanted. Shag as many hookups as he liked, leave dirty dishes in the sink with impunity, walk naked as a *bairn* through the entire place. In some ways, this was the student experience he'd dreamed of his whole time at Gray's. Sure, he'd partied plenty at art school, had made friends, a few enemies even, been inspired by some lecturers, bored by others, but living at home was yet another thing that had grown old long ago. Bringing boyfriends back to his childhood room? Nursing a hangover while his little sister jumped on his head? And as for his mother...

Seat of learning.

No, this was good. This was the freedom he deserved. Hell,

he might even be able to jimmy the lock on one of the dorms to convert into a makeshift studio. He could imagine himself now, light jazz tinkling from his phone, a fag glowing at the edge of his lips, and chiselling, carving and filing long into the night, a series of interconnecting lines emerging on the surface of a piece of wood, maybe even stone, grooves deepening with each stroke until finally, when he stepped back, it would be a beautiful artwork. Something ancient and symbolic. Something indelible yet beyond meaning.

A breeze reached him as soon as he unlocked the dorm door. *Shit*. He'd left the window open. A glance from wardrobe to chair to bedside table revealed all his belongings accounted for. He berated himself, then suddenly tensed.

Something was on the bed. A small dark form twitched. He flipped on the light.

A black cat, one leg pointed ceiling-ward, blinked up at him with amber eyes. It made a small *mew* then buried its face back down in its pink bum hole.

IV.

The wood were darker than the previous night, but for some reason Duthie didn't feel the same fear. The cat had let him stroke it on the bed, even nuzzled into his hand. The affection was unexpected and comforting. 'Where's your owner, eh? Where's your spooky friend?' he had whispered. He had been met with a purr and a swish of tail.

Now, standing three steps deep into the woods as he had the previous night, the cat one step deeper, he felt emboldened, beckoned by its amber gaze. So he took a fourth step, then a fifth, then onwards. The trees curled at the edge of his vision. As his eyes adjusted to the blackness, he noticed some had broad and tall trunks with knuckle-like roots to tread on, while others were wiry, their branches jutting out at odd angles. The thinnest of breezes made it through them, rustling leaves and conveying green smells. The only other sound was Duthie's feet, soft crunching on twigs.

How long had they been walking? The woods were a perpetual 'now', a forever night. At that thought, he lost track of the cat. Disorientation suddenly disturbed, the evening's heat clung to his body, the question of what the hell he was doing tightened in his chest.

A new sound broke the spell of panic. It was a whispering at first, then louder, morphing into a babble, then a rush. The river! He had been following the course of the Don which moated the north and western banks of Hillhead. Duthie could see a path at the edge of the flowing water. He started towards it but a *meow* drew him back to the darkness.

They continued their journey together, over root, around trunk, through tangled branch. The cat chose the wildest route, avoiding a rose garden here, a sign reading 'Seaton Park' there. Then, without warning, it stopped and looked up. Through a gap in the canopy, Duthie could see the moon, pale and bright. But that wasn't what the cat was looking at. Peeking just above the trees was a pointed roof. No, a turret. The cat disappeared into a thicket. Duthie tried to follow but the trees had converged too densely. Their branches poked at bare arms.

"Isn't there an easier way?" he called into the blackness, but heard no reply. He pushed onwards, ignoring scratches and snags, drawn by closer glimpses of the turret. He could now make out the shape of the building, a tower attached to a large rectangular house. A light was on inside the tower, and in the window...was that...? His view was obscured by a gnarled branch. He held it away, felt its resistance and then –

A *skrawk!* pierced the night directly above his head, then a ragged flap of wings. Duthie lost his grip on the branch and it sprang at him. It hit like a punch then clawed at the left side of his face. He felt a twig scrape his eyeball, another slashed his eyebrow and cheekbone. The pain was immediate and excruciating. He pressed a hand over his eye and tumbled forward.

"Fuuuuuuuck," he howled and rolled on the ground. The searing sensation continued to bloom, hot and beating. *Thoom, thoom, thoom!* As it grew louder, he realised the sound belonged to something else: feet pounding towards him. Then a voice.

"Well now," the voice said. "What have we here?"

Duthie raised his head and grunted at fresh pain. Through his undamaged eye he could make out a tall form. Clear blue eyes looked down from below a crop of hair that shone silver in the moonlight.

What followed was a blur. The pain in Duthie's eye clouded his ability to form full awareness of what was happening. Mechanically, he obeyed each suggestion made by the silver woman. *Get to your feet...press this towel to your eye...dinna be stupid, chiel, it's okay to get it bloody...climb into the car...sit back, that's it.* The only thing that punctured the red haze was her voice, husky and grounding. She didn't seek to soothe him with words, but he was glad of her instructions.

He understood they were heading to the hospital. He hadn't

been at Aberdeen Royal Infirmary in years, not since he was a scrawny teenager cradling a broken hand. *'Totally worth it'*, he had told his appalled mother. *'Should've seen the bully's face. Didn't see my fist coming'*.

The bright lights of Accident & Emergency and the bustle of medical staff brought his focus back to the here and now. Blue scrubs, stethoscopes, gurney and gauze. The adrenaline leeched from his body just as the painkillers kicked in. His face still hurt like hell, but with the blood cleaned up and the sutures in place, there was a boundary to the pain. He sat alone in a cubicle, a huge cotton pad over his left eye, mouthing a line from an old pop song as a distraction, waiting for the doctor's verdict.

"Is that you blind then?" asked a husky voice from the corner of the room.

Duthie started at the sound, which was followed by a slurping noise. He twisted his head and saw the silver woman, leaning against the wall.

"How long you been standing there?" he said, a tingle going up the back of his neck.

"Wee while," she said, blowing steam off the top of a plastic cup. "So. Blind?"

"Don't know. Hope not."

"Worse things, eh?" she yawned.

Duthie realised this was the first time he'd seen the woman properly. She was tall and angular, he had known that, but now he could take in her slimness, slender neck but strong shoulders. All this he could tell despite her loose, simple clothing. She was old – wrinkles on her face, silver hair – but there was a vitality to her stance that made her difficult to pin a number on.

She looked around the cubicle as if it was the most unremarkable thing, as if she'd just wandered in to have a *lookie* before heading back home.

"Cheers for helping me," Duthie said, in case he hadn't on the way here. He tried to suppress the flush dawning on his cheeks – something he'd never mastered his whole redheaded life.

"Morgan," she said.

"What?"

"That's my name. Morgan. I'd shake your hand, *Red*, but I think we're past that."

Red. He'd heard this plenty his whole life too. Better than *ginger*.

"Duthie," he said, attempting a smile but retreating at the prickle from his cheekbone.

"You enjoy a'wandering the woods at night? That your thing?" The question didn't seem framed to embarrass.

"Uh," Duthie started, the events of the evening rushing back to mind. He wasn't sure he could even explain it to himself. "Your cat. It was in my dorm at Hillhead. I wanted to make sure it found its way home."

Morgan raised her eyebrows then took another slurp of the drink. "*My* cat?"

"Yeah, the black cat. Isn't it...?"

She released a little huff of laughter. "You think just because I'm an old woman that I own cats? Crazy *al' cat wifie* living in a castle?"

Duthie felt another wave of heat blossoming on his freckled cheeks but it stopped short at a new feeling. *Enough of this bashful bullshit.* "Why were you in the woods last night, then? I saw you when I was walking to my room. The cat was at your feet."

"In the woods? Was I?"

"You looked right at me."

"Interesting," Morgan said quietly then shrugged. "What can I say? Crazy *al' cat wifie*."

A doctor in blue scrubs pulled back the curtain and walked in.

"Mr Duthie," she said, looking down at a clipboard "How are you feeling?"

"Okay thanks," he replied, peeling his gaze away from Morgan's self-satisfied expression.

"Good, good. You should be a little swollen for a day or two, but just keep taking paracetamol and it'll calm down nicely. Have you got some at home, or do you need a prescription?"

"I've got plenty thanks," he said, recalling how he'd decimated the medicine cupboard at Northfield Place before leaving for Hillhead in preparation for daily hangovers.

"The lesions to your eyebrow and cheekbone are fairly shallow, so sutures were all that was needed. Just leave them in place for five to seven days. And here's some antiseptic and gauze to clean…"

She handed Duthie a paper bag. Over her shoulder, Morgan was unsubtly reading down the clipboard. She mouthed Duthie's full name and shot him a cartoonish look of being impressed.

"…and as to your eye itself," the doctor paused. Behind her, Morgan's face fell into sadness. '*Blind*', she mouthed to Duthie. His heart quickened, eye darted between her and the doctor.

"…thankfully it just looks like a bad scratch to the cornea."

Relief swept over Duthie, followed by a spark of anger which he directed at Morgan. She chuckled in response.

The doctor continued unabated: "Time and eye drops should do the trick. In the meantime you'll need to protect your eye with this."

She held up a plastic package.

"An eye patch?" said Morgan. "Fantastic!"

The doctor spun round to her, as if noticing her for the first time. "Um, yes. It'll help protect the eye while nature takes its course. I'm sorry, are you...?"

"Moral support," Morgan smiled and gave her a wink, then nodded at Duthie. "Come on then, *Pirate Red*. Your galleon awaits."

The doctor fitted the patch and led Duthie and Morgan to the waiting area. As the pair made their way outside, Morgan looked down at Duthie's hand

"Can I have that paper bag? I've got an errand to run."

VI.

Duthie's mouth was dry, his eye throbbed.

The Volvo cleared the cobbles of Don Street, transitioning to smooth asphalt. Duthie looked behind for any sign of a hopping, shitty-footed Professor Alasdair Seaton, then breathed a sigh when one didn't appear. Morgan was still hooting with laughter in the driver's seat.

"What the hell was that?" Duthie said, fixing her with his good eye.

"Ah nuthin'," Morgan said, wiping a tear. "Just a little payback."

"For what? Do you know who that was?"

"Of course I bloody know who that was. Calm yersel doon will ye? Your face is getting redder than your hair."

"Would you shut up about my– Look, why were you pranking Professor Seaton?"

Morgan mouthed the name then spat out the window. "You know Wee Ali, do you? The Professor. The Great Wizard of Skene."

"The Wizard? What kind of name is–? He's my adviser."

Morgan barked with laughter. "Good luck to ye, then."

"Why d'you say that?"

"He's a pain in the arse," she said, swinging the car into Hillhead and up the driveway, past halls of residence, their windows all dark.

"How do you know him?" Duthie pressed.

"Och God, who doesn't?"

"Would you stop avoiding... Just pull up here, okay? Stop!"

Morgan obliged by stomping on the brake. The force jolted them both forward in their seats. Duthie's covered eye twinged.

"Aya!" he grunted. "What is your problem?"

"I have not a problem in the world," she said, her husky voice lifting into song. "As for you?" She considered him for a beat then smiled. "Actually, I take it back, this anger suits you. You'll need it."

"For what?"

"Life," she said, wide-eyed and serious before a grin broke out on her face. "Okie dokie, out you pop."

She reached across Duthie and opened the door. Mechanically, once again he followed her directions, too confused to act otherwise. He closed it a millisecond before the engine roared and Morgan sped off towards the turning circle.

"Hey!" Duthie cried, patting his pockets. "Give me back my lighter!"

The old car's tyres squealed round the circle and back onto the driveway. Duthie leapt out of the way just in time to catch a glimpse of Morgan, in her mouth one of his pre-rolled cigarettes being sparked by his Zippo.

She was gone before he could say or do anything more.

He held his hands wide then slapped them down. It was unbelievable. This evening, this whole day, was one convoluted and inexplicable mess. And now he'd had his special lighter *knicked* by this ridiculous old woman who speaks in riddles.

Trudging up the deserted driveway in the direction of Esslemont House, he checked his wrist. Two twenty-two in the morning. By the time he reached the dorm, fatigue was dragging at him. He chucked the keys on the bedside table and caught himself in the mirror. "Arrrrr!" he whispered to the reflection in his best *pirate*. He didn't look half bad, actually. It was a bold look, sure, but he could make it work.

He fell on the bed, twisting at the last second to avoid hitting his face on the pillow. Sleep claimed him immediately, sucking him down into dark places. He dreamed long and deep, of black cats with question-mark tails, ragged crows coughing smoke from their beaks, and suicidal wizards dangling from towers. And through it all: a voice. Male and wailing, borne on the wind from far out east, calling his true name.

Part Two
Jock o' Northfield Place

I.

"It says here that your name is *'Rune'*," said the Professor. His bespectacled eyes were dotting around a stapled collection of documents which he hadn't looked up from since Duthie had arrived in the Cromwell Tower office. "*Rune* Duthie. Right on the nose for someone keen on ancient symbology, no?"

Duthie's voice caught on his throat. Of all the things he thought they would talk about, this was not it. On his way to campus the events of the previous night had whirled in his mind. He had no cigarettes to distract from them, and the mantras didn't seem to be working this morning.

"*Rune* like Moon, or Run*e* like Moon*a*?"

"Moon," Duthie croaked.

"Mmm" the Professor muttered. The documents *thwhipped* as he flipped between them.

"It's Thai," he added, though he wasn't sure why. "It means 'happy'."

"Thai," the Professor said, "well yes. Indeed. That would explain the–"

He looked up and his nose crinkled. He touched a hand to his own left eye. "You had two when last we met, yes?"

"Oh," Duthie said, mirroring the Professor, which caused a prickle behind his patch. "Had an accident last night. Lost a fight with a branch."

"Yes of course," he said, nodding solemnly. "I guess we both had unusual nights."

Duthie winced. "What? I mean, sorry?"

This was it. This was when the Professor would say he'd noticed Duthie in Morgan's car.

"Ignore me," he waved and smiled.

Relief spread through Duthie's stomach.

"So, Thai eh?" the Professor said, raising his chin. "You'll know all about *Patpong*, I presume? Bit of after hours fun in Bangkok's red light district, eh?"

"Excuse me?" Duthie said, thrown by the salacious waggle of the Professor's eyebrows.

"You're not *that* Thai then, I suppose," the Professor chuckled.

Before Duthie could form outrage, the Professor pointed at him. "You're in good company, by the way. Tiresias, Höðr, Manasa, Horus."

"Eh?" Duthie blurted, struggling to keep up.

"Mythology. It's full of characters losing their eyesight. Often just one eye too."

"Right," Duthie said, confused.

"Of course for most, losing sight isn't a big deal. Tends to be replaced with a deeper, supernatural insight on the world."

"I look forward to it," Duthie said.

The Professor *thwhipped* a final page. His gaze rested on an image of a white monolith with abstract faces inscribed on it.

"It's a six-foot polystyrene slab," Duthie said, peering over the desk. Finally, a chance to discuss his work. "I carved into it with a hot knife. The centrepiece of my degree show this year. Those faces are people I know, friends and family. I had a series of pieces in the collection, actually. Some in clay, some in wood. I was kind of exploring the idea that–"

"Your red hair," the Professor said, nose crinkled again, this time to such a degree that his glasses were nudged up to the bridge. "The pale skin."

"Is there a question?" Duthie said, agitation building once more.

The Professor shrugged and headed for a bookshelf near the door. He toppled a tower of boxes and books on the way past, but seemed oblivious to having done so. Duthie crouched to tidy it up. Hunkered on the ground, he was suddenly met by his own reflection on the screen of an old television set. The eye patch, the flushed cheeks, all were distended in the domed screen. The television set looked decades old. He must have missed it yesterday, obscured behind the mound of crap. A fraying cable led out of its rear, snaked along the ground between academic detritus littering the office floor, and disappeared into the wall near the window – the window that the Professor had been dangling out of yesterday. *'Bloody aerial. Always needs a waggle.'*

So much for his 'suicidal professor' hypothesis.

Duthie got up, dusted his hands and cleared his throat. "Is it possible to discuss the internship any time soon? I'm keen to get started."

The Professor seemed to ignore Duthie entirely. He hummed as he looked along a bookshelf, then up one shelf higher. "Ah here we are. Would you mind?"

He pointed to a small stack of academic-looking texts teetering on the edge of the top shelf. Duthie went up on tip toes and lifted them down.

"Quite tall too," the Professor said. "For an Asian. Well, part Asian."

Duthie tried to suppress the flash of irritation, but could feel his neck redden. He placed the books on the desk and sat down in the seat opposite the Professor.

With satisfaction smeared across his face, he disassembled the stack and selected the biggest book, a large hardback with faded gold writing on its spine. He picked up an empty mug next to it, sniffed inside, then walked out of the room.

Duthie sat there stewing, picking at the frayed edge of his shorts. He let out a hiss between his teeth at the same moment a vibration came from his rucksack. Just as he reached for it, he heard clanking from the corridor and the Professor saying something about 'carving'.

"I guess I'm supposed to follow?" Duthie muttered, ignoring the buzzing phone to head in the clanking direction.

In the corridor the Professor was searching around a cupboard, his fingers waggling over cups, teapots and containers. "Coffee, coffee, coffee," he said as if conjuring it into existence.

Duthie reached into the cupboard and pulled out a clearly-labelled jar.

"Ah good lad," the Professor said. "Black. One sugar."

Duthie made a small noise of exasperation, but when the Professor didn't react (nose stuck in the old book) he sighed and tipped coffee granules into the cup.

"Stone is a lot harder than polystyrene," the Professor said into the pages.

"Yes," Duthie said, unclenching his jaw. The non-sequitur rhythm of the Professor's conversation was maddening, but he was becoming accustomed to it, as if learning a dance. If he could just find a way to get ahead of the beat.

"Mmm hmm," the Professor said.

"But not impossible with the right tools," Duthie said, clicking the kettle on. "If the Picts could do it thirteen hundred years ago, I'm sure I can make it work."

"'*A Pictish-inspired artwork for modern times. Reaching back, through stone and symbol, into the past*'," said the Professor. The dry tone didn't indicate much love for Duthie's application form, but at least he'd read enough to be able to recite.

"That's the idea," Duthie said, filling the murky cup.

"Faces on rock."

"Not necessarily. I'm open to new things. That's why I applied for the intern–"

"The mystery of the Picts is part of the appeal, you realise?" The Professor looked over the rim of the book at Duthie. He put emphasis on 'mystery', as if he'd coined the word. "A whole civilisation, a fierce face-painted people, forming for a short seven hundred years, building great settlements on hilltops, fending off the Romans. Only to disappear with barely a trace. It's the *mystery* that enthrals us."

"Absolutely, and it's their *art* that grabs us most of all," Duthie said. "Art is how we know about the Picts. Only their stone carvings remain. Art is our thread to the past."

He pushed the cup into the Professor's hand.

The Professor either blew or sighed across the top of the coffee. "The Picts are not my area, dear boy," he said, looking out a stained-glass window towards a sun-scorched playing field.

"But the Placement Team suggested–"

"Oh well then, if the Placement Team suggested," he said, snapping the book closed. "The Celts, lad! They are my subjects. Mythology and history. Cú Chulainn and The Morrigan. Queen Medb and King Ailill. Not your carved standing stones. No, they were–" He cut himself off then loped back towards his office.

"The Picts were your wife's specialism," Duthie said before he could suppress it.

The Professor stopped but didn't turn round, just waved the book and disappeared into the office. By the time Duthie made it to the room, he was back behind his desk. He pushed the book across the table.

"This will teach you more than I can," he said.

Duthie inspected the book. The front and back were empty, its corners were dog-eared. It had clearly been separated from the cover long ago. He ran a thumb along the spine which read: *'The Picts: A Forgotten People? Dr Mary Seaton'*.

"Take it," he said.

"Really?" Duthie said. "Thanks. I'll take good care of it."

"I wouldn't worry," the Professor said. "I've got the original at home."

"On Don Street?" Duthie asked. He had been so engrossed in the worn edges of the book that he hadn't been aware of what he'd said.

"Excuse me?"

"Nothing. I just thought, uh, senior staff lived on campus? Like the houses on Don Street?" Duthie said, sliding the book into his backpack. Another vibration came from its depths. A call or a text?

"Indeed," the Professor said, his dubious expression levelling out. "But no. Digs on Don Street are hardly a place to hang your hat permanently. My proper home, well, Manor is probably more accurate, is in Skene."

The Wizard of Skene. Morgan's words from last night mingled with the puffed-up, prideful countenance.

Duthie attempted a smile. "Skene's a lovely place. Do you live by the loch?"

"The book is yours to keep," the Professor flicked his fingers. "My gift to you."

"Thanks. Looks great."

A strange expression went across the Professor's face. A micro expression, something fleetingly strained. "It has its moments. As I say, it will teach you more than I can."

Satisfaction rose once again. He pointed to the door. "The book; and also what's out there."

"I don't understand," Duthie said.

"Have you heard of the Aberdeen International Festival?" said the Professor. He reached for a pen and notepad and started scribbling. "It's a week-long celebration of music, dance blah blah blah. I've been on the steering committee since it started in the seventies. We bring in artists from across the world and tour their work around Aberdeen and the Shire. You've heard of it?"

"I'm not sure," Duthie said.

The Professor tutted. "It's the region's best kept secret. It starts in two days' time and who knows about it? The people of the North-East have become such philistines. Shame really, they'll miss it when it's gone."

"Sorry?"

"Gone, dear boy."

"No, I mean…you want me to perform in the festival?"

The Professor barked. "Ha! No lad. As interesting as carved

polystyrene is. No, no no. As your 'intern mentor'," he said, curling his lip, "I prescribe ten days of work *for* the Aberdeen International Festival."

He stabbed a full stop on the paper and folded it. He handed it to Duthie then stood up with a triumphant look on his face.

Duthie stammered. He couldn't believe this. It was outrageous. How had he so badly lost control of this opportunity? He was Rune Duthie, for Christ's sake. Rune Duthie was the guy who had convinced his art school Dean to raise his dissertation grade purely by incessant badgering. Rune Duthie was the guy who had *whammed, bammed and thank you 'manned'* his way through a good proportion of Aberdeen's gay population, and broken the hearts of the remainder. Rune Duthie was–

"But I'm supposed to study with you here for the next three weeks," he said, hating the whine in his voice. "To learn about the Picts, to feed what I learn into an artistic expression–"

"Follow!" the Professor said, marching out of the office once again.

Duthie grabbed his bag, his frustration now unrestrained and echoing down the stairwell. "Professor! This is not even slightly what I applied for. You can't just palm me off on some–"

"Best way to see the region and its people," he said, heading out the door and round a corner towards the quad lawn. "That's what this is all about isn't it? Faces in stone? Plenty of faces at the festival. And who knows, on your adventures around the north-east you'll be able to take in a standing stone or two, if you're lucky. Wouldn't that be nice?"

"But I–"

"And of course you'll be paid," the Professor added. "On top of the internship's accommodation and subsistence. Won't that be simply lovely?" He gestured towards an ivy-clad building where a plaque read 'New King's Building'. Another sign, wooden and staked into the ground at an angle, read 'Festival Office'. "Go in there and ask for Fedelm, she will see to your deployment."

"Fedelm?" Duthie spat the bizarre name. "But *you're* my mentor. You're supposed to–"

"Ten days, Mr Duthie," the Professor said, wagging a finger. "You have ten days. By the festival's end I expect you to have a...what did you say, an *artistic expression* summing up what you have learned."

"But–"

"I expect progress reports too," he said, turning on his heel. "That's the kind of thing mentors say, isn't it?"

"This is bullshit," Duthie said, loud enough for anyone to hear. Rage burned from his stomach to his cheeks.

He watched as the Professor disappeared from sight, back into his tower.

Duthie looked up at the New King's building and let out a fiery sigh. He considered its floor-to-roof ornate windows and considered smashing each and every panel.

He opened the folded piece of paper. The Professor's penmanship was predictably extravagant:

Another one for you.
D.

II.

A spotty teenager with face as fuchsia as his t-shirt was carrying a cardboard box down the stairs. His arms were pulled taut by the weight. A lanyard around his neck swung with each step.

"Hey, man. I'm looking for Fedelm?" Duthie said.

The teen looked a little surprised at Duthie. *Eye patch.* In his rage he'd almost become forgotten. "Uh...never heard of one," the teen said, then kicked open double doors, revealing a lecture theatre beyond and disappeared into it.

The inside of the New King's was very different from its exterior – the Linoleum and strip lighting telling a different story to the handsome granite outside. Duthie carried on up the stairs as more teenagers in pink t-shirts emerged from a room on the landing, also heaving boxes.

"Fedelm?" Duthie asked as they squeezed past. They served similar responses to their spotty friend but with the addition of a few giggles.

Duthie peeked into the room they'd come from. It looked like a seminar room which had been turned into a makeshift office – the desks, computers and photocopier at odds with the lectern and whiteboard. Yet more pink people were in there, milling around a mound of boxes in the centre of the room. A few of the desks were occupied with slightly older people, wearing lanyards but not the garish t-shirts.

"Sorry everyone, I'm looking for Fedelm?" Duthie said, trying for polite but sounding depleted.

A lady hunching over a spreadsheet looked up, squinted and said: "Who?"

Duthie looked at the piece of paper in his hand and sighed. "Fedelm? Am I not saying that right?"

"Can I help you?" asked someone behind him.

A young woman was standing on the landing, hands resting on hips. The logo on her fuchsia t-shirt read: 'Aberdeen International Festival'. Duthie recognised her immediately as the woman who he had seen carrying flags poles into Hillhead the previous night.

"Are you Fedelm?" Duthie said, catching the exasperation in his own voice.

"Technically yes," she said. She cocked her head and looked directly at his eye patch.

Duthie shifted from one foot to the other, part unease, part agitation. He attempted to counteract by leaning casually against the doorframe and ruffling through his hair.

Without taking her eyes off him, she called: "Guys, can you stop faffing about and get those brochures down to NK1?"

"Yes Eddie," said one of the pink kids. "Right away, Eddie. Three bags full, Eddie."

"Very funny," she replied, flicking a thumb behind her. "Shift your arses."

"Eddie," Duthie said. "Short for Fedelm."

"You're quick. Quicker than this lot. Look, can I help you? As you can see, I'm in the middle of herding teenagers."

Duthie handed over the piece of paper.

She read it, grimaced and muttered something about Jesus Christ under her breath. She looked at Duthie afresh. "So who are you, then?"

"Duthie. I'm doing an internship with Professor Seaton. Professor Alasdair Seaton? I'm guessing you know him?" He pointed at the piece of paper.

"Yep. Him I've heard of," Eddie said deadpan.

"Apparently he wants me to work at the Festival for my internship."

"Oh he does, does he?" she said, raising an eyebrow. "And don't you just sound ecstatic about it."

"It's just I'm confused about–"

"You and me both, kid," she said, wandering over to the whiteboard.

Kid? She looked only a few years older than Duthie.

"So what is your internship in?" she said.

"I'm an arts student."

"Well you've come to the right place, Duthie," she said, trying to erase an enormous cock and balls off the board. She whipped round to the pink kids. "Are you kidding me? It's been drawn with a Sharpie?"

The kids trooped out the door at pace, the weight of their boxes making them walk like monkeys. A gale of laughter bounced around the corridor.

"Whiteboard marker pen dissolves permanent ink," Duthie said. "You just need to scribble over it then the whole thing wipes off."

Eddie gave him a dubious look, picked up a couple of markers and commenced work on the giant member. "So. What do you imagine you can do for us, Mr Duthie?"

He looked around the office. The small fortress of boxes was piled in front of him. The worker bees at their computers remained bent over keyboards. Duthie's shoulders slumped, he rubbed the back of his neck.

"What do you need?" he said.

"Absolutely nothing," Eddie replied, gaze fixed on the board.

Her words were low and measured, spoken less at him than to the room at large. "I do not need a single thing."

"So I can't work here?" Duthie said. He got no response. "Wonderful. Just bloody wonderful."

He reached into his bag and fished out a phone. He spotted two missed calls from 'Jock', but fired past the notifications in search of the University of Aberdeen website, found a number then hit 'call'.

"Switchboard," a voice eventually droned.

"Hi. Yes. I want to speak to the Internship Placement Office. Now. Please."

"One second," said the voice.

Hold music crackled in Duthie's ear. *Greensleeves. Why was it always fucking Greensleeves?*

"Hello. This is the Internship Offi..."

"Hi I'd like to speak to someone about–"

"...ce. I'm afraid nobody is able to take–"

"Fuck my life!" Duthie said through gritted teeth and hung up.

"Phone a Friend not working?" Eddie said, stepping back from the board. The cock and balls were still there, not erased, but enhanced; veins, hair and a glowing red tip.

"You finding this amusing?" Duthie seethed, cool well and truly broken.

"Not at all," Eddie said, turning to face him. "I'm just not entirely sure what the wise old Professor had in mind when he sent you."

Spreadsheet Lady looked up and said, "Oh, has your father found someone to help out? That's awesome timing actually because I've just had a call from–"

"Hold on," Duthie said, eye boring into Eddie. Her expression darkened momentarily in the direction of Spreadsheet. "The Professor's your dad?"

Eddie folded her arms and jutted her chin.

Duthie laughed. "What the hell is this? I'm being passed about in some kind of family game?"

"This isn't a creche or a home for stray puppies," Eddie spat, the veneer of amusement wiped away. "I have everything under control, so you can go back to Professor Seaton–"

"Daddy," Duthie said under his breath.

"–and tell him I have all the help I need, thank you very much."

"This is just perfect," Duthie said waving a hand around the room. He could only imagine how beetroot his cheeks were by now. "You know, I didn't even want to come here and work for your stupid festival."

"Clearly," Eddie chuckled.

Duthie turned on the spot.

"Oh you're leaving?" Eddie called out. "Take a box with you? There's a dear."

Duthie ransacked his bag for anything resembling a cigarette, grunting with each compartment he unzipped, finding nothing smokable in any of them.

He thumped down on a stone wall intersecting the King's quad. No internship. No money. No cigarettes. No plan. Everything was crashing around him. In his mind's eye he saw himself trudging home, standing outside Northfield Place, staring up at the living room window, his family inside just waiting to pull him back into their tangled web. He scooped his hand through his hair and groaned at his shitty fate. This wasn't how his story was meant to go this summer–

Something leapt onto Duthie's back, pushing him on to the grass face first. The wind was knocked out of him. He tried to get up but the body on top of him had other ideas, knees and elbows pinning him to the ground. Little hands found their way to his flanks and started needling him, the fingers too sharp to accomplish a proper tickle.

Duthie roared and managed to twist around, dislodging his attacker. But as soon as he'd done so, the assailant made a big gasp and jumped on his stomach, winding him further.

"What's that?" the voice shrieked.

Unclenching his eye, Duthie could make out a halo of ginger hair and a wide row of teeth. He wailed, "Oh for God's sake. Kelly! Get off me!"

"Dad!" said the girl. "Come see! Rune's lost an eye!"

"Bloody hell," boomed a second voice from high in the sky. "What's happened, son?"

"Did a tiger bite it off?" asked the girl, bouncing up and down on Duthie's stomach. "Did something hit the back of your head and it came popping out? Did you hold in a sneeze too much and the pressure made it *ptoooooooooooooosplat!*?"

Duthie let out all the morning's aggression in one guttural howl then flopped back on the grass, panting, arms spread out wide.

"I think it was the last one, Dad," Kelly whispered. "The sneeze."

"Did ye get in a fight?" said the deep voice.

Duthie looked up. Silhouetted by the sun, head mingling with wisps of clouds was Jock.

"No," said Duthie. His throat felt tight. "Branch caught it."

"Where?" said Kelly.

"In my eye!"

"No, dummy. Where was the branch?"

"In a forest."

"A forest? Where was the forest? Were you scared? Can I see under the patch?" she said, already lifting it up and pulling a face of disgust.

"Aya! Quit it!" Duthie said, flicking her clammy fingers off. "What are you doing here anyway?"

"Dad called you," Kelly said, her voice straining as Jock lifted her by the chest off Duthie.

The Big Man smiled: "This wee one wanted to come see you for lunch. Had the genius idea of tracking you on the family mobile tracker app thingie."

"Lucky me," Duthie said. He'd been too focused on removing his traceability from his mother's phone, he completely forgot to do the same with Jock's.

"We missed you," Kelly said, pulling at the hem of her t-shirt and batting her eyelashes. Her ruddy cheeks and ginger curls were adorable. To anyone else.

"Plus I brought the tools ye asked for. They're in the car," Jock said offering a hand.

"Thanks," Duthie said, getting to his feet on his own. He looked up at Jock, who was a full head taller than himself. "You buying lunch, then?"

The Big Man beamed and squeezed his shoulder.

"Hello?" asked a voice from across the lawn. Duthie raised a hand over his brow and squinted. A Black man, laden with a huge backpack, was pulling an even huger case across the grass.

"Excuse me." The man's exertion flipped into a perfect smile as he approached. "I wonder if you could help me? I'm looking for the Aberdeen International Festival office?"

"It's just over there," Duthie pointed to the New King's building.

"Wow," Kelly breathed, taking in the intricate pattern on the man's top. Duthie nudged her.

"Thank you," the man said. "There?"

Duthie nodded. He felt himself staring, the guy was incredibly handsome, and that accent...

Kelly nudged back.

"I just arrived," the man said. He looked exhausted. "Someone from the festival was supposed to meet me at the airport I think, but no matter."

"Sorry to hear that. Though it doesn't surprise me–" Duthie started.

"I like your accent," Kelly said to the man.

"Thank you very much. I like yours too," he replied. "And your beautiful hair."

"Oh stop, sir. You'll make me blush," she said in a Southern Belle voice and feigned a swoon. *Where did she get this crap from?*

"Like the colour of the sunset. You're both lucky to have it," he said, his warmth transferring to Duthie, who couldn't help but return it with a dopey smile.

"Well that's settled, kind stranger," Kelly continued to drawl. "We shall accompany you to your destination."

"What?" Duthie said. Kelly's grip was surprisingly strong as she pulled him towards the building.

She turned to Jock and sang out: "You just wait here, butler. We shall return for lunch."

"Aye aye, ma'am," Jock saluted.

"So," Kelly shifted back to her own accent, sprang round to the man's side and grabbed his hand. "Where have you just arrived from? Somewhere very far away?"

The man laughed and said: "A city called Kampala."

Kelly's face scrunched. "Wherezat?"

"You have to guess."

Kelly gnawed her lip. "Australia?"

"Kel," Duthie groaned.

"Guess again," the man beamed.

"Africa?"

"Correct. From a country called Uganda."

"Wow," Kelly said. "Rune, can we go to Uganda?"

"There's no need to go right away, I just got here," the man said. "But you and your brother should go some day. It's a beautiful country."

"Oh, he's not my brother," said Kelly, pointing between her hair and Duthie's. "He's my dad."

The man looked at Duthie in disbelief. Duthie rolled his eye and shook his head.

Kel continued, "He was oh-so-terribly young when he had me. Merely a pup."

"My little sister enjoys playing with the truth," Duthie said.

"Ah," the man said. "A creative spirit. You and I are going to get on very well."

Kelly grinned.

"And this is us," Duthie said. They had reached the large wooden entrance to New King's.

"Why Rune, don't be so rude," Kelly said, back in her Southern Belle. "Escort the gentleman caller in."

Duthie fumbled some words.

"There's no need, really," the man said. "I'm sure I can find my way."

"Well if you won't, I will," Kelly said and ran into the building.

"Kelly!" Duthie sprinted up the stairs in pursuit, catching her just as she burst into the office. His heart froze as Eddie, standing bolt upright next to Spreadsheet Lady, locked eyes with him.

"Back so soon?" she said, surprise turning into what Duthie took to be a practiced nonchalance.

Kelly looked between them both in confusion and was about to say something when the clattering of wheels up the stairs broke the silence. She clapped her hands and shouted: "Preeeesenting, fresh from Aberdeen Airport, after a million-mile journey from Uganda, the one, theeeeeee only…uh…" She looked at the man in the doorway. "I don't know your name, sorry."

"Abel Okello," the man smiled, breathless. "Abe."

Eddie's expression cracked. Was that mortification splintering across it?

Spreadsheet Lady mumbled: "That's what I was trying to say. I got a call from him. He was at the airport so I explained how to get here and–"

Eddie crossed the room to shake Abel's hand. "Huge apologies, Abe. Obviously you were meant to be picked up by one of our Youth Team, um, but something must have…you had a safe flight?"

"The safest," he said. "I'm looking forward to performing in your wonderful festival. It's an honour."

"Well, I don't know about that," Eddie laughed, "but it's certainly great to have you here with us. We're lucky to have you. The people of Aberdeen can't wait to see you and your, um, you know, your…"

"Folk story-telling?" Abe said, smile not faltering one bit.

"Yes! Yes, folk story-telling. Of course."

Duthie didn't even try to suppress his glee at Eddie's discomfort.

She picked up a ring binder and flipped through the pages at a rate just shy of frantic. "Now, you must be tired after such a long journey. We'll get you taken to Hillhead Halls...of Residence to your...uh...dorm!" She poked a finger at the very last page in the binder and smiled with relief. Duthie could see an empty floor plan of a Hillhead apartment.

"Thank you, that would be great," Abel said.

"I think she forgot you were coming," Kelly said, looking up at him.

Duthie gripped her shoulder.

"Ow! What? She must have. Didn't you see her face."

Abel put a hand on Kelly's other shoulder and patted it, then looked back at Eddie. He said: "The welcome pack mentioned I would be assigned a courier?"

"A courier!" Eddie said, her colour rising. "Yes of course. Absolutely."

She darted a look at Duthie, desperation in her eyes.

Duthie cocked his head in imitation of the look she'd given him not twenty minutes before.

III.

Jock and Kelly were locked in competition. Unblinking, committed. There could only be one victor. The rule was simple: whoever's ice-cream dribbled down the cone fastest won. The prize? Aside from a sticky hand and the freedom to gloat all the way home, the prize was up for negotiation. If it was Kelly who won – and rest assured it would be – the prize was likely to be something horse-related.

The family Drip Race usually took a while, the record hovering somewhere around the 'let's-give-up-it's-bloody-freezing-outside' mark. But trips to Aberdeen beach were seldom this warm and so the heat, as the saying goes, was on. Jock stormed to an early lead with his Mr Whippy amid calls of foul play – *"Yours is leaning more than mine!"* – but Kelly made up for lost time thanks to a tumbling marshmallow forging a pathway for her melting chocolate ice-cream. It was neck and neck until drip and fist met, Jock's mountain-range fingers proving a far trickier terrain for the Mr Whippy drip to negotiate; Kel's slender hand shallow glens by comparison. Victory was secured two seconds later when chocolate blob met pavement and, thanks to Kelly's whoops of celebration, the whole beach esplanade knew about it.

Duthie's Rocky Road had been silently dripping on the asphalt for a good ten seconds beforehand. But this had stopped being his and Jock's game many years ago – eight to be precise.

He and the Big Man followed Kelly's gallops down to the beachfront. The tide was far out and the golden expanse was full of sunbathers with parasols and kids etching messages in the sand.

"So it's going well?" Jock asked through a mouthful of waffle cone.

"Sure," Duthie said, trying to fabricate a smile.

"You're going to be a tour guide for that African laddie?"

"Seems like it."

"But you'll get to do your art alongside?"

"The Professor said so. Gave me a book about the Picts to study. I've got ten days to do something arty. Plus I get paid by the festival. So it should all work out. I hope. Anyway, anything's better than…"

"Than home?"

"No, not that," Duthie said a little too fast.

Jock pinched Duthie's neck. "This'll be good for you, Wee Man. Meet some new people, make some art. Figure *oot* your next steps."

Duthie buried his response in Rocky Road.

"Proud of you," Jock said, looking out across the sea. When Duthie was small, perched on Jock's shoulders, he imagined they could wade out together and touch the horizon. Nothing was too big for them, he and his stepfather.

Duthie chucked the rest of the ice-cream away. Its sweetness had reached the point of sickliness. "Have you got a fag?"

Jock gave him a look of horror. "I thought we weren't supposed to use that word these days."

"Hilarious. I'm all out, and someone's nicked my lighter."

"Well your bad luck disnae end here, *loon*. I've quit."

"You have not!" Duthie exclaimed, mouth gaping.

Jock puffed his chest. "Six whole days. They say that's past the point of physical addiction. Say hello to the brand new, healthy me."

"How's that ice-cream going down, then?" Duthie inquired.

"Aye well. One step at a time, eh?" Jock said with a small huff of laughter. "It's funny, *she* wanted me to quit smoking ages ago. Hated the mucky habit, as you well *ken*. I could never seem to kick it. But now that she's gone?"

Duthie averted his eyes. Up ahead Kelly was using people as

obstacles in her imaginary dressage arena, her face as flushed and ecstatic as the day she was born.

"Have you been to see her?" Jock's deep voice broke the silence.

Duthie breathed in deeply and let it go in a sharp blast. "Nope."

"Still not talking?"

"Nope."

"She's not perfect. I know I'm certainly not. But she's still your mum. You should ta–"

"Have you buried Annie yet?" Duthie said. He felt a stab of guilt the second he'd released the words. From Jock's expression, it had hit the spot.

"Christ," the Big Man said. "*Dinna* say that name so close to Kel. I've just got her sleeping properly again. You know she wrote that dog a goodbye letter every night for a week? God, Annie's death was awful but it was at least a distraction for everything else that's been going on." He massaged his brow. "*Nae* a distraction, I don't mean that. It's the same with Kel's lying. I can handle that, you know? I get it. I just...I don't know. It all breaks my heart."

"Well that's Mum's forte," Duthie sniffed.

"Come on, that's nae fair."

"Why are you defending her, Jock? *She* left *you*. You shouldn't protect her, she doesn't deserve–"

"Rune! Rune!" Kelly galloped up, sand spraying from her bare feet. Chocolate was smeared all round her mouth like she was only three years old. "Ride with me!"

"Negative," Duthie said in a robotic voice.

"Please?" she whined.

"Denied."

"Aw c'mon..."

"Kelly, stop it."

"That's not my name," she stamped her foot. "It's *Kelpie*!"

"God, you're not still on with that crap are you?"

"Dad, tell him my name's Kelpie," she said, cheeks red with desperation. "He can't be the only one with a fancy name."

Jock ignored her pleas. "Where are your shoes, Wee Girl?"

Kelly shrugged. She placed a finger on her lip and surveyed the beach. Her eyes lit up and she rode off.

Jock shook his head and chuckled. Duthie looked up at his stepfather. The beard was half grey now, but he could still see the dark haired gentle giant behind it. The eyes, though, had lost some of their light.

"How are you really doing, Big Man?" Duthie said quietly.

Jock released a sigh then pulled his expression into one of pride. He patted a fist against his chest. "Six whole days, Runey."

IV.

Jock tapped the steering wheel in time to music as they drove up Tillydrone Avenue. They passed a sign for Seaton Park.

"You know, we used to come over here for picnics by the river when you were little. *D'ye* remember?" Jock said, leaning to Duthie.

"*I* don't remember," piped Kelly from the back seat. Her window was open and she had been tasting the air all the way from the beach.

"This was long before you were even a wink in my eye, Wee Girl," Jock said into the mirror.

"Gross," Duthie muttered, looking down at his phone. He was pinching and dragging a map on the screen.

"Gross," Kelly laughed and parroted out the window. "Gross, Dad. Gross!"

"We had a great time," Jock said. "Just you, me and your mum. Jack adores sunny days just like this, doesn't she?"

"Good story, Jock," Duthie said, eye flitting from the phone to the road. It must be somewhere around here. On the map he traced a finger along the undulating course of the River Don, from Hillhead down and round, through a blanket of trees that hemmed the banks.

"Ooh, look at that!" Kelly said, pointing out of the window.

"Dinna dee that, Kel!" Jock yelled. "You'll lose a hand!"

Duthie followed the line of his sister's finger and his heart leapt. There it was! A turret poking through the trees. They rounded the corner and the entire tower house was laid bare.

"Actually, I think I'm going to get out here," Duthie said, trying to keep his voice calm.

"But you wanted the long route back to Halls," Jock said.

"Nah, it's a nice day. I fancy a walk."

Jock flipped the indicator and pulled into the side. He said: "I'll get the tools out of the boot. Now, you'll look after them, yeah? I need them back in one piece. And that eye too, look after it, won't ye?"

Duthie saluted.

Kelly made a noise of complaint in the back seat. "I want to come too."

"Absolutely not, Kelly," Duthie said.

She kicked the back of his seat. "It's *Kelpie*!"

"Ouch! Okay fine, whatever. '*Absolutely not, Kelpie*'."

Jock reached behind and squeezed her leg. "Sorry, Wee Girl. We've got to get you packed up and ready for Mummy."

Her expression stilled. She bobbed her head silently.

Jock got out of the car. Just as Duthie was about to do the same Jock fixed him with a stare and tilted his head towards Kel. He left the pair alone

Duthie sighed, then turned to face Kel. He softened his tone. "I'll see you soon, okay? Promise."

"Will you come and see me at Mummy's?" she said leaning forward, pulling the seatbelt taut. "There's a stable where they're letting me ride one of the horses. It's really pretty. I'm not very good at it yet but–"

"I won't have time to get out the road, Kel," Duthie said. "I'll be busy for a few weeks, but I'll see you when you're back in the city. You'll be back before you know it."

"And then back out there. Then back here again," Kelly said, slumping back in her seat.

He tried a big brotherly grin. "It's fun. It's like you've got two houses now."

Kelly didn't respond immediately. When she did, it was in a whisper, "Why are you and Mummy not talking? Is it because she and Daddy have split up?"

Duthie leaned his cheek against the headrest. Kelly was almost entirely in his blind-spot but he could just make out the wetness of her eyes.

He shrugged.

"Is it because of the letter that arrived a while back?" Kel said.

Duthie imagined a range of responses, but he felt a tug of the promise he'd made his mother. Even now, after everything that had happened, he couldn't bring himself to break it. *"Kel can't know. Not right now."*

He settled for another shrug.

The passenger door opened and Jock held a battered duffle bag. Its contents clanked as Duthie took its weight.

On the pavement he reached up on tiptoes to give Jock a hug. "Thanks Pops," he said, his words compressed by the strength of the Big Man's returning embrace.

"Be good," Jock said. "And if you canna be good…"

"…be good at it," Duthie said.

Kelly curled her fingers in a feeble wave as the car peeled away. Her wee face disappeared behind the rising window.

Duthie headed back down Tillydrone Avenue, mentally trying to shuck off the conversation with his little sister. Then astonishment took over.

The castle loomed down from on top of a knoll. A sign at its base read 'Benholm's Lodge'. He counted the storeys: one, two, three of them. As he walked up the driveway, he could make out the building's form more clearly: a large rectangular body with gabled roof and two diagonally opposed cylindrical towers, both topped with slate turrets. On one tower, poised in a sheltered alcove, was the statue of a man, painted white. He was dressed in formal regalia and, at his feet, sat a faithful canine companion.

The stones of the building were of different colours and shapes: oval, angular, orange, blue-grey. The windows on the ground floor were boarded up, but those higher on the main body and towers were glass. In the daylight, Duthie couldn't tell if any lights were on inside.

His overall feeling was bafflement. He couldn't believe the house was so viewable from the roadside. Hidden in plain sight. When he had found it the previous night, stumbling through the thicket by moonlight, it seemed as if he had discovered a fairy-tale castle, an enchanted tower cut off from the world. But this was no fairy-tale. Castles didn't have names like 'Benholm's Lodge'.

The rear of the house was obscured by trees. After a full loop of the grounds Duthie found the entrance, a wooden door with wrought iron handle and knocker. He approached, held his breath, then rapped the knocker once, twice, three times. He stood back and waited. Nothing happened. No sounds from inside, no footsteps or turning keys. He tried again. Silence.

He sat on the ground and leaned back against the door. He peeled off his patch, but kept the damaged eye closed. The pain was minimal, more the expectation of it than the reality. He pulled out antiseptic cream and cotton pads from his bag and, using his phone as a mirror, treated the wounds.

His reflection was unfamiliar. Even with the swelling going down and the wounds no more than red lines and sutures, the effect was alienating. His face was a collection of parts rather than a whole: apple cheekbones, seeded freckles, almond eyes. As a child people had only seen the orange candy floss hair and vanilla ice cream skin. So it was all he saw too, or maybe he had just willed it so. But now he saw his otherness staring back, the parts of him that were not *ginger* and vanilla. His *Thai-ness*. Some people called it 'exotic', which he understood was meant to be a compliment, but sounded like something you'd say about a foreign cuisine. Either way, it seemed that, as he'd grown older, this reflection was largely what others saw. There was no hiding it. How Kelly hadn't spotted his Thai heritage was anybody's guess. She's still young, he supposed.

He replaced the patch – and an even newer face appeared. *Pirate Red* glared back. New thoughts too. They stretched towards him, reaching out like tangled branches. His sister's face, lost behind the car window. His mother and stepfather locked in battle, little Annie the dog killed in the crossfire. A secret letter arriving from half a world away, bearing sad tidings that Duthie had no idea how to process, so he hid it from everyone else.

The late afternoon sun glinted from a turret above his head.

"Twin turrets", he mouthed.

Twin turrets. Twin turrets. Twin turrets. The mantra helped a little, shielded him from some gnarled branching thoughts, but not all. He got to his feet, faced the door and without hesitation turned the handle. Somehow, he knew that it would give. With a squeal it turned and the door opened inwards. Inside was a small vestibule, an umbrella stand, a dusty pair of boots and an internal door. He tried this smaller handle but it was locked tight. At head height, taped to the door, was a leaflet of some kind. Taped to the leaflet was a rolled cigarette. And taped to the cigarette was a single match.

Duthie laughed. Tired and defeated. He peeled them off the door. With one sharp strike against the stone wall, he lit the match and drew deeply on the cigarette. He coughed, the unexpected taste catching in his throat. He looked at the cigarette with disbelief and more laughter trickled out of him. Morgan had rolled him a joint. A strong one too, from the glorious feeling that was already spreading through his feet. He sat in the doorway and sucked in a few more times. The feeling spread higher, up his legs, torso, arms. Up, up, and away.

He noticed a pyramid of logs half-covered in tarpaulin. Must take a lot of firewood to heat a place like this, he thought. He slid one log out of the pile and tossed it in his hand, alternating between the rough bark on its underside and its smooth golden face. At his feet lay Jock's duffle bag. He unzipped it and searched through his stepdad's clanking collection of chisels, files, rifflers and – what did he call this one? – a rasp. He held up the coarse file, thinking how much damage could be done with this stuff. He threw it back and felt his way down to a penknife. He levered out the strongest blade and began carving into the wood, at first without a plan, just to feel how the metal and wood spoke to each other, and then with purpose, with design. With each stroke a form in his mind revealed itself, unfurled its ragged wings and guided him towards its rendering.

Time disappeared beneath puffs of smoke and falling chips of wood. When he came up for air the sun was tickling the tree canopy, the heat of the day finally giving way. He looked at the creation as if for the first time, turned it in his hand. He chuckled afresh. The sound came freely and danced around the vestibule's stone walls.

He picked up the leaflet that had been taped to the wall. Its bawdy lettering leapt out at him, promising yet more distraction, making clear the next steps of this adventure.

V.

The Green looked sexy by night. Hidden beneath Union Street, occupying the stretch between the high street and the harbour, the old market had a sinister, subterranean appearance. Sinister but exciting. Its bougie cafes and restaurants did little to lessen this effect, especially by nightfall. The Green's shadowy alleyways and Victorian lamps were meant for the night, one could do mischief here and get away with it.

Cheerz revelled in this promise, its pink neon lighting delicious against the cobbles. To say Aberdeen only had one gay bar was perhaps unfair. There had once been more bars, some explicitly rainbow-friendly, others in a more coded way, secret havens for those who knew how to find them. But the city's wider acceptance of the North-East's queers came too late for some of its smaller hideaways. To some extent, things were better back then, or so many a drunken old queen had told Duthie, who always rolled his eyes dutifully.

But mainly it was true: Cheerz was the beginning and end of Aberdeen's gay nightlife. Duthie had avoided Cheerz in the past year, instead seeking sexual kicks elsewhere. He considered his adventures beyond the bar to be a natural graduation towards finding his own spaces to 'be gay'. In all honesty, he'd only journeyed as far as house parties and dating app hookups. Coming back through the rainbow archway of Cheerz, Duthie felt that mixture of resentment and fondness he imagined all people feel when returning home. He checked the duffel bag at the cloakroom – enjoying the attendant's surprise at the bag's weight, its dubious content, and the eye-patched owner – and made his way to the bar.

Alice down the rabbit hole, he chanted. They were all here, the Carrollian cast of characters: the pool-playing lesbians holding cues like staffs; the twirling twinks showing their dance moves without spilling a drop; the heterosexual tourists snatching anxious and occasionally hungry looks; and presiding over it all, the aged queens, perched like sages, tired eyes surveying the Scene. *Off with their heads*, Duthie mused.

A series of squeaks came from the stage at the far end of the room. A drag queen in a huge blonde wig and sequin gown was twisting a balloon into lurid shapes. The crowd delighted in the contorted expressions she made with each twist, ripples of laughter and alarm mounting as the balloons bulged with the threat of bursting.

Duthie approached the bar and curled a finger at a big, meaty man with a thick beard and a nose ring. The bear-man-bar-man squinted. He looked downright intimidating for a second until recognition dawned, at which point his face softened beautifully, grizzly to teddy in zero-point-six seconds.

"Hello stranger," the Bear said.

Duthie remembered how those soft pink lips tasted beneath the bristles.

"Hola."

"Nice look," the Bear grinned, pointing at the patch.

"Thanks," Duthie said, fingers combing through his hair. "Trying something new."

"What brings you back here?"

"Looking for someone," Duthie said, raising an eyebrow.

"Aren't we all," the Bear winked.

"No fair," Duthie pouted. "I can't wink right now."

The Bear reached a meaty hand over the bar and pinched Duthie's cheek.

"Poor wee *ginger* boy," he growled. He grabbed a dish towel and pretended to clean a glass. "So what can I get you, Slick? Something tall? Dark? Winsome?"

"Female," Duthie said in a stage whisper.

"Oh dear."

"And old."

The Bear tutted. "When you said you were trying something new..."

A shriek from the stage pulled their attention away. The drag queen had released a final balloon over the heads of the thirty-or-so onlookers. Shaped like an enormous cock, it hung in the air for a second and then was grabbed by an excited guy and duly popped. Applause and hoots rang out. The drag queen leaned into the mic, thanked the audience and tottered off the stage.

Duthie picked up a leaflet from the counter. It was the same as the one taped to Morgan's door. On it read: *'Cheerz Open Mic. Bring it. Sing it. Wing it.'*

"Thinking of doing a turn on the stage?" the Bear said.

"God no," Duthie replied, horrified at the prospect.

At the end of the bar a pair of women were waiting to be served. One of them, hair blow-dried into dramatic curls, *chapped* her credit card on the surface.

The Bear poured a large rum and coke and passed it to Duthie.

"Oh," Duthie said, searching in his pockets.

"Puppy, please," the Bear laughed. "We both know you've drunk more than you've paid for in this place. Why start now?"

"Bitch," Duthie said then sipped the drink through a tiny straw. "Thanks."

"Welcome home," the Bear said, then prowled in the direction of the *chapping* credit card, calling: "Yes, Daisy Duke, I see you. Patience is a virtue!"

Duthie propped himself up on a stool and took in the Scene, searching once more for the person who had beckoned him here. A mixture of smells drifted around the bar, cologne with a hint of toilet bleach. He breathed it in and wafted his shirt. At least the bar's air-con was working, bringing some relief from the stickiness outside.

On the stage, a young bottle collector placed a tall stool in the centre and lowered the mic stand. He placed a glass, with something looking like whisky in it, at the foot of the stool then walked off. The lights lowered a touch, making the cone of spotlight stand out more brightly.

Clomping slowly up the steps came a tall man wearing a dark suit with broad shoulders and patent leather shoes with bright red spats. He entered the spotlight, picked up the drink and settled on the stool, one foot touching the floor, the other on the footrest. A pencil-thin moustache framed the man's upper lip. His hair, silver as the sea, was slicked back like a wave, cresting at the forehead then rolling back, disappearing behind a high-collared shirt. The man leered at the audience, awaiting silence which, surprisingly, he received. He scanned the crowd and rested his gaze momentarily on Duthie. A familiar smile flickered at the edge of the moustache.

He opened his mouth. The voice was gravelly, full, but not male. It said:

"Once upon a time…"

Part Three
The Maiden Stone

I.

...there was a wee girl who lived in a croft at the foothills of Bennachie. She was as bonnie as the morn, red cheeks, ringlets in her hair. Her name, we shall say, was Margaret. Because it doesn't really matter what her name was, does it? Stories don't *really* need names, just people to move about in them.

Margaret was known far and wide among the people of the Garioch and Gordon for her talent: baking. Butteries, bannocks, and buns, on any given day you could see from far away the smoke rising from the croft's tiny chimney and, from just as far, you could smell the scent of fresh bread carried on the air. 'Oh fit rare. Fit fine,' they would all say, as country folk proclaim when something takes their fancy.

All day long, Margaret would bake for the men-folk in her life, to keep them strong. In particular her father, John, hard at work cutting peat from high up on Mither Tap, the most memorable peak of the Bennachie hills. (Memorable, of course, for its resemblance to a human *breest*. The Mother Tap.)

It was back-breaking work for John, cutting the peat and

pulling it downhill through the moss and bracken, a rough, treacherous pathway for him to tread upon. Each day, standing in the doorway of the croft, Margaret would watch as her father ventured out with the sunrise. She would catch occasional glimpses of him atop the breast-shaped hill, cutting into it, gouging and wrenching. She vowed to put as much effort into her baking, inspired by her father's labour. When her morning baking was done, she would walk half-way up the hill, just clear of the peat moss, where a beautiful juniper tree jutted out of the ground. There she would wait for her father, who at the sun's highest point in the sky would break from his work to join Margaret beneath the tree.

'You're a guid wee lass, Peggy,' her father would say. 'I'm fair blessed tae hiv sic a guid baker as yersel at hame.'

If Margaret had thought about it, she could be offended that her Dad seemed to only value her baking prowess. But characters in stories like Margaret never do think about things like that, so instead she would say: 'Och wheesht, Faither. I'm just deein' my part.'

And they would say no more about it, enjoying the view and their butteries from beneath their juniper tree.

I say Margaret was wee. And she was, physically, but not so young. She was actually fifteen, old enough to be married off. As if smelling her change, mingling with the scent of fresh baking, suitors began to call from all around the Garioch and Gordon – from down the glen, from the nearby villages, even from the other side of Bennachie.

Her father had warned her about hungry boys.

'Only the best fer you, wee Peggy,' he said. And by best, he meant the one with the deepest pockets.

Over the coming months the young lads stopped by one by one. Big and tall ones, short and squat ones, spotty ones and hairy ones. All with the same hunger growling in their bellies.

'Here, this bannock'll see tae yer hunger,' Margaret would say, chucking buns through the gate and clapping the flour from her wee hands. 'Now, awa wi' ye! There's nithin' else for ye here.'

And that would be that. Her would-be suitors would dander down the hill, tails between their legs and mouths full of baking.

If truth be told, if such a thing exists in Story, Margaret didn't know what she was waiting for. Many a hungry lad who stopped by seemed nice enough, fine for marriage, but none had truly taken her fancy. Which seemed to suit her father fine. Beneath their juniper tree, she would tell him of the latest young men who had come by the croft.

'Ah Peggy,' he would sigh. 'When ye know, ye know. Ae day a laddie will stop by and ye'll jist ken he's the een fer you. A nice, rich laddie. Jist remember, dinna gi yersel awa withoot my blessing. Ye hear me, quine?'

'I hear ye, Faither,' Margaret would say, and then they would part ways; she back to her chores, he up the hill to his back-breaking work. And Margaret held to her word. That is, until one morning, when I came calling at her croft.

I wore my finest attire that day. My dark cloak was adorned with a sprig of purple heather. I stood next to the gate, feet hidden by the low stone wall. I called a greeting and she came to her doorway. A buttery rowie, baked to golden perfection, was held in her flour-white hands.

"Can I help ye?" she asked and looked for a time at my face and person. "Ye hiv a look of hunger about you, sir."

"If I do, it's not from an empty belly," I said.

"I see," she said. "Then what do you hunger for?"

"Life," I said.

She looked somewhat befuddled. The golden buttery remained in her grasp.

"My name is Clove," I continued. "What is yours? I have heard many a tale of the Peat Cutter's daughter and her baking, but I have never heard a name."

She looked surprised. Perhaps because nobody had cared to ask such a question.

"Margaret," she said.

We spoke for some time as country-folk do, of the weather, the turning of the seasons, the coming and going of birds high in the sky. With each new topic Margaret took a step closer to me. In time she was in front of me, only the stone wall between us. The sun was reaching its highest point.

"I must awa, Clove," she said, looking up the hill towards her juniper tree.

I asked if I might come by another day to talk some more. "I've so enjoyed getting to know you, Margaret."

She nodded and offered me the buttery in her hand.

"Thank you," I said. "Would it offend if I shared your baking with the birds? For they have hunger far greater than my own."

She said it wouldn't, adding that her father told her it was a fine thing to share one's wealth with others.

I came by Margaret's croft many more times that summer. I would call to her from behind the wall and she would come. We would talk until the sun reached its peak, and sometimes we would walk together, our feet brushing through the long grass. The Wheel of the Year turned beneath our courtship, from

Beltane to Litha and beyond until, on the eve of Lughnasadh – the first day of harvest – it was time for me to feed.

"Will you marry me, Margaret?" I said.

She looked at me, then up to the hill. When her eyes returned, they were troubled.

"I cannot marry ye, Clove," she sighed. "My faither, he needs me. His days are hard, carrying the peat from Mither Tap."

"Am I not enough, Margaret?" I asked. "Fair? Healthy? Wealthy?"

"Aye, ye are. And that would please Faither well. But it is not riches he needs, though he may believe it."

"I understand," I said. "What if I were to build a golden pathway from the top of Mither Tap all the way down to your croft, so that your father could more easily go about his labour? Then would you marry me?"

She laughed and shook her ringleted hair. "A golden path, aye? You have a strange humour about ye, Clove. Aye, if you build the path I'll marry ye."

That night I came once more to the croft at the foothills of Bennachie, but this time I did not wait at the gate. I came to the doorway and called to Margaret. Her look of surprise greeted me. Behind her, a dinner table was freshly laid.

"Forgive my unannounced arrival, Margaret, but if we are to be married, it would only be proper to meet your father first. Will you invite me in?"

"Yes, of course," she said with breath, I do believe, that was taken away.

John the Peat Cutter rose from his seat and shook my gloved hand. He considered my face and my fine clothes, just as his daughter had when first we met. The promise of riches upon me was met with a glint of approval in the old man's eye. His hunger was clear to me.

"Ye'll sup wi' us, will ye nae?" he said.

"Very kind," said I.

There's many a slip twixt cup and lip, they say. But what of spoon and bowl? Upon the old man's last sip of his daughter's thin soup, he missed his mark and the spoon fell to the floor. I smiled at what was to come. For when John bent to collect the spoon and witnessed my feet, he sprang back from the table.

"Hooves!" he cried, looking at Margaret. "Yon mannie has hooves, reed the colour o' blood! I ken fa ye are, ye scoundrel. Ye're Cloven Hoddie. Laird o' Hel! Git awa fae my hoose and daughter. Git awa!"

"I'm afraid not, Peat Cutter," I said. "Your daughter and I are to be wed."

The old man looked at his daughter in disbelief and horror.

Margaret wailed. "Och Faither. I didna know. I promise! But wait, Clove, your proposal was in jest, wis it nae? You said you would build a golden path from Mither Tap to our door."

"No jest did I make," I said. "But I'm a fair Deil. Tomorrow at the rise of the sun, I shall begin building your golden path. If you can bake one hundred buttery rowies before I complete my task, I shall leave you be. But if you fail, you are mine for ever."

And so it was that, come the first shining threads of morn, Margaret and I began the race for her hand and soul. I laid a slab for every buttery baked, the first atop the very nipple of Mither Tap, and continuing down its softly-domed slope. I imagined the sweat on wee Margaret's brow, the fire in her heart as full and roaring as her oven. I arrived at her door, laying the hundredth slab mere moments before the final buttery emerged from the fire.

"No!" she cried.

"Please, sir. Ye canna tak her," the Peat Cutter moaned.

"But wait!" Margaret said, hope flickering in her eyes. "Ye said the path would be golden. Yon path is as broon as the very earth it is laid upon."

I waited silently, letting father and daughter witness my satisfaction. The sun reached its highest point in the sky and bathed the hill in its golden rays, reflected in the freshly laid pathway, burning a golden trail from peak to croft.

The Peat Cutter fell to his knees in despair. Margaret, however, found strength in her feet and ran out the door, through the gate and up the path towards her juniper tree.

She didn't make it far. My blood-red hooves, for all their unsightliness, are swift. I reached her right shoulder and held her in place.

She tried to move, but my spell was already taking effect, her legs turning to stone. With a wrench she turned and a piece of her stony shoulder came free in my hand. I tossed it far away and watched as Margaret's fine features and ringlets greyed and hardened.

She was mine for ever.

My Maiden Stone.

II.

Nobody clapped when the storyteller finished. They had been quiet all the way through the tale, but it wasn't an awed-silence; it was an impatient one punctuated by whispers and giggles in the darkness. The stool squeaked as the moustachioed storyteller moved it aside. She scanned the crowd once more, her expression, as it had been the entire story, was one of great satisfaction. Mission apparently accomplished, the storyteller clomped out of the spotlight, her bright red spats disappearing behind a door at the edge of the stage.

The young bottle collector slouched up to the mic and cleared his throat.

"Let's hear it for The Morgan. Another, uh, interesting performance."

A few slow claps. The bottle collector beaconed frantically to a corner of the room. The *click-clack* of high heels soon travelled up the centre of the room towards the stage.

"Did someone say they wanted more balloon tricks?" shouted the drag queen from earlier. The audience erupted with gratitude. Music and hilarity filled the room once more.

Duthie sipped at his rum and coke. Morgan's performance swilled through his mind. It had been a surreal moment. She was a drag king? At times it felt as if he was the only true audience member in the room. Where had she disappeared to, anyway?

Before he could ruminate further, he became aware of a pair of eyes from across the room, dimly at first, then unmistakable – they were looking directly at him. They were cat-like eyes, accompanied all of a sudden by a generous grin. In the half-light they seemed to float, the shape of their owner coalescing slowly as they approached, sliding through the crowd towards the bar.

"Hello," said Abe.

"Hi there," Duthie said. "Wow. What are…what're you doing here?"

Abe's smile broadened. All signs of long-distance travel were washed away. He was freshly shaven and the colourful patterned top he had been wearing on the university lawn was replaced by a simple shirt. However, the air of ease he had worn – or was it aloofness – was exactly the same.

"I'm here to see the sights," he said.

"And this place was at the top of your list?"

"Is this not a good place to have come?"

"No. I mean, yes…I…sorry I'm just a little…" Duthie fumbled, surprised at the squeak that had crept into his voice.

Abe seemed amused by the sound. He said: "I was talking to one of the Youth Team members."

"The pink kids?"

"Ha! Yes, one of the pink kids. They kindly checked me into my room at Hillhead. I asked where was good to go in Aberdeen at night, and they recommended here."

"They just happened to suggest here?"

"Of course," Abe chuckled then leaned in conspiratorially. As he whispered, his jaw brushed Duthie's cheek. "I believe this is a place for homosexuals."

He pulled away and glanced pointedly at the rainbow flags and neon all around. He mouthed: "I think this is the right place."

Duthie laughed. How had he missed the signs? "Well then, welcome! Can I get you a drink?"

"If you mean alcohol, no thank you," Abe said.

"I'm sure they have something milder." He caught the Bear's eye: "Can I please order a drink for my friend? I promise I'll pay this time."

"Wonders never cease," the Bear said with a smirk. "What'll it be for…"

"This is Abe," Duthie said. "He's here all the way from Uganda to perform in the International Festival. I'm his…um…"

"Courier," Abe said, reaching across the bar to shake the Bear's hand.

"Yeah, that's right," Duthie said, adding with a comedic flex: "I'm his courier. No need to brag about it but I'm kinda a big deal these days."

"And what, pray tell, does a courier do?" The Bear said.

"Y'know," said Duthie. "Couriers?"

The Bear looked at Abe. "God help you with this one."

"I'm in good hands," Abe replied without missing a beat.

"You are indeed. He's surprisingly decent in bed," the Bear said with complete nonchalance. "Great sense of timing."

Duthie tried to send him the stinkiest of looks, but undermined his efforts completely by wrestling a grin. Abe smiled pleasantly as if he'd been told he simply must try the Chef's special. He was either oblivious to – or totally unfazed by – this kind of chat. *Curiouser and curiouser.*

"So what can I get you, Oh Traveller to our fair Granite City?" said the Bear.

"Get him one of those," Duthie said, pointing towards a glass-fronted fridge.

The Bear brought over a bottle of something bright orange and poured it into a glass where it fizzed with an aggressive intensity. He handed it to Abe and said in a grand tone: "I present to you: The Elixir of Scotland."

Abe took a deep glug of the Irn-Bru. The Bear stole a wink at Duthie, nodded towards Abe and made *kissy* lips. Duthie rolled his eyes, but felt his smile widen.

Thirst quenched, Abe met Duthie and the Bear's expectant faces with a look of confusion.

"And?" Duthie said.

"The drink's nice?" Abe said. "Thank you?"

"Well, I hate to disappoint, pal," said the Bear, "but that drink's as good as it gets in this country."

Over the following hour Duthie commenced his duties as courier with gusto. He gave Abe a tour of the bar's key spots: the corner he'd first puked in after too much Blue WKD; the stairwell he'd had his first sexual dalliance on; the upstairs nightclub where he'd regularly lost himself, through drink and poppers. Abe maintained the same gentle smile through each tale. His moves on the dance floor were similarly smooth; shoulders grinding together and apart, feet tapping in and out of a small invisible circle on the ground. He was rhythmic and measured in his motion with no waste of energy. All the while he continued to sip on his orange fizz and took regular looks at the surroundings.

Duthie on the other hand was beginning to sweat. He opened a further button of his shirt, letting it gape wide. He quickly learned that some of his wilder moves could elicit a smile from Abe, so he peppered the performance accordingly. He found it to be a lovely sight, Abe's smile, and enjoyed the game of teasing it out.

He had almost completely forgotten why he'd come to Cheerz in the first place, had become so close to losing himself, but on a particularly wide twirl he spotted a familiar face in a booth at the back of the room. The events of the past few days came tumbling back to mind.

"I'm just going to say hi to someone," Duthie said to Abe over the music. Abe nodded and carried on dancing.

Duthie pushed through the crowded dance floor. The drinks

he'd scrounged were hitting pretty hard on his empty stomach, but they emboldened his stride. He reached the booth and sat down, throwing one leg over the other.

"I liked your story," he said.

Morgan was dappled in the disco ball's light. She rested an arm over the back of the booth, her knees spread wide, neck tie loosened just so. The once-slicked back fringe fell in a kiss-curl over her brow. The edge of the pencilled-on moustache was sharp. "Well that makes one," she said.

"They were listening. Just maybe not the vibe they were looking for."

"Never is, Red."

"Sad about it?"

She puffed out her chest. "I'm fabulously unpopular round these parts."

"Oh?"

"Aye. Never really know what to do with me, this lot."

"Maybe if you told a dirty limerick. Or a naughty poem. Or, y'know, something more current than a centuries-old Scottish folktale?"

She flashed him a look of disgust then gazed back out at the crowd.

"You've heard it before?" she said.

"The Maiden Stone? A version of it. In the one I heard she was engaged to a local boy. A real sweet guy. He had to race the Devil back to her home, but the Devil won. Same ending."

She upturned her mouth like a New York gangster and shrugged.

Duthie continued: "I've never seen the real thing, though. The stone."

"Never?" Real surprise seemed to bloom on her face.

"I know. Terrible."

"Weel," she said, her accent thickening, "she's nae awa tae sproot wings and flee aff onytime soon, Red. I'm sure ye'll get yir chunce to look upon her stony face."

Duthie let his gaze linger on Morgan a while. Had the toothpick been in the corner of her mouth when he had sat down?

He sighed. "So what is all this?"

"What?"

"This. I mean, what are you? Some kind of sleep-walking-in-the-woods, living-in-a-castle, dog-shit-pranking, leaving-me-cryptic-messages-and-doobies-on-your-front-door, story-telling-drag-king?"

"Too much for a business card really, isn't it?" she said.

Her continued chicanery should have pissed Duthie off, but for some reason he found the humour in it. Or maybe he'd given in to it. Maybe it was exhaustion at the twisty-turny day he'd just lived through. Or some deeper acceptance of the pawn-like, unquestioning role Morgan seemed to have cast him in, like Margaret and her Devil. Maybe it was just the booze.

"How's the eye," she said.

"Itchy. The sweat isn't helping," Duthie said, tugging at the elastic band that stretched around the back of his head. The hair beneath was damp.

"You'll be fine. Bit of time it'll be good as new. You'll be seeing the world with a new eye."

"Cheers to that," he said, clinking an imaginary glass against her equally-empty fist.

"In the meantime, you're in good company," she said.

"Eh?"

"Horus, Manasa, Tiresias, Höðr. All of that mythological lot lost their eyesight."

"Often just one eye too," Duthie recited, the words coming to him in a ghostly recollection. "You're the second person to tell me that today."

"Really? How strange," she said without expression, then looked up at an approaching figure. "And who's this?"

Abe held out his hand and introduced himself.

"A pleasure," Morgan said.

"Oh no, the pleasure is all mine," Abe said. "I very much enjoyed your tale."

"Well that makes two," she said, nudging Duthie.

He looked up at Abe's face and enjoyed the view. "He's a storyteller too."

"Interesting," Morgan said. "And that accent, I'm nae an expert but I would guess...Ugandan?"

"Very good," Abe smiled. "Your story reminded me of a few Bagandan tales from home. It shared some similarities of structure and message."

Duthie had no idea what *Bagandan* meant but liked the way Abe said it with such fondness.

"Ah," Morgan said, placing stretched hands behind her head. "Scratch an old folktale and you'll find the miles it's travelled."

"I agree. Do you have many tales like this one here in Aberdeen?"

"We do indeed. Tales of trickery. Tales of greed. Tales of lust. Tales of need." She patted the space on the banquette next to her which he duly filled.

"You remind me of the Elder who taught me. You don't mind being compared to someone old, I hope?"

"Wouldn't be much use if I did," Morgan said. "So tell me, you'll be performing some of your stories here for the International Festival?"

"How did you know?"

"Ah laddie, there have been many like you who have come before. Travelling from far and wide to our wee pocket of the world from far and wide to share their artistic wares."

"Of course. And I'm happy to follow in their footsteps," he said.

He paused then chuckled. Morgan tilted her head in question.

"Nothing," Abe said. "Just something my Elder used to say to me. *Ettuufu ligwa wala*. An old Luganda phrase. It means 'What is good is always far away'."

"True," Morgan said and patted Abe's shoulder. Her eyes softened in a way Duthie hadn't seen before. "I hope we're far enough for you, lad."

Abe seemed taken aback for a moment. She patted his leg and he seemed comforted. "I do too," he said.

The pair carried on talking this way, in gentle communion, for some time, trading epigrams and ancient words of wisdom. Abe was a natural, he seemed to fall so easily into Morgan's enigmatic way of speaking. Morgan appeared to welcome him as an equal, she wasn't just throwing riddles his way, didn't seem merely amused by his presence, she was actually listening.

Duthie felt himself melting into the background. An initial curiosity in this new side of Morgan slowly turned sour. The more the pair leaned into their bond, the more it irked him. He protested with a wide-mouthed yawn.

"Shall we go, my friend?" came Abe's voice.

"Only if you're ready," Duthie said. "You must be exhausted after travelling so far."

"I am. Though your orange soda is keeping the worst of it away."

"Come awa, the pair o' ye," Morgan said, slapping their thighs. "My car's out front. I'll gie you a lift home."

She strode ahead, her gait morphing into something more languid and masculine with each step.

III.

The old Volvo trundled up to the turning circle. Despite the lateness, Hillhead was practically buzzing compared to the silence of the previous night. People were dotting to and fro between residential blocks, others were emerging from the main building with a few-drinks-down sheen on their cheeks.

"Looks like the festival's ready to begin," Morgan said.

"Looks like it," Abe said, getting out of the car. "Thank you for the lift, Morgan. It was lovely to meet you."

"Couldn't agree more," she said.

He stepped towards the main building and began introducing himself to fellow artists.

Duthie leaned into the driver-side window.

"I have a feeling he's one of those 'makes friends wherever he goes' kind of guys," he said.

"Aye," Morgan said.

Duthie reached into the duffle bag and pulled out the wooden carving he'd made that afternoon outside Morgan's tower.

He handed it through the window. "I made you something."

Morgan turned it in her hands, inspecting the sharp features. She placed the pad of her finger on its beak and along the spiky ridge of feathers. She didn't say anything, but Duthie thought it met her approval because for the merest of seconds her expression softened as it had with Abe.

"Can I have my lighter back," Duthie said.

Murders of crow's feet formed at the edges of her eyes. "I've got something you need much more than that."

"It's my lighter," he said, tiring of the cat and mouse.

She jutted her chin towards Abe. "You and your man there. You'll be travelling all around the North-East, will ye nae?"

"Suppose so," Duthie said. Yet another logistic of the couriership that he hadn't realised. "Why?"

She reached out the window and patted the door panel of the Volvo. "She's yours if you need her. She's a bit old and *crabbit*, but she'll get you where you need to be."

Duthie searched for a witty response but failed to find one. "That's actually very nice of you."

"Just stop by my *hoosie* when you need her."

"*Hoosie*? It's a castle, Morgan."

"A lodge, technically," she said, pinching finger and thumb to diminish the concept.

"*Benholm's* Lodge," Duthie said, remembering the sign. "Morgan Benholm?"

"At yer service," she said.

From this vantage point Duthie could make out capillaries breaking up the whites of Morgan's eyes, the deep shades of her sockets. He felt a fondness towards the woman at the sight, as if finally excavating something real beneath the sardonic exterior.

"Your moustache is rubbing off," he said.

She felt along her top lip. "Aye, the spell's waning."

"So I can't have my lighter?"

"Have you even thought of a cigarette all night?"

He searched inwardly for the familiar pull, only to find it buried deep.

Morgan cast her eyes across the turning circle towards Abe. He was shaking hands with a small group of Asian-looking people.

"You see?" Morgan said. "You've had something far more enticing in your midst."

"Don't know what you're talking about," Duthie said with a grin, but his words were drowned out by the thrum of the car as it turned away into the night.

Duthie walked up to Abe and the small group. He was laughing at a joke made by one of them, a man with jet black hair. Duthie recognised him immediately as South East Asian, possibly even Thai.

"Ah, and this is my courier," Abe said, patting Duthie's shoulder. "Rune Duthie."

"Rune?" the man said.

"Duthie's fine," Duthie said, shaking his hand.

"Kit," he said then gestured to the two women beside him. "And these are my friends Naowarat and Anchalee."

Duthie tried repeating their names but fumbled, immediately feeling hot in the face. The women graciously waved it away, though he noticed one of them – Naowarat, maybe? – staring at his eye patch.

"We're going to The Moon," Kit said, pointing to the main building.

"Sorry?" said Duthie.

"The bar on campus, my friend," Abe said. "You really haven't read your welcome pack, have you?"

"Not a single page, dude," Duthie said. "I'm up for a nightcap if you are?"

Abe replied more quietly: "I think I have a different idea."

Duthie felt a tingle in his stomach that rippled downwards.

"Sounds good," he said, suppressing a smile. He turned to Kit and said: "Maybe another night? It's pretty late."

"Of course," said Kit, who was already stepping towards the main doors. "*Fan dii na*."

"Eh?" Duthie said.

"I said 'good night'," Kit chuckled.

"Oh. G'night" Duthie said. He knew Kit was just being friendly, but he couldn't escape feeling like an imposter.

He looked at Abe who, once again, was taking in his surroundings with an unreadable expression.

"So," Duthie said, poking Abe's foot with his own. He felt his pulse quicken in his throat. "Your place or mine?"

Abe laughed but continued to look around. Duthie took it as a hint to begin heading towards Esslemont House. He felt a thrill when Abe followed.

"Must feel strange, being so far away from home," Duthie said.

"Mmm," Abe smiled.

"First time away?"

"Outside of Africa, yes."

"Is it what you expected?"

"I don't know. Warmer than I expected, maybe."

"Don't get used to it. This isn't normal for us."

The moon was high. It cast a silver glow over Abe's features, his strong jaw, kind eyes, soft lips.

Duthie said: "You know, when we met this afternoon, I didn't realise you were…y'know."

Abe's eyebrows scrunched together.

"Gay," Duthie said. The word felt electric on his tongue.

"Ah," Abe said and looked up at the moon.

Duthie couldn't read Abe's silence, wasn't able to tell if it was awkward or simply the end of the conversation.

"I think I always knew," Duthie said. "About me, I mean. Guys just always did it for me. How about you?"

Abe blinked, eyes still up high. "I accepted it as my story a long time ago."

"I like the sound of that," Duthie said. "'My story'."

The entrance to Esslemont House was shaded from the moonlight. Some bedroom lights were on higher up in the block, but the ground floor seemed as dark as it had been the past few nights. Duthie led Abe to the main door.

"Well," he said.

Abe met his gaze. His expression remained still, but his eyes examined Duthie. Each place they rested felt like a kiss. A jingle pierced the silence. Abe had a keyring in his hand and fed a key into the lock. The door opened and Abe stepped through, holding it for Duthie to follow.

"Coming?" Abe said.

Duthie stood in confusion, then felt the outline of his own keys in his pocket. He followed Abe through the vestibule and across to Flat 3. The crunch of another key turning.

"What the–?" Duthie began, but Abe placed a finger on his lips.

The pair entered the flat's central corridor and closed the front door behind them.

"You're staying here?" Duthie whispered.

"Yes," Abe said, a hiss of laughter escaping his teeth. "I thought you knew?"

"I…" Duthie said, turning his palms ceilingward.

"A few of us moved in this afternoon. This is your room?" Abe said, pointing at the first door on the left.

Duthie, still stunned, nodded.

"We're neighbours," Abe said, pointing at the door next to it. He grinned. "Okay then. Goodnight, neighbour."

Before Duthie could say anything more Abe had disappeared into his room, closing the door softly behind him. Duthie stood in the corridor, dumbfounded, casting around the darkness for a witness to this turn of events. He breathed out in exasperation and shook his head. He entered his own room and flipped on the bedside light. The rucksack thudded and the duffle bag clanked as he chucked them down. He batted a pair of socks off his bed and lay down.

He could hear Abe's movements through the thin walls, the sound of his feet up the corridor towards the bathroom and the sound of their return a few minutes later. Duthie waited, staring at the ceiling, hoping for a small knock at the door. But it never came. The flicker of hope extinguished with the sound of a light switch clicking off.

The pulse in Duthie's neck was subsiding but the sensation in his crotch was unabated, the initial tingle now a throb. He shuffled out of his clothes, intending to break the pressure the old-fashioned way. He even removed his underpants and took himself in hand, but within a few strokes he knew it wasn't going to happen, it felt teenage and cheap. His tension deflated into a worm of disappointment.

His eye twinged, a reminder of his need to care better for it. He unzipped the backpack, took out the antiseptic cream and gauze, then set about cleaning the scratches. On the way back to bed he spotted the hardback book inside the bag. He took it out and propped himself up in bed.

He ran a thumb over the spine, and along the golden writing, as he had in the Professor's office. 'The Picts: A Forgotten People? Dr Mary Seaton'.

He opened the cover and took in the book's scent. It was surprisingly fresh considering the 1986 print date. He flipped past the contents page to the introduction.

'*A Celtic people. A painted people. A tribal people.* Through the centuries, Picts have been named many things, their description ever rendered by those on the outside.

A fearsome people, so named by the Romans who they fought on the foothills of Mons Graupius, with faces painted blue and weapons raised high.

A heathen people, so named and treated by the Christian missionaries who sought to convert them from their pagan ways.

'We academics have continued in this naming tradition, bestowing the Picts with labels such as *a mayfly people* and *a silent people*: the former on account of their being a tribal confederation of Celtic people who appeared in 300AD and disappeared a mere six centuries later; the latter for having no written language with which to scribe their mark on history's page – beyond, of course, their inscriptions on stone.

'Having a taste for naming, we academics have continued with gay abandon. *A lost people*. What do we mean by this title, so laden with ennui and tragedy? I for one find it ill-fitting. The Pictish stones which still stand today

– their arrangement across the north and east of Scotland delineating the footprint of Pictavia, their rocky faces still carrying the carved marks of their artistry – are testament to this people having never been lost. On the contrary, they knew precisely where they stood.

'*A forgotten people?* On the face of it, surely not. Do we not still write and talk about the Picts today? Although, this title is perhaps accurate from an alternative viewpoint: for what is memory, when describing the duration of an entire people? If the only remnants of a civilisation are etchings in stone, their meanings as enigmatic as a language with no apparent alphabet, can we consider those people 'forgotten'?

'Current thinking would have the Picts suddenly disappear in 900AD, a chasm across which no single Painted Person stepped. I stand in opposition to this narrative, due to many years studying the artefacts of the Picts, delving first-hand through historical accounts of them, and getting my fingernails crammed with dirt on archaeological digs. In the course of this book, I argue that they did not suddenly disappear, ripped from history and memory alike, by some unknown cataclysmic event. The reality was far less dramatic, but no less fascinating: a blurring of the boundaries, rather than a rending of them. The kingdom of Pictavia blended with the Gaels of Dál Riata, ultimately becoming one with them, trading their independence for threads within the wider tapestry of an emerging nation. No longer Picts, but Scots.

'I ask again: are the Picts a forgotten people? To some extent, yes. In so far as their culture, their rites and rituals, their very identity blended into their surroundings. But I believe that, in doing so, these proud people, these fearless people, these mysterious people, joined the wider fabric of Scotland, and gained a form of immortality in our collective memory.

'In this book I shall...'

Duthie felt his naked skin prickle at Mary Seaton's words. They sounded like a rallying cry, he imagined them being spoken aloud atop a hill, met with hollers of approval from a crowd of people with blue designs painted on their faces. He flipped to the back cover, hoping to find a photograph of the author but didn't find one there. He thumbed backwards, the book naturally splaying open at glossy pages with black and white images printed on them. An array of grey stone slabs was displayed, each marked with etchings, some offering clear illustration, others too weathered to make out. In the carvings he could discern people in combat, some on horseback, others on foot. One soldier was having his eyes pecked by a raven.

The names of the stones leapt out: the Aberlemno Stone, the Picardy symbol stone, the Rhynie Man, the Dunnichen Stone. The academic descriptions of the symbols also caught his eye: *triple discs and cross-bars, double disks notched with Z-rods, crescents and V-rods, arches, flowers, wolves, bulls and deer.*

What was it about the Picts that held his fascination so firmly? Even now, he couldn't exactly express it. But he knew Mary shared it.

Here on a page of its own was a familiar stone. Tall, slender and rectangular with symbols inscribed on its surface: a centaur below three faded figures, a rectangle and Z-rod, a mirror and comb, and directly above it a Pictish beast with smooth features and a wild eye. The stone was complete except for a notch on its right shoulder.

It was the Maiden Stone. Duthie read the extended caption, once again conjuring Mary Seaton's voice in his mind, imagining she would have sounded energised, passionate, awed:

> 'When I discovered the missing shard of the Maiden Stone, it was a wet and windy day. My fellow archaeologists had fled, seeking refuge in the tent, but I was barely aware of the rain. It was as if I knew to persevere. When my fingers and brush finally met its smooth surface, I have no shame in saying, I wept. For here was a piece of the puzzle. A forgotten chunk of the past, pulled from the depths of memory, back into the world.'

Duthie turned the page and saw the shard. It was long, triangular and slim with smooth edges and a face unmarked by carvings. He flipped back and forth, looking at the notch in the Maiden Stone's right shoulder, and imagined the shard slotting into place. It didn't seem nearly big enough to fill the gap.

He removed his eye patch to take a closer look. Carefully, he blinked open the lid. The binocular vision disorientated him at first, his covered iris strained against the meagre lamplight, but in time the page came into focus. He felt his eye beginning to water, but held it on the image of the stone as long as he could bear.

There, a slight crease in the notch. That's where the shard would fit, he could see it now. It wouldn't fill the whole crevice, but it could complete the picture of the centaur's hoof. He inspected the picture of the shard once again, a thick tear now running down his cheek. He searched its smooth face but couldn't see any markings, the image too grainy to tell for sure. But the shape was unmistakable, he could hold it in his mind, rotate it and place it in the stone's notch, guiding it home.

He returned to the opening section but stopped himself before turning down the corner to mark his place. The book was too precious for such casual misuse. He searched for a suitable bookmark, a scrap of card, a tissue, but nothing seemed appropriate. Only the letter on the bedside table seemed right. He had read the letter each night at Esslemont, and each night before that for two weeks, ever since it had arrived in the post at Northfield Place.

Perhaps just the envelope would do as a bookmark? Its cellophane window crinkled as he lifted it, but the red stamp and typed address exuded a bureaucratic coolness.

No, it would have to be the letter itself.

He slid the letter out. The top section splayed open, revealing the first few words...

Attn: Mr Rune Duthie, Mrs Jacqueline Duthie

This letter is to inform you of....

But for the first time, Duthie didn't feel the need to read it. Had he finally read it enough? Or was there simply no longer need – its exact words transferred from the page and permanently imprinted on his mind? He pressed the letter flat, placed it in Mary Seaton's book and closed the cover.

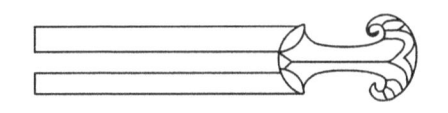

Part Four
The Dreaming Prophetess Fedelm

I.

The shower came in fits and starts then settled into a lukewarm gush. The tiled cubicle was separated from the rest of the bathroom by a curtain but, no matter how Duthie tried, he couldn't position the mildewed thing in a way that covered the entrance fully. Through the gap he could make out the row of sinks on the opposite wall. They stared back in horror with stainless steel eyes and cracked porcelain mouths.

On the way to the bathroom, he had noted Abe's baritone voice in conversation with others, maybe as many as three, in the kitchen. Clearly Duthie was no longer alone in Flat 3, Esslemont House. The lack of locks on the bathroom door should have bothered him, but it didn't. He imagined Abe coming in and seeing his nakedness through the gap in the curtain. He would peel it back and join him.

Laughter issued once more from the kitchen. He turned the shower dial from gush to permanent drip, wrapped a towel around his waist and pulled back the curtain.

He found himself eye to eye with Fedelm Seaton.

"Jesus!" he shouted.

Her flash of surprise was swiftly replaced with a smirk.

"Not quite," she said. She was also wrapped in a towel. She had a bottle of shampoo in one hand and a loofah in the other.

"Uh hi Fedelm," he said, squinting with his sore eye closed.

"Try again," she said, seeming to enjoy his discomfort.

"Eddie."

"Bingo. Done in there?"

She stepped aside so Duthie could get out of the cubicle. He skidded but managed to stay upright.

"Whoa there! Whatever happens, hold on to that towel, buddy."

She scanned his whole body, from feet upwards. He was sure it was to increase his humiliation, but on the contrary, it emboldened him. He liked being looked at, even by the likes of the Professor's snarky daughter. He considered dropping the towel to see if he could shock the smirk off her face.

Her scan ended on his damaged eye. "That looks painful."

"It's getting better," he said, reaching for the eyepatch and stretching the elastic round his head. "So, you're living here too, then?"

"Looks like it," she said, raising up her shampoo and loofah. "I spotted you had a flat all to yourself and we needed some rooms. Handy, you dropping by the office, really."

"Meant to be," Duthie said, willing some gravity into his voice. "But I'm sure you could've had your choice of any flats. Big manager, and all that. Slumming it in Esslemont House?"

The steel in her eyes wavered. "Yeah well, one of the group leaders needed an en suite so..." She stepped into the cubicle and pulled the mouldy curtain across the entrance. She pulled it to the left, only to have the right side gape, pulled it to the right and the left side wafted open. Duthie did nothing to suppress his smile.

"Gonna stand and watch?" Eddie said, fixing him with a glare from between the gap. She then whipped off her towel, giving Duthie a slice of naked flesh. He pivoted away, embarrassment blooming up his neck in a hot wave. He swore he could hear Eddie chuckle over the hiss of shower water.

Across the hall, laughter was still ringing from the kitchen. Duthie was met by the sight of Abe holding court with three people: a woman with chocolate brown skin and a halo of curly hair streaked with grey was sitting on the kitchen counter; beside her perched a sleepy-looking guy, with a generous belly peeking out from under his t-shirt; and, leaning awkwardly against the stove, was a tall blond man. Abe seemed to be finishing a story about his journey to Scotland and his difficulty understanding the Customs officers in Aberdeen airport.

"...was a crash course in the accent," he said. The group laughed in response.

The sleepy guy on the counter said, "Tell me about it. I'm only from Glasgow and I cannae understand hauf of whit they say up here."

The woman tilted her head to the doorway and beamed at Duthie, "Hello."

Abe jumped in, "Ah good morning, my friend. Everyone, this is Rune."

"Duthie," Duthie said with a wave to the room. "They could really do with a table in here, huh?"

"None of the Esslemont kitchens have tables," said the woman, shaking her head.

Abe touched Duthie's bare shoulder and motioned round the room.

"These are our flatmates. Celia," he said, holding an open hand towards the woman. "She is the courier for an entire orchestra that just arrived from China."

"Wow," Duthie said. "Guess I got it easy with just one person to look after."

Celia brushed the comment off. She spoke with a Latin accent, but some words came out pure Aberdonian. "It's nae bother. When you've couriered at the festival as long as I have, it's 'the more the merrier'."

"And this is Fraser," Abe continued. "He is the conductor of... now hold on...*Kale More?*"

"Pretty much bang on, pal, though it's more of a *Keel*," Fraser said. He turned to Duthie and spelled out 'Ceòl Mòr'. "It means 'the great music' in Gaelic. We're basically a trad Scots band that does modern music."

"I can't wait to hear it," Abe said then carried on along the line. "This is Georgiy. He is the leader of a Ukrainian culture group. I'm sorry, my friend, I will need to practice its name."

The tall blond guy shook his head: "No worries, man. It's the Svyatkuvannya Culture Group."

Georgiy's accent was not at all what Duthie expected. As if reading his confusion, he said: "We're *Canadian*-Ukrainian."

"Oh right, cool," Duthie said.

"And we have one more flatmate who just headed to her room. She is called Vlada, and she's the dance captain of *Rusalka*, a group from Slovakia."

He looked to Celia for confirmation, who said: "Full marks, Abe. I'm very impressed."

She switched to Duthie and scrunched her nose. "Did that hurt?"

Duthie touched the eye patch. "Did. Not so much any more."

"No, I mean the piercing," she said, pointing to his chest.

He looked down at the steel bar with balls screwed at either end that framed his nipple.

"Ah right," he laughed. "A bit. To be honest, I always forget I had it done. Thought it was dead cool at the time. Very 'art student'. Everyone else with them has probably taken them out by now."

"Art student?" Celia said, looking impressed.

Duthie shrugged, aiming for nonchalant but feeling a little twist inside at the moniker.

"Well, I like it," Celia continued. "It's super sexy. Maybe I should get my nipples done, then I could blind people when the light bounces off them. The Venezuelan Vigilante! Pow! Pow!"

She jerked from side to side, as if firing bullets from her sizeable bosom, then let out a glorious laugh.

"So much noise," said a silky voice behind Duthie. It belonged to a young woman with a willowy frame and poker-straight hair that hung below her shoulders.

"Vlada?" Duthie said, holding out a hand which she took in a bony grasp. "I'm Duthie."

"Pleasure," she said in a manner that was neither pleased nor displeased. Her fingers walked a little dance in the air. "Are you not going?"

Celia looked at her watch and hopped off the counter. "Shit, yes. Eddie will kick our *bumbuns* if we're late for the first meeting."

"Correct!" Eddie called from the corridor. She was already

dressed, damp hair scraped back in a severe ponytail. "Chop chop, people."

"You're gonna need some clothes," Celia said to Duthie on her way past. "S'later everyone."

"They're not coming?" Duthie asked.

"Couriers only," Celia said.

Duthie looked at Abe. "You'll be okay without me?"

"*Musajja gyagenda-gyasanga banne*," Abe said, clapping his hands then opening them towards Georgiy, Vlada and Fraser. "'A man finds friends wherever he goes.'"

"I like this one, can we keep him?" Celia patted Abe's cheek, then turned to Duthie. "You're gonna need his positivity when the festival takes over your life."

"Can't be that bad," Duthie said.

"Buckle up, *mi amore*," she cackled.

II.

The following two days hit like a wave. At first gentle and lapping, covering only the ankles of Duthie's consciousness. But the more he became aware of the festival, its churn of characters and cultures, the greater he felt its force. The further he waded into its depths, the more powerfully it slapped, eventually sweeping him in its current.

He barely registered the people at first, absorbed as he was in his sketch pad or the words of Dr Mary Seaton's book, but then, quite despite himself, he started to notice them. There were one-hundred-and-fifty performers at the festival, he was told in his first courier meeting. He could well believe it, for they were everywhere he looked: dancers flipping, musicians tuning, theatrical-types serenading, choirs harmonising. They seemed to stick to their enclaves at first, huddled together in long tables in the canteen and walking in separate groups. In one particularly cute case, Celia's Chinese youth orchestra, they walked in crocodile lines, hand-in-hand as they made their way across campus. He saw something of Kelly – *Kelpie*, whatever – about the children, a shade of her playfulness in their faces. The recognition caused a spark of guilt which he did his best to extinguish.

The performers reacted to their new surroundings in different ways: the youngest among them were wide-eyed at the austere halls of residence, then wider still at the ancient cloisters of the university campus itself; the older ones seemed to explore more gregariously, introducing themselves to other groups, pausing at the leaflet stand in the main building and pointing out castles and other sights to visit in their downtime; and then the teenagers, apparently the same wherever they came from – the Bahamas, Norway, Algeria, Thailand – more absorbed in each other and their phones than their new environment.

The lunch queues were fascinating, like an Olympic procession where the podium is a strip-lighted food serving station, and the medal an overcooked fish pie.

"I wouldn't have that," Duthie had said through the corner of his mouth to a Bahamian teenager. "Curry is the safer option."

The kid had grinned, then pointed at the tray of sweaty-looking salad leaves.

"Definitely not," Duthie had grimaced.

The couriers, too, were a strange collection in many ways. A decent percentage of the thirty-or-so couriers were ages with

Duthie, or thereabouts – university students, postgrads, even some early career folk. Then there were the handful of older ones, the seasoned few who had many festivals under their belts. These 'elders' seemed to take it upon themselves to explain the finer points of couriership that had been missed in the broad-brush briefing notes and meetings. Like sages in a village, people like Celia were besieged by younger couriers seeking advice. From behind his sketch pad Duthie overheard many an impromptu counselling session: how to deal with the difficult choir leader who demanded an early dinner spot for his group and bottled water for their precious throats; or strategies for dealing with the festival transport manager whose buses are always running late to pick up your impatient dancing troop from campus. The advice normally came down to the same simple rules: use your common sense, have faith in your resourcefulness, establish your authority.

Initially Duthie had lots of free time. Abe's performing didn't start until they were on the road in a few days, so he spent many hours capturing the festival's myriad faces, the kaleidoscope of expressions, his pencil on paper rendering youthful awe and adult indignation. He filled many pages with their smaller features alone – the delicate fold of eyes, the kinked slopes of noses – the smorgasbord of nationalities offered him endless inspiration. And then, the clock of his internship ever ticking at the back of his mind, he set about transmuting them to be ready for carving. He sought ways to simplify the sketches, to establish their archetypes, reveal their inner shapes somehow in a way that could at some point be etched into wood. Who knows, maybe even stone? If he was successful, he imagined the people's likenesses would be unrecognisable save for the *truth* of them.

"What doing?" a little Chinese boy had said, leaning on Duthie's shoulder.

"Drawing. Want to see?"

The boy peered at the page of sketches, shrugged then tottered off. *So Kelpie.*

The rest of the time he was absorbed in the pages of '*The Picts: A Forgotten People?*' Dr Mary Seaton took him on a journey through the ancient civilisation's history. She taught him about the language they spoke, a version of P-Celtic, itself a form of Britannic, and how that language was ultimately lost to time – replaced by Gaelic, the language of the Dalriada Scots. She read to him Saint Bede's legend of the Picts' origin: that they landed in Ireland from Eastern Europe but were unwelcome, so moved on to Britain where they finally settled. And she told him the phrase *Rex Pictorum*, the King of the Picts, held most famously by Cinead mac Ailpin, the great leader who united Dalriada and Pictavia. '*Not a forgotten people, a merged one*'.

In time Duthie began to look up more often, and started to notice the knitting together of the festival's diverse peoples. The spark of community became apparent to him in inklings: in the joke shared between a Sri Lankan puppeteer and a Chilean breakdancer; the Norwegian choir girl's curiosity about the Algerian's stringed mandole; flirtatious exchanges between the Slovak and Bahamian principal dancers. He saw it all from afar, in rehearsal rooms and across dining tables. It all began melding in his mind, the more he sketched and the more he read Mary Seaton's book, the more he started to consider this unlikely conference of peoples as the birthplace of a tribe. Hillhead halls, fort-like, moated by the River Don, offered safe haven, a place to come together and explore the 'we' that they might become.

Duthie didn't feel part of it, not yet. But he felt the stirrings of community. It felt surprisingly good. He had to remind himself to be pissed off, that this was not how his summer was meant to turn out. But as distractions went, this wasn't terrible.

If a fondness for this strange collection of people was kindling within Duthie's heart, the flames were truly fanned at the opening ceremony. It was held in Aberdeen Music Hall to great pomp, the immense auditorium, ornate ceiling and golden walls gave the ceremony a feeling of majesty and stateliness. Ceòl Mòr was arranged on the stage in a wide curve, their clarsachs, bagpipes and fiddles looking grand beneath the organ's golden pipes. The auditorium was alive with colour, the horseshoe balcony that hemmed its full depth was adorned with the flags of each attending nation at the festival. Performers filled the north and south flanks of the balcony. They wore traditional tartan attire and their faces brimmed with pride.

By comparison the audience below was threadbare. The seats of the stalls were half-filled, and those sitting in them were largely old and expressionless. At the very front of the stalls sat a row of men and women wearing rumpled suits and dowdy skirts, uniform in their flinty stares and pursed mouths.

They were the festival's Steering Committee, Celia explained. Mostly elected overlords, city Councillors and such like, who held sway over much of the festival's trajectory and fate – and all under the chairmanship of one Professor Alasdair Seaton, no less. Not one of the committee could give a shit about the festival, Celia had whispered. To them, the festival was just an expensive party that the City Council saw less and less value in, as the years rolled on.

The Professor was immediately recognisable to Duthie, brown tweed stood out, a shade warmer against the regiment of grey. He sat in the centre of the front row, head turned upwards, scanning the balcony. From the back row, Duthie guessed the Professor would be unlikely to spot him, so he focused fully on the older man's face. But the Professor's expression was unreadable. Only when it reached Eddie did it waver. He paused, seemingly waiting for her to return his gaze but she didn't. Comparing the two, Duthie saw something of the Professor in Eddie's face, the pointed chin, perhaps, or the arched eyebrows, but there was also something undeniably different. He wondered which parts belonged to her mother, Dr Mary Seaton, proud historian of the Picts. It's so sad, Celia had whispered, following Duthie's eye line between the Professor and Eddie. He didn't get a chance to ask what was sad because the national anthems had begun.

Ceòl Mòr performed each anthem in turn, their melodies foreign but the sound made almost recognisable to Duthie's ears thanks to the Scots orchestra; every song sounds familiar when haunted by bagpipes. The performers emanated respect. They stood at the first notes of their homeland's music, many placing hands on hearts. Duthie found it endearing to see such honest love for one's country, to hear the fluency of their words as they sang along, to feel the enthusiasm with which they cheered for others when their anthems came.

No-one caught Duthie's attention more than Abe. The band had no music for the Ugandan national anthem, an administrative error that showed itself in a twitch on Eddie's face. Abe was resplendent in ceremonial attire, sashes of beads criss-crossing his bare chest, an ornate headband with a huge white feather jutting out of its base. Without pause Abe stood and sang *a cappella*.

The sound of his voice, so full and broad, filled the cavernous auditorium.

Oh, Uganda! the land of freedom,
Our love and labour we give;
And with neighbours all
At our country's call
In peace and friendship we'll live.

When he finished, the hall was silent, caught momentarily in the echo of his song. Then the balcony erupted; voices hollered, hands pounded, feet thundered. Abe's smile lit up in triumph.

It was a different tale in the stalls. The steering committee clapped politely, as they had between all the anthems, but they didn't join the cacophony from the balcony. Only when the Professor took to the stage for his welcome speech did the committee show any life, and even then only a mild deference at his words. He opened his palms on either side of the microphone stand. The warmth of his expression towards the performers looked rehearsed, Duthie thought, so he was surprised when the Professor's first few words came out choked.

"When we started this festival nearly forty years ago, my wife and I," he said, coughing once into his fist. "My wife and I had barely an inkling of what we were creating. We issued a call into the ether, a message to the artists of the world. We waited for a response. To our surprise and delight, the response came. Musicians. Dancers. Folktellers. They came from all corners of the globe and shared with us their talent, their energy, their culture. It brought fresh life to our humble city. My wife, Mary…"

Without realising it, Duthie had taken Dr Mary Seaton's book out of his bag. He sought out Eddie down the row of seats next to him. She had the look of someone who felt the eyes of the world on her; eyes unblinking, the tendons of her neck protruding. Duthie willed for something to crumble on that rigid face, to show something real, but it didn't come.

"...she had a word for the festival," the Professor continued. "A word for the performers, the couriers, the audiences. That word was 'Family'."

A whoop came from somewhere in the balcony, which set off a ripple of responses. Duthie couldn't help but lend his voice to the wave. He leaned forward to look at the front row of the stalls but again only found a coolness on the Steering Committee's grey faces. *To them the festival is just an expensive party.* He wondered how they must feel towards the noisy hordes above their heads. It burned him that they seemed so uninvested, so unmoved.

The performers seemed oblivious, or maybe defiant; they were the only audience they needed. As Duthie perceived it through his undamaged eye, this was a matter of upstairs versus downstairs, performer versus committee, *us* versus *them*.

"And now, four decades later, here you are," the Professor carried on, the power in his voice rising with each sentence, as if laying foundations. "Like the many who have come before you..."

Duthie quietly opened the book and the pages parted two thirds of the way through at his bookmark – the folded letter continuing to do its job well. He thumbed back a few chapters and found the passage that had come to mind: Mary Seaton's account of The Battle of Mons Graupius. The battle, she explained in the passionate style he had come to love so much, was 'a great clash of arms' on north-east Scottish soil in AD84.

'The fearsome Roman General Agricola and his army stood in waiting at the foothills of Mons Graupius. The mountain's exact location has been lost to history, but the battle itself has been burned onto memories for millennia hence.

'A native Caledonian horde – the forebears of the Picts – stood on the mountainside, arranged in horseshoe formation, ready for battle. Their fearless leader Calgacus addressed his 30,000-strong horde of barbarians. He vowed that Rome would never take the Highlands:'

'We, the choicest flower of Britain's manhood, were hidden away in her most secret places.

'Out of sight of subject shores, we kept even our eyes free from the defilement of tyranny.

'We, the most distant dwellers upon the earth, the last of the free, have been shielded until today by our very remoteness and by the obscurity in which it has shrouded our name.

'Let us then show, at the very first clash of arms, what manner of men Caledonia has kept in reserve.

'On, then, into action; and as you go, think of those that went before you and of those that shall come after.'

III.

The performers' roars swelled out on to Union Street, heralding their imminent arrival. And arrive they did: they marched out of the Music Hall, beyond its granite columns and on to the street, armed with wooden poles, flags of all nations waving from their spear-like ends. The avenue had been cleared for their procession, now was the moment for the festival to announce in earnest its presence to the people of Aberdeen.

The sun blessed their exultant faces, catching the fine detailing of traditional garb in its rays, enhancing the brilliance of grinning mouths, the joy of energetic stances. They waved and danced and sang, pouring electricity onto the shopping high street and their onlookers, willing them to be caught in the festival's spell. They were met with a mixture of responses from the Friday afternoon shoppers who hemmed the pavements of Union Street: some waved back with glee, others peered in confusion, some grimaced in frustration at their route being blocked by some inane celebration.

A group of Sri Lankans got separated from the procession, too busy delighting a child hoisted on her mother's shoulders. The little girl clapped and squealed at the attention she got from the troupe. Duthie spotted this and walked up to the performers, clapped along for a moment then gently suggested they rejoin the parade. Just as his coaxing began to work, Eddie pounced, hawklike and sharp. She instructed the performers to get back in line and warned Duthie that his responsibility was to Abe and Abe alone. Duthie's response was lost in the noise but he was sure Eddie got its meaning.

By the time he had caught up with Abe, the parade had reached its terminus. Performers spilled around the Castlegate, flowing in excitable groups at the foot of the Salvation Army Citadel, many gazing up to admire its impressive turreted peaks. Abe was talking to the Professor at the bandstand in the centre of the cobbled square. His Ugandan flag fluttered on the breeze. He pointed towards it, then motioned at the throng of performers. Duthie approached carefully at first, gauging the reception he was likely to get from the Professor. He recalled his own departing words from two days back. *'This is bullshit!'* Embarrassment prickled up his neck, followed swiftly by the annoyance that he still felt towards the Professor. He couldn't quite understand this mixture of feelings. The festival was turning out surprisingly engaging, but the nagging thought that he was not in control because of that self-satisfied man still burned in his gut.

"...a wonderful celebration," Abe said.

"Yes indeed," the Professor said, seemingly mollified by Abe's positivity, but not holding much eye contact with him either. His gaze was out on the crowd. "And you're being looked after well I trust?"

"Oh yes," Abe said. "Very well thank you. Actually, I was hoping I might talk to you in private at some point if that's–"

"Ah the one-eyed Seer approaches," the Professor boomed, locking on to Duthie. "How fares it, Intern?"

"Fine thanks," Duthie said, aiming for easy-breezy. "Good speech."

"Why thank you," the Professor doffed an invisible cap. "Time for a progress report?"

"I've been sketching a lot, actually," Duthie said, then fished into his bag and flipped through a few pages of the sketchbook. The Professor barely gave them a glance, his eyes sifting through the crowd once more. Duthie felt a twist of annoyance.

"I've been reading your wife's book," he said, bringing the hardback out. "It's good. Really good."

"Well there you go, dear boy," the Professor said. "I told you she would be a far better teacher than I."

"I didn't realise she co-founded the festival," Duthie said.

"Founded really," the Professor's tone softened a touch. "It was her baby."

"It would have been great to meet her," Duthie ventured, needling for a response. For what exactly, he wasn't sure. "It's a shame."

"Yes well," the Professor's voice trailed, his face fell.

"You must miss her very-," Duthie began but halted at the look Abe gave. It was a mixture of puzzlement and warning. Frankly it was nice to see something other than unreadable placidity on the Ugandan's face.

The Professor appeared to bounce back to a well-practiced ebullience. "Say, have either of you two squires seen my daughter Fedelm?"

"Yes, I think I saw her behind us a second ago, yes over there," Abe pointed.

"Do excuse me," the Professor said and made a beeline for Eddie. She was mid-sentence with Celia, Fraser and a gaggle of youth team members when he tapped her shoulder. Duthie watched the exchange with fascination. Eddie gave the Professor a courteous smile then attempted to turn back to the group. Something he said, jovial but direct, made the team disband, leaving him alone with his daughter. Duthie saw the makings of anger on Eddie's face but she brought it swiftly under control, her eyes darting around, perhaps in case it had been spotted. The Professor leaned in, his fingers wrapped gently around her upper arm.

"You were a little direct with Professor Seaton, my friend," Abe said.

"Was I?" he mumbled.

What was the Professor saying to Eddie? His demeanour seemed somehow apologetic, or was it more the way a parent speaks to a toddler? Yes, that was it. His head was tilting from one side to the other, as if placating a child. Eddie tried a few times to break his monologue but was unsuccessful.

"Do you know him well?" Abe said.

"The Professor? Nope. I know what he's all about though."

"Oh?"

"Being stuck right up his own arse," Duthie said, craning his neck the better to see the Professor and Eddie. She seemed to have finally broken through and was saying her piece. A rosy hue had begun to bloom on her cheeks, her mouth stretching into a tense line.

"He's your intern supervisor?" Abe said, his soft tone humming at the edge of Duthie's attention.

"Lucky ol' me, eh? Stuck under the thumb of that old fart."

Eddie had started to bring her hands into the equation, her finger pointing to the ground to punctuate what she was saying. The Professor seemed amused by this, even chuckled a little. Eddie's eyes lit up in response.

"I think you judge a little too strongly," Abe said. "The poor man's grieving."

"What?" Duthie said.

"His wife."

"She died years back."

"No she didn't. She only died six months ago."

Duthie wrenched his attention back fully. "Eh? But I thought... how do you know that?"

"We have Google in Uganda," Abe said with a snort of laughter.

"Shit," Duthie said, the beginnings of guilt germinating in his stomach. "I don't know why I thought...wait, why were you Googling that?"

Something flickered on Abe's expression, but was quickly smoothed over. He shrugged. "I was learning about the festival."

"You were just saying something to the Professor about wanting to talk privately with him. What about?"

Abe smiled at Duthie's probing stare. "You understand what *private* means?"

"Hmm," Duthie said, cocking an eyebrow.

He looked back towards Eddie just in time to see her marching by. She caught him looking.

"What?" she said. Her cheeks were now blood red.

"Nothing," Duthie said, holding his hands aloft.

She locked eyes with him. "Afterparty at our flat. Spread the word. I need a fucking drink."

IV.

The fuchsia t-shirt teenager, who Duthie first met carrying a heavy box at the foot of the New Kings building, had the same look of strain about his face as he ran past. He made it to a nearby tree then vomited spectacularly. It looked mostly liquid and bright blue.

"*Ah si*," Celia said with a knowing look. "Some things are launched with a bottle of champagne smashed against them. This ship? We do it with the puke of underage drinkers."

She got up from the grass with a heave, leaving behind her plastic cup of wine.

"And what have you learned, *muchachito*?" she called as she approached the kid.

Duthie shared a look of amused disgust with Abe and Fraser.

The sounds of the Flat 3 party drifted out each time the doors wafted open – throaty singing and the strum of an acoustic guitar. There must have been thirty people crammed into the humid kitchen. At the sight of the guitar being brought out, half of the gathering had spilled out to the grass surrounding Esslemont, taking their warm discount beer and own-brand vodka with them. The sight of people drinking in the warm night air had been a magnet for passers-by, and now scores of office staff, couriers and performers mingled, some in circles, some lying flat to watch stars winking above.

At the farthest away point, over towards the North Court tower, was the largest group. To Duthie's eye they all looked Asian, mostly dark-haired, a few dyed bright colours. He had identified three of them as the people Abe had been speaking to in the turning circle when Morgan had dropped them off. The one who had introduced himself that night – Kit, that was his name – had waved over when the group first arrived, unloading large cases from a van. The group had taken odd-looking bamboo contraptions out of the cases. Duthie continued to watch as Kit had lifted one up and shaken it front to back, at which point it had made a noise somewhere between a rattle and a musical trill like a xylophone. Duthie was transfixed at the sight and sound as more and more of the instruments came out of the bags.

"What do you think of that?" Fraser said next to him.

"Hmm?" Duthie said. Fraser was motioning towards Vlada and Georgiy. The pair were huddled in deep conference nearby. Georgiy was running his fingers through Vlada's waterfall of hair.

"They move fast," Duthie said, then took a swig of vodka.

"Jealous?" Abe added.

"Not in the slightest," Fraser sniffed. "Gimme that vodka."

Abe chuckled. "So, it seems the festival is quite an amorous place?"

He had been drinking lemonade all night, and his speech was crystal clear. He'd changed out of his ceremonial outfit and Duthie was missing unhindered visual access to his bare chest.

"God yeah," Fraser grinned. "It's awesome. Seriously, it's like the United Nations of Sex."

Duthie laughed. It seemed true; already he had witnessed flirtations across multiple national boundaries, and now with the booze flowing through the community, it seemed diplomatic dialogues were becoming full blown treaties.

He glanced at Abe, hoping for another of their silent moments of connection, but he was smiling back at Fraser. It was a mild smile, the kind one gives when being a good audience, if not entirely onboard with the conversation.

"Hello stranger," said a voice from on high. *Whatshisname* towered above their three heads.

Duthie blanched. "Oh hi," he said, suddenly glad Abe's eyes hadn't been on him or he might have spotted the flicker of surprise.

"How are you?" *Whatshisname* said then looked around the grass at the pods of people. "Quite the party."

At that moment a Chilean breakdancer, eyes bleary with drink, burst onto the lawn and shouted 'FestFam!' Half the seated crowd held their drinks aloft and returned the phrase. Beaming, the dancer wobbled straight back indoors towards the singalong. The word, *FestFam*, had become common parlance among the community ever since the Professor's 'family' speech.

Whatshisname looked perplexed. "This is your internship?"

"Kinda," Duthie said. "This is just downtime."

"Cool, cool," *Whatshisname* said. He looked at Abe and Fraser, who smiled back up at him. "So..."

A beat too late, Duthie said, "Want to join us?"

"Nah," *Whatshisname* said. "Just going to head in to do some studying. Maybe see you round?"

His voice trailed upwards. Duthie felt Abe and Fraser staring at him.

"Sure thing, mate," he said. "See you round."

He looked down at his vodka to break eye contact with everyone. When he looked back, *Whatshisname* was gone.

"Hi there," Fraser said under his breath, nudging Abe. "I'm Fraser, and this is Abel. It's nice to meet you. Duthie, won't you introduce us?"

"Shut up," Duthie said.

"*Friend* of yours?" Fraser said, his tone musical and mocking.

"I've never asked his name," Duthie shrugged. "To be fair, he doesn't know mine either. We never got round to that bit." He cringed, immediately regretting how the last part made him sound like a 'player'. But hey, maybe he was. Why did it bother him what Abe thought?

Fraser laughed at the caddish remark, but Abe didn't – his gaze was still in the direction *Whatshisname* had gone in. When it returned and rested on Duthie it was with something typically unreadable. Though it felt like judgement.

Duthie flustered. "I'm...going to take a piss. Can I grab either of you a drink?"

"Not from the toilet. Gross," Fraser said.

"Very funny," Duthie said. He got to his feet, suddenly feeling the effects of wine and vodka. Having one eye covered seemed to exacerbate the dizziness. He looked down at Abe before turning away. "You okay?"

"I'm good," Abe smiled.

Duthie felt awkward, panicked almost. He wanted to wipe away Abe's enigmatic smile, for it to become something tangible, to be sure there was no judgement in it. "You, uh, got a phrase for me?"

"Sorry?"

"Y'know, one of your phrases. 'A man finds friends wherever he goes'," he said, immediately regretting the imitation.

"Nothing comes to mind, my friend," Abe said, face still placid.

As Duthie walked towards the flat, he imagined all kinds of emotions that lay underneath that calm exterior.

V.

The corridor was dark and still when he walked in, as if all light and sound had been dispelled from the world. It disorientated Duthie, heightened the drunken fug. A small orange glow at the end of the corridor beckoned. It caught the curled edges of pages stuck to each bedroom door. On every page was one of Duthie's drawings – simple line sketches of his housemates' faces – which he'd ripped from his pad and glued earlier in the evening. Now, in the half-light, the likenesses seemed warped, more sinister than he remembered. Their eyes peered at him, a silent gallery of onlookers.

A voice split the silence. Husky but beautiful, it rang out. A siren call, its words clearer with each step.

...upon Ireland's green hills,
A tale of doom, foreseen and foretold.

Cruel Queen of Connacht – Medb – would surely find,
When avarice and ego are combined
With jealousy and love more like to hate,
That lust for riches leads to bloody fate.

Her King owned equal riches to this Queen
As well as one possession clearly seen –
The White Bull, Finnbhennach, the pride and joy
Of King Aillil – so Mebh devised a ploy.

The song was unaccompanied, the melody, which he didn't recognise, stripped back. The singer took time with each line, letting it hang in the air.

The fine Brown Bull of Cooley matched the White,
Donn Cuailnge, he alone, had equal might.
'To Ulster!' Medb decreed 'We ride in line.
The great Brown Bull of Cooley will be mine!'

Duthie opened the door as quietly as he could, for fear of breaking the spell. The kitchen was packed, faces upon faces – some high above the kitchen top, some gazing up from the floor – all outlined in the flicker of candlelight. They seemed entranced.

They rode, enlisting men prepared to fight,
Through provinces, with Ulster trained in sight,

*But slowed when mist and light began to fall –
A gold-haired figure loomed and did appal!*

The voice belonged to a solitary figure who leaned against the fridge. The whisky in her glass glinted and swirled with each movement. Duthie's eyes adjusted further. For some reason he wasn't surprised when he realised the source of the song was Eddie. The gravel in the voice, the piercing truth of it, could only have belonged to her.

Her expression was mournful and distant as she sang, summoning a misty past.

*Two stallions drew the chariot she did ride
A sword, so long and sharp, was at her side.
Her eyes had irises both cleft in three
And glared at Medb – so frightening to see.*

*'I am Fedelm, from Alba o'er the sea,
That land of heather and the honey bee.
My power of foresight, imbas forasnai,
Must warn you that a multitude shall die!'*

*'It cannot be,' Queen Medb did then respond.
'Your prophecy is worthless, foolish, fond.'
But, at Fedelm's next words, she had to quail.
'Alas, I know your quest is bound to fail!*

*Since, guarding Ulster and the strong Brown Bull,
There is a warrior hero, brave and cool.
The Hound of Culann, he is hailed by men -
Cú Chulainn is his true name, you may ken.*

*If you should reach the North, then you will meet
This enemy, so powerful, hard to beat.
Your army cannot win, you should learn well –
They'll fall beneath his sword, I can foretell!"*

Duthie felt a shoulder nudge against his. "Sorry," the person mouthed, as he leaned to see inside the kitchen. It was Kit, the South East Asian guy who had been playing the bamboo instrument outside. He smiled in recognition. Duthie waved *hello* and was about to turn back to the song when he spotted Abe next to Kit. Already, the Ugandan looked entranced by the song, his fascination clear in the candles' orange glow.

*'You jest, foul witch," Queen Medb, she snarled and spat,
'How can you be so very sure of that?'
Fedelm gazed back with triple-irised eyes.
No jest did Queen Medb see, to her surprise.*

*'He's guided by a goddess,' Fedelm said,
'His heart is pure and steadfast, Ulster-bred.
'The raven goddess – Morrigan's her name –
Has him in thrall, she is the one to blame.*

*She beats her ragged wings to drive him on,
Her beak caws ghastly sounds at dusk and dawn.
These noises, full of violence and hate,
Force Cú Chulainn to boldly meet his fate.*

*'Your future, too, Queen Medb, she does ensure.
Towards it you are rushing, without cure.*

I see it crimson and I see it red.
A sea of blood descends upon your head!'

Intensity increased as Eddie's voice and her stance grew stronger. Duthie could see only her, the candlelit audience blurring into orange mist.

'Turn back, proud Queen, before you step too far!
Control your greed, be content as you are.
Forget the Bull and save your woeful men –
Or face the Morrigan and Cú Chulainn!'

Yet Medb marched on to meet the fearsome foe.
Alas, her powerless army was brought low.
The Hound of Culann left them hacked and red –
Medb's quest had failed, so many men lay dead.

Beware Feldelm, the Alban Prophetess!
If not, I fear that you will lack success.
She hears doom like the calls of distant birds –
Be wise and heed her dreadful warning words!

Eddie stared at the spirit in her glass, then tipped it all down her throat. Enthusiastic applause broke the silence yet her exultant stance diminished at the sound; shoulders slumped, gaze cast down. When she spoke, there was no hint of singing power, as if the tale had left her spent.

"Told you it was a bit of a downer," she said in a drunken mumble. "Anyone got a happier one?"

The room began to regain its former buzz. The guitar was

passed around and requests for pop songs and power ballads were thrown about. Eddie leaned against the fridge, lost in the noise.

"That was beautiful, wasn't it?" said Kit, looking from Duthie to Abe.

"I did *not* expect that from her," Duthie shook his head.

"Beautiful," Abe said, clearly caught in his own thoughts. He walked into the kitchen and made a beeline for Eddie. He reached her and started speaking. Duthie couldn't hear the words, but by the way Abe's hands moved in the air between them, the words were effusive. Eddie seemed initially frosty, but a small smile soon broke the ice.

"Having a good night?" Kit asked.

"Uh sure," Duthie said, turning to face him. The guy was looking at him intently. "Are you?"

"Yeah, great," he said. "We had our first concert tonight. Just got back."

"I saw," Duthie said, recalling the strange-looking instruments. "Big bamboo things."

Kit laughed. "Bamboo things, yes that's right. Me and the *angklung* orchestra have been touring Europe for a few weeks now."

Angklung. Duthie noted the word. It sounded interesting in Kit's accent. His English was perfect, and there were some words that sounded almost American, but for the most part his accent was one Duthie had heard so many times before: in YouTube videos, in the chatter of waiting staff at Thai restaurants, among tourists walking around the city. But to speak to someone with that accent, to actually speak in person, gave him a thrill. "You've come from pretty far away, huh?"

"*Khap pom*," Kit said. The curiosity in his expression took a playful glint.

"What?" Duthie said. The words had been alien, but he sparked in recognition of their tone.

"I said 'Yes, sir'."

"In Thai," Duthie said.

"*Khap pom*," Kit grinned, then his eyes narrowed as if he was examining something very closely. "Y'know I've been wondering. Abe calls you Rune."

Duthie felt a flash of warmth, first at hearing his name in Kit's accent, then at the thought of Abe talking about him to other people.

"It means 'happy'," Duthie said.

"I know," Kit said. "You have some Thai in you?"

Duthie's normal reaction would be to evade this question. As a child it had rarely come; people only saw the ginger hair, the freckles, the pale skin. But as he'd grown older, it seemed as if his Thai heritage had risen to the surface, becoming more apparent, and the question came more frequently. It was galling how brazen people were in asking it, as if it was their right to look directly into his eyes and ask: 'What are you?' But this felt different. Coming from Kit, his accent, that curiosity, the question seemed to be motivated by a desire to reveal similarity rather than difference.

"My dad," Duthie said. The word felt strange in his mouth, cold like a pebble.

"That's so cool," Kit said. "I knew it."

"How did you know?" Duthie said.

"Mostly your name," Kit said. "But also your smile. Very Thai."

"Oh right," Duthie said, feeling the warmth creeping further up his neck.

"Your name," Kit carried on, "it's the same as my uncle. It's quite a rare name in Thailand actually."

"Really?" Duthie said. "People here think my name's super weird. That it has something to do with the ancient alphabet."

Kit gave a confused squint.

"Runes?" Duthie waved a hand. "Basically, in English my name sounds hippy-ish."

Another look of confusion.

"Anyway. Nice to have someone recognise it for what it is, I guess."

"What's he called?" Kit said.

"My dad?"

Kit nodded. Duthie felt that cold pebble slip to his stomach. At that moment the kitchen exploded into song, an acoustic rendition of The Proclaimers' 500 Miles. Duthie had never been so grateful for the Scottish duo's anthem.

"Has he taken you to visit Thailand, your dad?" Kit shouted over the sound of the hollering.

Duthie shook his head.

"You must," Kit said. "It's a beautiful country."

"Well, at least I'll know someone now," Duthie said, pressing a finger against Kit's chest.

"I'll show you around." Kit held out his hand. "Deal?"

Duthie took it. "Deal."

Kit didn't let his grip slacken. In fact, it tightened.

"Your tour starts now," he said, and pulled Duthie towards the front door.

VI.

"No, no, it's like this," Kit said, holding a large *angklung* at chest height. "Light and quick, back and forth. Like this."

The bamboo instrument trilled loud and true. Duthie laughed in surprise. His reaction was met with glee by the orchestra members who sat on the grass around him. Their angklung came in a vast array of sizes, but their shapes were the same; A-frames with two or three bamboo cylinders jutting up from their bases. They looked a little like musical bar charts, Duthie thought. He held two of them, one in each hand, one larger in size and deeper in tone than the other.

"No, you're still waving it side to side," Kit said. "For the Thai angklung, like the ones you've got, it's front to back. Here."

He placed his angklung down and shifted along the grass, positioning himself directly behind Duthie. He reached both hands around him and placed them on Duthie's wrist – the left hand appearing out of nowhere from Duthie's blind spot.

"Oh hello there! Bit intimate," Duthie said, casting another look of surprise around the group, this time for comedic effect. The group creased up at the joke, much to his satisfaction. He recognised the two women from the previous night, Anchalee and Naowarat, but there must have been fifteen or so members in the circle. Not all were Thai, Kit had explained, some were Indonesian – where the angklung originated – and some Malaysian. Duthie looked along the faces and wondered which ones he looked like most. The sound of their laughter was infectious, so joyful that Duthie couldn't help but feel his own 'Thai smile' widen.

"It's like this," Kit breathed into his ear. He gripped Duthie's hand and shook the angklung back and forth. It gave out a glorious sound once more.

"Oh wow," he said. Kit let go and Duthie continued in the method he'd been shown, letting the note fill the air between himself and the group. "It's kinda like when an LP record skips. One note held for ever."

"Well, that's why we play in orchestras," Kit laughed. He gestured round the group. "More notes. So, what do you want to play?"

Duthie searched the faces once more. Their expressions wrapped around him, he felt their warmth as much as the ambient heat of the night air. He looked up to the cloudless sky and smiled.

"Maybe something that will finally make it rain?"

Kit grinned, looked round the orchestra and, in a piercing voice, began to sing the opening verse of Rihanna's *Umbrella*, and they spontaneously joined in with their instruments, perfectly in time and tune.

Kit conducted, his hands thrusting round the semicircle of angklung players. He guided Duthie to shake the angklung at the right times.

By the time the chorus came round a second time, everyone outside on the grass was singing along, drunken people of all nations, cups waving in the air, arms cast around each other. The angklung of all pitches rattled on high to mark the conclusion. Duthie did the same, raising his bamboo instruments to the sky. Kit flopped back on the grass, his face pink with the exertion. No water came from the sky, but it rained with applause and laughter.

The party disbanded soon after, a result of the campus warden shooing people off to their beds and also the genuine tiredness of most revellers. Duthie helped Kit load the remaining angklung into the van. The pair sat in the opening of the vehicle, its double doors hiding them from the last few people who still sat on the grass.

Duthie still felt the buzz of the impromptu concert, as if the trilling music had awakened something in his bones. The vibration was in his bloodstream, dancing with the alcohol that was also singing in his veins. He hummed and swayed in time to both. Kit's voice was a descant on top of the thud of Duthie's heart.

"–and then we go to Leipzig, then to Prague and then home," Kit said.

"Pretty long tour," Duthie said. "What will you do when you get back?"

"I teach music," Kit said. "In a school in Bangkok. If you come visit, I'll show you round. You really should come see the city. The whole country too. Up north to the jungle, south to the islands."

Duthie could see them in his mind's eye, the pictures he'd looked at online so many times in his life now becoming animated, three-dimensional. Palm trees swaying in the breeze on white sand beaches, pigeons flying past sky-scrapers in the city as the sun dipped on the horizon, leaves crunching underfoot on a trail through the northern jungles. He could feel the humidity of that foreign land on his skin, smell its strange scents on the air.

"Can't believe he hasn't taken you yet," Kit said.

"Hmm?" Duthie mumbled, caught in a daze.

"Your dad."

"Oh."

"You'll love it. I promise. It'll be like coming home."

The word sounded full in Kit's mouth, but suddenly empty in Duthie's ears. The idea of this far off land being any kind of home to a Scottish lad was so fantastical he almost laughed. But the cold pebble in his stomach quelled any giddiness.

"His name's Somchai Bunsong," Duthie said. He saw the name in front of him, recalling it as letters printed on bureaucratic paper. "My dad."

"What's he like?" Kit said.

"Never met him," Duthie said.

He looked at Kit. A crease formed on the Thai guy's dark brows.

"Really? Why?"

Duthie manufactured a smile. "Busy guy, I guess. Anyway–"

"He would be proud of you, Rune," Kit said then patted his knee.

Duthie felt his pulse bubble. What Kit had said should have made him want to cry, as should the look of empathy. Duthie didn't know what to do with either, but he didn't want them to end. He studied Kit's face, the kind eyes, the button nose, the stubbled chin. All of Thailand seemed to breathe through those features. A call from afar sang through those friendly lips. Duthie leaned forward and pressed his own against them. Soft at first, and then with intent.

Kit jerked backwards. Duthie opened his eye and saw alarm.

"Whoa," Kit said, rubbing his mouth. He made a thin laugh. "Sorry dude, not really what I was going for."

Duthie felt his lips go cold. "Shit sorry, don't know what I... think I'm just drunk."

"Don't worry about it," Kit said, but his body language said otherwise. He hopped off the van and wiped the hand that had been on his lips across his shorts.

"Please, just forget I did–" Duthie said, scrambling to his feet.

A throat cleared in the space between him and Kit. Abe stood a few feet back from the van's double doors. Duthie's mind raced. Abe's expression was mostly still, but there was definitely surprise somewhere in the combination of his features.

"I just wanted to say goodnight," he said with a voice that was deep and smooth. He raised a hand. "I hope you both sleep well."

"Night Abe," Kit said, his voice twittery and cracked by comparison. "Yeah, I better head off too. Night Duthie."

Duthie shifted out of the way, allowing Kit to close the van doors. The sound was abrupt against the quiet of the night.

Duthie whispered: "Kit, I'm really sorry–"

"It's absolutely fine, buddy," Kit said quietly and gave him a playful punch on the arm. He then walked away into the night.

Duthie turned to Abe. There was no way Abe hadn't seen the kiss, but there was no query in his expression.

"Had a nice night?" Duthie said, scratching the back of his neck.

"Very nice. You?"

The eyes. Duthie had never properly noticed their honey colour until now. They seemed to shine like an echo of the sun that would return with the dawn.

"Sure," Duthie said.

"Sleep well then, my friend," Abe said.

"I'll see you in the morning, yeah? Our first adventure on the open road."

Abe gave a nod and a smile. He blinked and walked away, taking the warmth of his honey eyes with him.

Duthie considered following him to Esslemont House, but his feet wouldn't budge. He looked at the space which Kit had vacated and let out a groan. He scuffed the sun-browned grass with his foot and whispered under his breath:

"Well done, Duthie."

VII.

Fedelm 'Eddie' Seaton sat on the steps outside Esslemont House. Her eyes, dull beneath heavy lids, followed the lit end of a cigarette as she waved it from side to side.

"Please say I can have one of those," Duthie said.

She looked up at him. He saw the bloodshot evidence of alcohol and exhaustion. The line of her mouth bowed downwards. She kicked the packet across the concrete. Duthie sighed then bent to pick it up, and was immediately pleased to find it full of cigarettes. Eddie held hers upright, the glowing tip pointing skywards. Duthie crouched, held a new cigarette against it and pulled in a few quick drags, then a long, steady one. The initial hit made his head spin and he slumped gently on the ground.

He released a sliver of smoke between his lips and recited in a low, ominous tone:

"I see it crimson and I see it red. A sea of blood descends upon your head."

Eddie grimaced. "Oh piss off."

Duthie enjoyed the sound of her swearing at him. It was just what he needed.

"No, I liked it, seriously," he said. "Wish I had a song written about my name."

She considered him a moment then said: "Write it, then. I did."

"You wrote that song?"

She followed the glowing end of the cigarette once more.

"I'm impressed," Duthie said.

"'S an old Irish legend. But I wrote the lyrics."

"The Prophetess Fedelm," Duthie said, drawing deeply on his fag. "An ancient Irish legend. What a name. The old Prof didn't even give you a chance, did he?"

Duthie saw a retort kindle within Eddie but it died as quickly as it had sparked. "'Lucy' would've been fine," she eventually said. "Or 'Susan'. Maybe 'Debbie'."

"Try being called 'Rune'."

She chuckled. "He really hates 'Eddie'. Despairs any time someone says it."

"What were you two arguing about earlier?" Duthie asked. "After the parade."

Eddie considered him again. Whatever the test was, he passed it once more. "He and I have very different ideas about what's going to save this bloody festival."

Duthie chose silence, confident she'd carry on. So he worked on his cigarette.

Eddie continued, words heavy with drink: "*He* thinks we need to maintain a calm and steady course, do exactly what we always do, as perfectly as we can. Give the steering committee no single thing to pick at. All those fucking useless councillors. Wouldn't know art if it bit them on their shrivelled pancake arses."

Duthie eyed the packet, deciding how many fags he could get through while sitting there, but the gentle nausea from the first one was already hitting.

"But me? I don't think we have the luxury of time."

"You've got time," Duthie sighed.

Eddie cackled. It was a brittle sound. "This could be the very last festival. And it's going to crumble under my watch. What a kicker, eh?"

Duthie leaned back. "Well, shit. I knew the festival was on its arse, but I didn't think it was so close to death."

Eddie widened her bloodshot lids. "Yep. It's going to take something much bigger than a 'calm and steady course'."

"Like what?" Duthie said.

"Wish I knew."

"C'mon," he growled. "I saw the way you were arguing with your dad. There's no way you're this angry if–"

Her expression soured. "What is this? A pep talk or an interrogation?"

"It just reminded me of how I am with my mum," Duthie said. "We fight all the time these days, so I know how it is, believe me."

"Does she think you're a prick too?" Eddie said with lopsided delight.

"Y'know, I think she probably does," Duthie laughed. "And in return I think she's a bit of a bitch. Probably a bit of a crappy mother too."

Eddie squinted.

Duthie did his best Dolly Parton singing voice and spelled out '*D.I.V.O.R.C.E.*'

Eddie didn't seem sure what to do with this. Neither did Duthie. He was surprised at his own honesty. Long seconds passed between them. He stared into the middle distance and said softly: "The Prophetess Fedelm. Oracle of Esslemont House. Tell me then, what do you see on the horizon?"

"Doom," she whispered.

"Doom," Duthie echoed.

"It's going to take a hero to save us."

"A great warrior," he said, reciting her song. He looked into her eyes. The cigarette's light was perfectly reflected in her irises. "Where do these visions come to you?"

"In dreams," she said, almost wistfully.

"Tell me about them."

"You want to hear my dreams?"

"Sure."

"Then what?"

"I dunno. Then maybe I'll know you better."

She laughed. It would have been a cruel laugh if not for the dark circles under her eyes, the defeat in her voice.

He nodded at her cigarette. "You not going to smoke that?"

"I don't smoke."

"Then why…?"

"I just like to watch it burn."

"So dramatic."

"Drama runs in the family," she sniffed.

Duthie lit another cigarette from the embers of his first. "Look, Eddie, I don't know what you're so worried about. Your dad's head of the committee, isn't he? He can be your great hero. I'm sure he'd love that."

She jutted her chin out. It looked momentarily like pride. "He's doing what he can."

"But it's not his festival," Duthie said, comprehension dawning. "It was your mum's baby."

He wondered if he'd stepped too far, and maybe he had, but Eddie looked too tired, so he carried on: "I'm reading her book.

Your dad gave it to me for the internship. The one about the Pi–"

"She only wrote one."

"Really? Why?"

"Let me hop in my time machine and find out," she bristled.

"I love it. Genuinely. The way she writes, so passionate and alive. She talks about the Picts like they're real people, I mean, not just some ancient history."

"Well, there you go," Eddie said emptily.

"Sorry to hear about her death," Duthie said.

Eddie just bobbed her head, didn't meet his eye.

"What was she like?"

"She was..." Eddie began. "She was here. And now she's not."

"What's it feel like?" Duthie felt his pulse beating in his throat.

Eddie didn't move.

He added: "What does it feel like to have a parent die?"

She finally looked up at him. He hoped she read the sincerity in his face.

"Pretty creepy question," she said.

"That's not what I–"

"You trying to figure me out? Asking about my dreams. Telling me about your crappy mother, asking about my dead one?"

"Sorry," Duthie said. The booze stifled a blush but he felt its beginnings.

"We best friends now? This mean you're going to draw a picture of me too, eh?"

He had considered drawing one of Eddie and hanging it on her bedroom door as he had with the other flatmates. He'd even begun one, but no matter how he positioned the pencil, he couldn't figure out where to begin, how to capture her likeness. Was it steel in her eyes, or maybe despair? Fire or ice? She seemed to change in his mind's eye from moment to moment. She was infuriating.

Duthie shook his head, lit a cigarette and passed it to her. She crushed the original under her foot and began watching the new one smoulder.

She cleared her throat. "How's the internship?"

"I have absolutely no idea," Duthie said. "Tried showing your dad some of my sketches at the parade but he was too distracted."

"Yep, that's him," she said.

Duthie considered for a split second telling her how important this internship was to him, how vital it was to his plans to never place one foot back at home, a stepping stone to a new future. But the idea of handing her this kind of power seemed like a bad idea.

"And Abe?"

"What about him?"

"Are you doing a good job couriering him?"

Abe's honey-coloured eyes flashed in his mind.

She pointed the lit cigarette at him. "Pop quiz: what's his surname?"

Duthie searched. The name was there, just out of reach.

"And where's he from?"

"Uganda," Duthie said.

"Aye, but which city?"

Again, the information was just beyond his fingertips.

"Thought not," Eddie said, settling back with a look of amusement. "You think you're the first courier to lust after your artist?"

"I don't–"

"I've seen you looking at him. God, I've been part of this festival my whole life. It's nothing new. Don't get me wrong, he's a beautiful man. But he's your ward, not a piece of eye candy."

"Does pomposity run in your family too?" Duthie muttered.

She seemed to enjoy this. "I'm actually quite serious, Duthie. Do better. This festival is hanging in the balance. I can't have any dead weight."

Duthie pushed a breath between his teeth. As if *she* could berate *him*?

She shrugged, but Duthie caught something dangerous in her eyes. "If you can't do it for me, then do it for your precious internship. If you lose sight of your job here I have absolutely no qualms telling my father and getting you booted off. Goodbye festival? Goodbye internship."

He felt like the wind had been kicked out of him. It must have shown because Eddie looked pleased. She flicked the cigarette away and stepped on to the grass.

"Not going in?" Duthie said, trying to recover his cool.

"Nah," she said, stretching her arms. "There's a Chilean skateboarder who's been giving me the eye all night. Going to see if he's up for a nightcap."

"I thought artists weren't just pieces of eye candy," Duthie said, hearing petulance in his voice.

"What can I say, *Red*?" she said, flashing him a grin. "Drama, pomposity, hypocrisy. They all run in the family."

As she disappeared into the night, Duthie's mind came alive, drawing lines from one thing to another: Eddie's changeability, her performances of cool and hot, the ever-present knowing glint in her eyes. Where had he seen it before?

An echo in his mind. *'What can I say, Red?'*

He looked past Esslemont House towards the forest, the darkness that loomed within. A mirthful laugh escaped his chest. "You've got to be fucking kidding me."

A midnight dram between stories

"She was your sister!" Duthie panted on the doorstep of Benholm's Lodge. "Mary Seaton was your sister."

Morgan adjusted her pink silk robe as Duthie, flushed and sweaty from running through the forest, brandished in her face the hardback copy of 'The Picts: A Forgotten People?' by Dr Mary Seaton.

She peered at the book. The angles of her cheekbones and nose were sharp in the vestibule's light. She looked not the least bit surprised at his two-in-the-morning visit. "Guess you better come in then," she said and wafted through the inner door. "Shoes off."

Duthie kicked off his dusty trainers, triumphant at gaining entry to the castle. Two sensations hit him first: the hardness of the stone floor and the coolness of the air. These were swiftly followed by a smell somewhere between the mineral scent of earth and something more human, bread perhaps? He wasn't sure what he'd expected from the castle's interior, but the modest kitchen underwhelmed him. In the dim light he could make out various shapes and appliances – a wooden table with rickety chairs, a bank of counters with cups strewn about their surfaces, a stove straight out of the sixties, a freezer big enough for a body.

Morgan said something from the stairwell behind him. He couldn't see her because the stairs wound upwards in a tight circle; this must have been the turreted-tower that scaled the full height of the building. Of the ten or so bulbs lighting the staircase only a few worked, the remaining ones dusty and inert. More remarkable was what hung on the walls: dangling from iron stakes above every second step was an array of what Duthie could only assume were costumes. Ballgowns, ceremonial robes, tweed suits, police uniforms, fairy wings, red cloaks and more lined the stairwell. They floated like ghostly sentinels, hems skimming the stone steps.

"Good exercise," Morgan called from the top of the stairs.

"Could do with a lift, this place," Duthie said, his voice bouncing up the tower. He felt the weight of booze in his system, it wanted him to go home and sleep, but it was overridden by curiosity.

He stopped halfway up at the sight of an oak door on the first floor landing. The door, studded with rusty bolts, gaped ajar, revealing a huge room beyond. Moonlight painted the room, revealing yet more costumes, some arranged along rails, others spilling out of boxes. In the centre of the room – or perhaps *hall* was more accurate – was a long dining table, big enough for ten people. The centre of the table cried out for a pig's head with an apple between its teeth, but instead it was adorned with piles of books, a vanity mirror, and who-knows-what-else scattered about the surface.

The winding staircase topped out in a cosy-looking snug; two high-backed armchairs facing a window that was set into the tower wall. A humid breeze whispered through the open window, a reminder of the summer that clung to the castle but didn't enter.

He heard some business behind him, glasses clanking and the scrape of chair legs on wooden floor. The room behind was as big as the hall immediately below. It was open plan, filled with a flat's-worth of things; a four-poster bed in the far corner, a three-piece suite, Persian rug, and of course yet more costumes. However, these garments were different. They were far grander. Each was displayed on a headless mannequin. In one corner was the pin-striped pant suit Morgan had worn at the gay bar; in another stood a fur coat with a bushy-tailed stole; next to it was a jet-black gown, voluminous with panels of satin and something more textured. Great plumes of dark feathers sprouted from its shoulders.

And opposite Duthie was another long dark outfit, but this one more familiar – black robes topped with a white barrister's wig. He lifted the wig off the mannequin's headless stump and placed it on his head. The pale horsehair tendrils that spiralled down from the back of the wig felt rough against his neck.

"Your honour," Morgan said behind him. Something cool was placed in his hand.

"I don't drink whisky," he said, looking down at the crystal glass with a generous slug of hay-coloured liquid in it. It smelled of rubber plimsolls. He tossed the barrister's wig back on the mannequin and ruffled his own hair.

"Rude not to accept a gift from your host," Morgan said. She settled on the sofa and rested a glass of the same drink on the leather arm. Her silk robe was draped about her, its sheen luxurious against the worn leather. The whole effect was ridiculous.

She looked like someone ready to share their memoirs with a scribe. Her supercilious expression completed the look; it rekindled the fire that had propelled Duthie through the forest.

"You have to give up this 'home' bullshit," he said, pointing towards the centuries-old stone stairwell. "It's a castle. And as for these?"

He motioned to the costumes.

"You like my friends?" Morgan said.

"I think they're crazy. And creepy. And I think you are too."

He waited for the force of his words to land but they didn't.

"You're nae the first to say so," she smiled gently, much to Duthie's annoyance.

He planted his feet. "Look, who *are* you?"

"Morgan Benholm," she said, as if singing the words of a clever little ditty.

"No, I...what is all this?"

"This?"

"For God's sake: this!" He threw a hand in the air. "It's all too weird, too coincidental. You just happen to turn up in my life out of the blue at the exact time I come across the Professor. He gives me a book written by your sister. Her daughter – your bloody niece – is now my boss? I just can't fit it all in my head. What's your game?"

"Yer nae *makkin'* sense, loon," she said,

"Oh stop with the–" he groaned at her sporadic use of Doric words. "Is everything a performance with you? Be honest: are you stalking me?"

"If that's what you'd like to believe," she laughed. "Makes as much sense as anything, I suppose. Although if we're being 'honest' it seems *you're* the one coming knocking on *my* door in the dead of night."

Duthie let out a dismissive puff, though he couldn't deny her logic.

Morgan continued. "I'll admit I was surprised when I discovered the connection. But real life's far more coincidental than fiction, don't you think?"

"You see? This is just the kind of Tartan Yoda shit you've been pulling since we met. Do you drive everyone insane?"

"You've already met my friends," she chuckled, pointing to the mannequins.

Duthie muttered under his breath and paced the room.

When Morgan next spoke, her tone was soft, pitying. "I know you would like this all to be some big plot. I can see it in your eyes...well, eye. You like things to be all neat and in a row, arranged in a pattern of your choosing."

"Oh, you know me, do you?" Duthie spat. "You know every little thi–"

"She used to be like that," Morgan raised her voice and pointed at the book in Duthie's hand. "*'This is a 'this', that is a 'that', she's just a downright 'this', he's a perfect 'that'.'* That was Mary down to a tee. Thinking there's great power in the naming of things. I hear the same in you. Maybe it's the sculptor in you talking."

She looked at a chest of drawers. On top was the wooden carving Duthie had made for her. He felt a twist inside; it didn't look nearly as impressive and intricate as when he'd carved it. All he saw were the clumsy strokes, the caricature features.

She continued softly: "Etching the world in a way that seems right to you. There's nothing wrong with that, of course, but not every story is made by hand. So I promise you, Rune, our meeting is just one of life's mysteries."

He was quiet for a beat, gaze resting on a faceless mannequin. "Everybody seems to be calling me that these days."

"Rune? It's your name, isn't it?"

He took a deep breath. It was as if the sound of his true given name in Morgan's voice stripped him of all defences. He snapped back to the matter at hand. "Okay fine. Just one of life's mysteries. Tell me something real, then. What do you do?"

"Retired," she said.

"Before that?"

"Costume store manager for Aberdeen City Council. And a few other things."

"Oh," Duthie blinked. He pointed at the be-garbed mannequins. "And these are…?"

"Also retired."

"Stolen?"

She raised a finger to her lips.

"What a surprise. Married?"

"How dare you," she smirked. "The very thought."

"Gay? Straight? Bi?"

"Indeed," she beamed.

"Drag king?"

"Sometimes."

"Queen?"

She shrugged.

"Mad?"

"Rude. Aren't we all?"

"God you're infuriating."

"Was that a question?"

"Just a fact."

"*This is a 'this'. That is a 'that'*," she sang.

"Whatever. Truth: how is all this yours?"

"Simple," Morgan said, shifting up in her seat. "We Benholms go very far back. Things get handed down from generation to generation, and here we are."

"I like what you've done with the place," Duthie said, running his finger along a dusty mantlepiece.

"And fit wid you dee wi a '*castle*' o' yer ain?" she said, making air quotes with her free hand.

"Dunno. Maybe some chandeliers? Chuck some shields and swords on the wall. At least hang a family crest somewhere prominent."

"I see," Morgan said, taking a sip of whisky. "A *man's* castle. Well, I'm afraid the Benholms were shit oot o' luck there. Only us *quines* left."

"Mary was your only sibling?" Duthie asked. "And Eddie the only offspring?"

"Cheers to the end of patriarchy," Morgan winked.

"Now *that* I'll drink to," Duthie said. He clinked glasses and settled down next to her. The whisky tasted every bit as rubbery as it smelled, but quickly melted into something altogether different; a sweetness at the tip of the tongue and a life-affirming burn in the throat. Morgan saw the transformation and a satisfied smirk formed on her lips.

Duthie rested Mary Seaton's book between them and considered Morgan afresh.

"What was she like?" he said.

He watched as her expression broadened. Something of the storyteller from the gay bar returned to her countenance. He saw a story blooming there, a hundred stories maybe, and observed as they danced across her recollection like stars in the cosmos, but then winked out one by one.

"Was she like you?" he tried again.

"In some ways," she said. "Couldn't be more different in others. Siblings are like that; they try so hard to be separate but underneath it all they share the same bones."

An image of Kelly's cherubic face flashed before Duthie's eyes. He often wished to see a full connection, but their genetic bond – only their mother's side – seemed tenuous, brittle. "I'm not so sure about that."

Morgan now seemed to consider *him* afresh. "You'd be surprised. For all our arguments, Mary and I were more alike than different. Both fascinating creatures, of course."

Duthie laughed. "Growing up in a place like this would do that, I guess."

"You don't know the half of it. Aye, we shared a lot. Too much, maybe."

Duthie's eyebrows knitted at Morgan's darkened expression.

She shook it off. "Both headstrong, one might say."

Duthie cleared his throat. "I'm sorry she's dead."

She held his gaze. "Thank you. I am too."

"Were you there when she died?" He felt the pulse in his neck.

"No, I wasn't afforded that chance," she said, then looked at him curiously. "Have you known death, Rune?"

He broke eye contact. He waited for something to happen, a lump to form in his throat, eyes to sting, voice to waver, but nothing did.

"I don't know, I'm just a little..." he trailed off, looking down at his hands. "Death. It's a lot, isn't it?"

"Aye," Morgan breathed. There was something so accepting, so knowing, in the sound. *Aye*. Duthie pulled the ancient word into him, accepted all its meanings. He tapped the book cover. "I like the way she writes."

"She was good at that kind of thing, was our Mary." She smiled and quietly intoned: "*'This is a 'this', that is a 'that'.*"

"I told Eddie I liked the book and she couldn't have clammed up quick enough."

"It's all still so fresh, I expect," Morgan said.

"Expect?"

"Can't say I've seen wee Fedelm in a while," she shrugged.

"You don't spend any time with her?"

"Oh we see each other from time to time. But it's nae the same. The closeness we shared when she was a kiddie, that's mostly gone."

"Why?"

"Why do you think?"

"Mary's death?"

She tilted her head in partial agreement. "Try again."

"The Professor," Duthie curled his lip.

She raised her eyebrows then drained the glass of its whisky.

"What happened between you two?" Duthie said.

She stood up, the folds of her silk robe smoothing out. She stepped into the landing at the top of the stairs and motioned for Duthie to follow.

"What do you see?" she said.

Duthie tracked her gaze out of the window, over the dark rooftops and glowing streetlights of Tillydrone Avenue. At the farthest reaches of his vision was the blackness of the North Sea. Halfway between them and the sea was a golden crown; the tip of King's College chapel lit from below, and to its left, Cromwell Tower.

"This is how it's always been," Morgan said. "Him in his tower – filled with dusty books and clever words – and me here in mine."

"You and your castle, filled with your 'friends'," Duthie whispered.

She let out a little laugh. "He's wanted Benholm's Lodge his whole life. From even before, you might say."

"What d'you mean?"

"Tell me, Rune, what's the name of the park we're right next to?"

"Seaton Park," Duthie said, then mouthed: "Professor Alasdair *Seaton*."

She stared at the Old Aberdeen campus in the distance, her eyes unblinking. "The Benholms have always been locked in war with the Seatons. Ever since we Benholms sailed from Ireland and trekked across this heathery land from west to east, and staked our claim on this grey granite rock. Our family lodge has been a piece of grit in the Seatons' eyes. A constant reminder that they can't have it all."

Her expression grew exultant. Duthie felt the heat in her words mingling with the warm air coming in the window.

"So, when he married Mary..." he began.

"Aye, he sunk his claws into her well. I remember the look on his face in our doorway, back when he began courting her all those years ago. He looked hungry, famished from the tales his family had raised him on. When he proposed to her? Ha! Well, naturally he thought Benholm's Lodge would come to him. And it would have too."

"Why?"

"Our parents were dead by that time. Mary and I were orphaned by our mid-twenties. There was precious little stopping Wee Ali Seaton from claiming everything."

"But you stood in his way," Duthie grinned.

"The deeds were in my name," she said, eyes sparkling. "The privilege of the first-born."

"And the responsibility," Duthie nodded.

"Clever lad," she patted his arm. "Keeping this pile of stones in the Benholm name has been a terrible responsibility. It drove a wedge between us, Mary and me."

"But surely she wanted it to stay in the family too?"

"Family," she laughed, but there was disgust in her expression. "The word took a new meaning under *yon* Professor's wing. 'Family' now meant him and the wee bairn. No, Mary forgot the name Benholm the moment she said 'I do'. People become wilfully blind when it comes to having children, Rune. They think family is something that can be built, when really it's something that comes *before you* as much as it does *because of you*. I wouldn't let Wee Ali erase my lineage for the sake of his. I knew the day I was born that nobody would chisel the name 'Seaton' onto our home. You saw the statue on the wall outside?"

"The man with the dog?" Duthie recalled.

"Aye, that's my ancestor, Oisin Benholm and his watchdog Orla. I see that statue every day. And every day I think it looks a little more like me. Watchdog and owner, both. That's my role, my responsibility."

Morgan may as well have been holding a fist against her heart, Duthie mused. Her words were grand, rehearsed almost, but they stirred Duthie nonetheless.

- 149 -

"What happened after they married? They cut you out of their lives?"

"Oh I had my visiting rights. Diplomatic access, you could say. For the sake of Eddie. She was born into the middle of our squabble, but it wasn't her fault. She was just a bairn. Our wee girl. Family, you see? The true meaning of it. She stands to inherit so much. Not just all this." She looked around the stone walls. "But our fight too. None of us wanted that, so we played peaceably for years."

"What changed?"

Morgan's face became as stony as the walls. "Peacetime only lasts so long, doesn't it? Even the most indelibly-written accords can be ripped up and tossed in the fire. Greed, no matter how dormant, always boils back to the surface eventually."

"The Professor?"

She pursed her lips, her eyes shone outwards to Cromwell Tower like a searchlight. "That man. That hungry, foolish man. He took everything from Mary. Her family name. Her career."

"Eddie said she didn't write any more books."

"No more writing. No more archaeology. No room for any of that when it comes to building the next generation of the Seaton clan."

"But the festival. She founded it." Duthie reflected on the myriad of young artists lining the balcony of the Music Hall during the opening ceremony. He could see their faces shining as they marched out to the streets of Aberdeen.

"Oh *that* he allowed. A folly. Nothing she did with the festival was any competition for his academic career. No, no. There was only room for one Professor in that tower."

Duthie tried to marry the image Morgan was painting with

the voice in the book. It didn't seem to entirely fit. "She can't have just accepted it. The woman who wrote that book wouldn't have given up."

"Well, I suppose it didn't help that her own academic peers turned against her. That book was the beginning of the end."

Duthie mentally scanned through the book, searching for any hint of what could have harmed her reputation. His mind came to rest on an image of a slim, angular yet smooth stone.

"The shard of the Maiden Stone?" he muttered.

"You've read that far, aye?"

"Nearly finished the whole book," he said. He fetched it and found the passage describing the moment Mary Seaton discovered the shard – the missing notch from the shoulder of the Pictish standing stone. He read aloud:

'When my fingers and brush finally met its smooth surface, I have no shame in saying, I wept. For here was a piece of the puzzle. A forgotten chunk of the past, pulled from the depths of memory, back into the world.'

Morgan was perched on his shoulder, peering over the image of the shard. "Her whole thesis rested on that thing. And do you know what her peers called it? Those fusty *al' mannies* with their gowns and their mortar boards? They said it was just 'a rock'. Nothing more."

"Was it?"

Morgan tutted. "She believed it was real, and that's good enough for me. Mary *Benholm* was nothing but thorough, a more dedicated archaeologist you wouldn't find. Mary *Seaton* though? Well, she didn't have the same fight in her. She gave in to her critics, accepted their ruling as fact. And wee Professor Ali Seaton just patted her hand, *'There there, never mind'* and led her away from her life's passion."

Duthie let the weight of Morgan's words settle to the ground. He let them build a new image of Dr Mary Seaton in his mind, of a young woman, bright and full of vigour, turned grey and slow at the touch of her husband.

Morgan's gravelly voice broke the silence. "To this day, the shard of the Maiden Stone sits gathering dust in his house. The thing she was most proud of, that connects all of us to that ancient past, demoted to a paperweight."

"In his flat in Don Street?" Duthie said, recollecting the shit-in-the-paper-bag prank.

Morgan's laugh was loud and rueful. "You think that's the house of the great Seaton Clan? Och no, laddie. There's a reason they call him 'The Wizard of Skene'. His true home is a grotesque pile of bricks at the banks of the Loch of Skene, way out in the countryside. Talk about a man's castle: you'll find your chandeliers there, boy. Shields and swords aplenty, a family crest above every doorway."

"Wow," Duthie breathed. He had become transfixed by Morgan's steely tone.

"Aye. But it's a modern monstrosity. Nothing like this old castle," she patted the walls. "But that's where our Mary's shard remains. In that bloody man's fake castle."

"You should do something about it," Duthie said. "Go steal it. Doesn't belong to him anyway."

Something sparkled in Morgan's eyes, like moonlight rippling on the surface of a black pond. She grinned. "Now there's an idea."

"Me?" Duthie said and stepped backwards. "I'm not breaking into his castle."

Morgan held her hands out. "Your words, not mine."

"Oh, hell no!" Duthie squealed. "I'm already in deep enough with your family. More than enough, thank you. And now you want me to steal the shard?"

"Oh *wheesht*, I want nothing of the sort," Morgan said, wandering back to the living area. "I was just tellin' ye a story."

"About some old rock?"

She whipped round, eyes blazed with warning. "You watch your words, Rune Duthie!"

Duthie was taken aback. Hearing his name between her teeth, seeing the crackle in her gaze, doused his temper immediately. He took a deep breath. "Do you know what your niece said to me before I came here? She said if I so much as stepped one foot wrong at the festival, she would go straight to her daddy and get me kicked off the internship."

Morgan shook her head and chuckled. "That's the Ali Seaton in her talking. I wouldn't let it worry you."

"Of course I fucking worry about it! It's easy for you to say, sitting up here in your *literal* castle, nipping out to do naughty wee pranks at the Professor's expense. But as much as it makes me sick, I need his approval. I need this internship."

"Why?" she said.

Duthie became aware of warmth that had risen in his cheeks. "It...doesn't matter. Look, I better hit the road–"

"Why?" she pursued.

"Because it's my ticket out of here, okay?" he said, arms wide.

"I see. Trouble at home?"

"You could say that," he laughed. The sound was thin and pathetic.

"Mummy and Daddy issues?" she said. He looked up, expecting ridicule on her face but was surprised to see something far softer.

"That obvious, eh?" He turned away from her and faced the chest of drawers. His wooden carving stared back at him, its beady eyes and lopsided beak forming a gormless expression. He turned it over in his hand, considering it from each angle, hoping with every rotation that it would somehow look better, that the skill in its creation would magically become apparent, but all he saw were more flaws. A hopelessness formed in his throat and, quite in spite of himself, tears fell down his cheek. He felt some get caught in the eye patch, and groaned at the ridiculousness of it all. Death, he couldn't muster a single tear for. But this?

"What's so funny?" Morgan breathed behind him.

He wiped his nose. His voice was thick. "Let's just say it's time I found a way out of Aberdeen."

"And art is your ticket out of here?"

He put the carving back. Its ragged edge left a splinter in his thumb. He bit at it. "I mucked about in uni. 'Too much fun, not enough focus'. Came out with second class honours. No Master's programme will accept me on that alone. But the internship?"

"Ah," she said.

He turned back to her and was startled by what he saw. She seemed troubled, her forehead a river of creases.

"So, the whole interest in the Picts?" she said.

"What about it?"

"It's just a ticket?"

"No, I like it," he said and picked up Mary Seaton's book. "It's really good."

"That's fine then," her brows slackened a little, but the worry seemed to remain. The electricity in her eyes was gone.

"Morgan. I can't be part of…whatever this game is. Not any more than I already am."

She blinked, as if coming back to herself. "Of course you can't," she replied.

She reached into her robes and pulled out something smooth and metallic. "Here. Be free, Rune."

He rubbed a thumb over the dull surface of his Zippo lighter.

"And also," she crossed to a row of small hooks and threw a set of car keys to him. "Let the wind from my wings speed you on your way."

"Thank you," he said. "I'll look after her. Promise."

He made his way down the circular staircase. He was nearly at the bottom when she called to him a final time. The boom of her voice, the way it echoed down the tower, it was as if he was being addressed by a god.

"You don't *need* to be an artist, Rune," the voice said.

He looked up at the dark stairway and smiled. "And you don't *need* to leave flaming bags of shit on people's doorsteps."

Deep laughter trickled down the stone steps.

Part Five
The Bard of Kampala

A dream...

The Prophetess Fedelm approaches the castle.

Her visions have led her here, through forest and misty lake, bracken and briar.

Back to the tower of her childhood

The Shard. It waits for her at its top, singing its mournful song:

"I am here. Here I am."

She has seen this before, heard this countless times. There is precious little that can surprise a prophetess, one with imbas forosnai, all-seeing knowledge.

So she takes the first inevitable step.

Up she climbs, up and up, closer and closer.

The threnody becomes clearer with each stride, the voice more familiar, as she knew it would:

"Here I am. Where have you been? I have waited."

She reaches the top of the tower, following her destiny, until she can go no further, for she has arrived.

Now is the time, the time is now. The Shard need wait no longer.

The Prophetess Fedelm knows what will happen, yet she plays her role as if this is new.

Ever the dutiful daughter, following the path that has been laid out for her.

She lifts the Shard. It is glass, brittle and lovely. It reflects her own eyes on its surface.

But at a tilt, another face appears.

The face of the Mother. A face to match the song.

The Prophetess Fedelm knew this would happen, but still she feels a stab of pain.

"Why did you die, Mother? Why did you leave me?"

Her hand trembles. The glass Shard slips.

Down it falls, end over end over end, until it hits the cold floor...

...with a thud.

For it is not glass after all.

Merely a piece of rock.

Dead and cold.

A rock without meaning.

The Prophetess Fedelm leaves the Shard and the tower.

She denies the Shard's song.

It was never anything but a hollow wail.

It is just as she knew it would be.

All-seeing knowledge gives certainty.

But it does not lessen the hurt.

I.

Okay my friends, here is how this will go...

When I begin my story, I will always say: '*Olwatuuka ngambalabira...*'.

Do you know what this means? Oh, you don't speak *Luganda*? I thought everyone from Aberdeen did. Ha! No, I am only making a joke.

Doric? Oh yes, that is what you speak, not Luganda. This is my mistake, of course. In that case, please don't worry, I will translate for you.

It means: 'Once upon a time I saw...'

Now doesn't this sound enticing? But I don't wish to tell you my story if you are not interested. I don't want to be a bore. So you need to tell me that you want to hear more.

You must say the following phrase: '...*nobulabibwo*'.

No-bu-la-bibwo. Got it? Say it for me.

Very good. And do you know what this means? It means '...with your very own eyes'.

So, now do you see how it works? I call to you: 'Once upon a time I saw...' and you reply '...with your very own eyes'.

And then we can begin. So here goes:

Olwatuuka ngambalabira!

And you say?

Ha! That is close enough for me. Well done, my friends. Very well, I shall begin my *enfumo*. That is the Luganda word for 'folktale'. And here it is:

Have you heard the story about how Hare saved her own life?

She is a very clever one, Hare. Very tricky. Always one step ahead of everyone else, just out of reach.

Now, one day Hare was very hungry but she had completely run out of food. She checked everywhere for even a small scrap. On top of the *akatandalo* rack above the fireplace? Maybe in the *ekibbo* dish?

"What am I going to eat?" Hare said. And then she had a clever thought. "I know! I will go speak to my friend Elephant."

Elephant lived down by the opening of the jungle with all his very big family. Everyone in his family was very big, and there were very many of them, but they never seemed to go hungry. There is strength in numbers, you see. And so Hare asked Elephant if she may have one of his cows.

"I have run out of food. I will, of course, pay you back with another cow as soon as I am able," she said.

"My friend," Elephant said loudly into the sky, "of course you may have one of our cows."

And so Hare, happy as the sunlight, took the cow away and ate it.

It took a very long time for Hare to eat the whole cow. She barbecued it, stewed it, fried it, dried it, cooked it and souped it. But after many days, she ran out of meat. And she was nowhere close to having a cow to replace the one Elephant had given her.

What was she to do?

Ah yes, excellent suggestion. She could grow some food. Some yams or bananas maybe?

She could catch her own cows? Well yes. Hare is very fast, and could outrun a cow. But Hare is also very lazy and also very clever. If there is a way for her to succeed without running, she will preserve her strength.

"I know!" Hare said. (Her belly was grumbling so she had to say it quite loudly to be heard.) "I will go ask Buffalo if he can give me a cow."

The next day Hare went up to the great plain to ask her friend Buffalo if he would give her one of his cows to eat. Buffalo's farm was very big, and he had many cows.

(What's that? Why no, I don't think it's strange that Buffalo kept cows for food. But they're the same? Oh dear, don't let Buffalo hear you say that. He will be very upset!)

"I will pay you back with a cow as soon as I can," Hare said.

"Well now," said Buffalo, low and humble to the ground, "what kind of a friend would I be if I didn't help in time of need?"

And so Hare skipped away with one of Buffalo's cows, ready to be barbecued and stewed, fried and dried, cooked and souped.

Many days later, Hare was still no closer to repaying either Elephant or Buffalo with replacement cows. She could maybe try to hunt for wild cows, but she was only one person, and that would take a lot of energy. She would need a cleverer solution.

And do you know, one came to her in the very next thought...

II.

It was the little girl with the long brown hair in Turriff who said it best. She stared up at Abe, all six years of her, wide-eyed and chubby-cheeked, and whispered: "You must be really tired!"

It was the perfect response. The only response, really. By the end of every performance, the Ugandan storyteller was out of breath and glossy with sweat, his smile filled with pride.

When they first arrived, audiences were agog at Abe's ceremonial attire; the sashes of cowrie shells draped across his bare chest, the tall feather sprouting from the rear of his headband. Many tittered at the sight. A group of teenagers in Woodend Barn were in stitches, and were summarily booted out of the hall by the staff. Abe didn't even bat an eyelid at the ridicule, his focus was on those who remained.

And those who did were immediately captivated. Here was a man, as dark-skinned as anyone they had ever seen, transforming their community space into a world of wonder and music.

Abe didn't simply tell stories, he brought them to life. He pulled the audience into them, wove them into the fabric. This wasn't story-time where the teller is nestled behind a book, his audience cross-legged on the floor. It wasn't theatre, with the actor on stage and the crowd in rowed-seating. This was full-bodied, full-hearted performance, where the storyteller moved among the audience, issuing call, listening for response.

Wherever Abe and Duthie travelled, the Ugandan spun magic: first through voice, changing pitch with every character; second with body, leaping and scuttling, inhabiting the form of every creature in his tales; and third with music, filling these Aberdeenshire village halls and community centres with Kiganda, the music of Baganda – the mellow beat of the drum, the flexing of the tube fiddle, the twanging of the lyre, the bird-like twittering of the flute. Audiences delighted at the instruments' names, and repeated them with hungry tongues: *ngoma, endingidi, endongo, endere.*

The adventures of Hare, Elephant, Buffalo, Leopard, Frog and Dog bewitched them.

They shrieked when the tale demanded it, laughed when comedy ensued, grew wistful and silent when the morality lessons followed through. Trickster Hare became their antihero, their favourite of the Bagandan pantheon. They chuckled at how she tied a long rope between Elephant and Buffalo, convincing them that their replacement cows were at the other end. They slapped their thighs with delight at the fruitless tug of war that took place between these two colossal creatures, and clapped when both gave up, deciding to simply gift the cows to clever Hare.

And the moral?

"Strength is good," Abe would say with a knowing grin, his amber gaze casting around the audience, "but intelligence is better."

At the end of each day, it was all Duthie could do to peel Abe away from his adoring fans. They wanted him to stay, to repay the favour with stories of their own – stories of the seal-like selkies who swim ashore wearing skins the shape of women, and of the two giants of Bennachie forever locked in war, hurling great rocks at one another.

The locals offered not only stories, but also home-cooked meals and pints of beer in the local pubs. Duthie had never seen or heard such north-east hospitality. '*Musajja gyagenda-gyasanga banne*'. A man finds friends wherever he goes.

But in time the light in Abe's amber eyes would flicker, the electrical thrum of the storyteller dimming to a crackle. Now Duthie could finally step in, say the thank you and farewell, and courier his artist home.

Safely stowed in the passenger seat of Morgan's old blue Volvo, the long road back to campus ahead of them, Abe would drift off, ripe from sweaty exertion and replete with accomplishment. And Duthie would hum quietly the whole way home, singing the melodies of the *endingidi*, *endongo* and *endere*.

III.

Olwatuuka ngambalabira!
Nobulabibwo!

Did you know that Hare and Leopard used to be best of friends? Quite unlikely, isn't it? One small and tricky, the other powerful but perhaps not so smart. But maybe that isn't so strange a friendship: one smart, the other less so; one cunning, the other trusting. A perfect friendship for a trickster, at least.

One day, Hare and Leopard...

No, wait! Let me see if we can bring this a little closer to home. What is a Scottish animal that is small and clever, always just out of reach?

A mouse? Yes, that's good, but mice can be found everywhere in the world, can they not? Maybe we should think of something you only find in Scotland.

Something is funny over here. Tell me, don't be shy. What is making you giggle, my young friends? What's that? A 'haggis'? Ah yes! I have heard of this. You eat it with potatoes and yams? '*Neeps*'? What are they? Oh, I see. But haggis is food, no? It's not an animal.

Oh, really? Well then, Haggis sounds perfect: a small animal, as you say, that lives in the hills, very difficult to find, one leg shorter than the other so it can run on a steep circular surface in a straight line, but only clockwise. Very clever.

In that case, Haggis shall be our Hare!

And what of Leopard? Do you have any big animals in Scotland? Hmm, yes, but I think the Loch Ness Monster is perhaps a little too big.

A wildcat? Very nice.

Haggis and Wildcat. Best of friends.

And so, one day Haggis and Wildcat were in search of food. They were hungry, and liked to hunt together.

"Why don't we sneak into a nearby farm?" said Haggis. "The farmer has lots of food, and would surely not notice one or two things going missing."

"Great idea as ever, Haggis," said Wildcat. He always followed her ideas without question.

Tell me, my friends. What did Haggis and Wildcat steal from the farmer? A 'Buttery'? Oh I see, it is baking. Yes, you're right, I must try it. Well then, Haggis and Wildcat stole many Butteries and took them back to Haggis's home in the hills.

But do you know what Haggis did? Just as she and Wildcat sat down to eat, Haggis pretended she heard a noise outside.

"Oh no!" she said, "I think I hear the farmer outside, looking for his Butteries. Oh please, Wildcat, I am too small and weak to fight off the farmer. Can you help?"

"Do not worry, Haggis," Wildcat said. "I will frighten the farmer away".

Wildcat left the house in search of the farmer. Haggis jumped off her seat and ran outside the back door and hid in the nearby trees. With a voice as big and farmer-like as she could manage, she shouted words of warning, with little arms as strong as she could make them, she shook the branches.

Wildcat was very scared at the sound and sight, and he ran away.

And what did Haggis do? Yes, that's right! She went back home and ate all the Butteries herself.

The next day, Haggis was very thirsty. She went to ask Wildcat if he was too. And he was – after all, he had run away very fast from the farmer. So they went to find something to drink. They went to a pub on the other side of the hill. There, the pub owner had a big selection of lovely things to drink.

Tell me, what did they drink?

Beer and whisky? No, no, no, my friends! Haggis and Wildcat are too young for that. Don't worry, I know precisely what they drank. What is the name of your orange soda? I like it very much. Irn Bru! That is the very one. Haggis and Wildcat managed to steal many bottles of Irn Bru without the pub owner noticing, and they took them back to Haggis's house.

But do you know what Haggis did? Ha ha, that's right, how did you guess? Are you telling me my stories are predictable?

Haggis banged on her pots and pans, and made her voice sound as much like the pub owner as she could. And Wildcat ran away again. Haggis went back home and began to drink the Irn Bru. It was the perfect thing to drink after eating salty Butteries.

But Haggis's luck was about to run out.

"Wait a minute," said Wildcat stopping in his tracks. "That voice wasn't really the pub owner. It was more of a Haggisy voice."

He made it back to Haggis's house just in time to see the little one drinking her third bottle of Irn Bru.

"Oh my goodness!" Wildcat shouted through the window. "You greedy little haggis. I shall chase you and chase you for tricking me!"

And he did! Wildcat chased Haggis up to the top of the hill, down to the bottom, and around and around the middle. He nearly caught her a few times too, but Haggis was always too quick and tricky, always just out of reach. Haggis managed to get quite far ahead just as she arrived at the river.

"There's nowhere else to go," she said. "I guess I better jump in the river and hold my breath."

From under the water Haggis could see Wildcat walking up and down the edge. She couldn't hear him, but could read his lips: "Haggis! Oh Haggis! Where are you? When I find you I will thump you and gobble you up! You tricky little Haggis, oh!"

Haggis's little Haggisy lungs are not very big, so she was soon running out of air. There was nothing else for it, so she popped her head out of the water and took a deep breath.

Wildcat looked at her long and hard. Haggis's heart began to go very fast.

"There you are, you greedy little thing," Wildcat called from the waterside.

And then Haggis, always one step ahead, had an idea.

"Hello Mister Wildcat!" she waved. "Can I help you?"

"Don't be silly," Wildcat shouted. "I have found you Haggis, and I will now thump you and gobble you up."

"I don't know what you mean. I am not Haggis."

"What? Yes you are."

Haggis swam to the waterside and stood on the bank next to Wildcat. Her legs, one shorter than the other, dripping with water.

"No I am not. I am *Wet Haggis*. But you are looking for *Haggis*."

"Oh," Wildcat said, and scratched his furry head. "I am sorry, Wet Haggis. Did you see where Haggis went?"

"I saw her run away into those woods. If you leave now, you may catch her."

"Thank you very much, Wet Haggis," said Wildcat, and ran away into the forest.

To this day, Wildcat is still looking for Haggis. Whenever he sees her he chases and chases. But he never catches her.

They are no longer friends, which sometimes makes Haggis sad. But then she remembers that Wildcat is probably better off without her friendship.

As we Baganda people always say: *Bwoyita n omubbi – nawe bakuyita mubbi.*

If you befriend a thief, you will be called a thief.

IV.

A troupe of dancers in ethereal clothing snaked among the gutted interior chambers of Slains Castle. The clifftop ruin was bathed in sunlight and gulls hovered on the breeze high above. An audience stood and admired the performance and haunting scenery.

"Y'know, there's a big myth about Cruden Bay," Duthie whispered to Vlada. "Ask any of these villagers and they'll tell you Slains was the inspiration for Castle Dracula. It's a neat story: fourteenth century ruin, perched on a cliff edge above the North Sea, very imposing, very scary, crashing waves blah blah. And sure, Bram Stoker actually stayed nearby when he was planning the novel. But ask me? I've always thought the myth was bullshit. I mean, I've read the book and watched the 1992 movie, so y'know."

He shrugged. He wasn't sure why he was saying all this, but somehow, breaking Vlada's stony expression rose like a challenge within him. "I mean, sure, Bram Stoker visited Slains. Big whoop! But what about Bran Castle in – oh, let's see now – *freakin'* Transylvania? Or what about all those creepy castles in Whitby where the actual novel is based?"

Vlada looked at Duthie with utter disinterest. The Slovakian dance captain was observing her troupe, Rusalka, as they performed among the castle's central chambers. The dancers floated and pranced among the ruins, like Shakespearean nymphs cavorting in the late afternoon sun. Vlada did not match the audience's expressions of delight. Her look was cool at best, her near-translucent skin and razor-perfect features were vampiric in the extreme. If it hadn't been daylight, Duthie could swear one of Stoker's creations had risen from the pages and flown to Aberdeenshire to cut a bitch with that stare.

She cast her gaze up through the roofless chamber and sighed something Slovak through her teeth.

Well, she breathes at least. "Not happy?" Duthie asked.

She pointed to one of the performers, one in particular whose arms were held aloft, gossamer material draped from her extended hands. "I've told Gabriela so many times about the line of her arms. And don't get me started on Dušan. Did you see the way he lifted Lenka in the first dance? Sloppy."

"Looks perfect to me," Duthie said.

Vlada considered him and smiled. It was a sharp thing full of ice. "You dance?"

He grinned back. "Like nobody's watching."

She considered him as if watching a seagull take a shit. She jutted her chin. "You look like a Pirate. Do you know that?"

"A *sexy* pirate? Sure," Duthie said

She made a '*mmm hmm*' sound and resumed tutting at her dancers.

Duthie was currently off the clock. Abe had recently finished his Haggis story, and so both he and Duthie had melded into the back row of the audience. Duthie was enjoying the break.

Rusalka's performance was a feast for the eyes, and he was even looking forward to the chamber ensemble from Celia's Chinese orchestra which was up next. He surprised himself, how much he cared for the performers and this ridiculous festival.

"'Scuse me," said a child, looking up at Duthie. The kid could barely have been five years old. The sheen of snot on his upper lip proved it. "Can I play with that?"

He motioned towards a moss-covered wall where Abe's *endongo* lyre was propped against the bricks. The kid's father gave a wave of encouragement.

Duthie leaned down to the kid's level. "Well, you'll have to ask Mr Okello very nicely first, okay?"

Abe was at the back of the chamber, chatting with Celia. They seemed deep in conversation. The pair had greeted each other like long lost friends when they had arrived at the clifftop castle – despite having seen each other that morning at breakfast.

The young boy tottered over to Abe, who greeted him with a pat on the shoulder. In moments he was crouched down with the stringed instrument in his hands. The kid beamed and reached out for it.

"Children," said Vlada with the same critical air she had used on her dancers. "Just looking at them makes me want to wash my hands."

Duthie barked with laughter, attracting the attention of a few disapproving audience members.

"I think I might love you a little bit, Vlada," he whispered.

"It's only natural," she said, dry as dust but a twinkle in her eye. She then squinted at the back wall. "What do you suppose they're talking about?"

Abe and Celia were back in quiet conference, their expressions more sober than they had been seconds ago.

"I have no idea," Duthie said, his words low and drawn out.

"They do this a lot, you know," she shrugged.

Duthie stepped forward. "Maybe I should see if everything's okay."

Vlada touched his arm lightly. "Wait, it's the final number. They've been rehearsing this with the orchestra for days."

Her look of anticipation was warranted. The performance was breath-taking. The Chinese ensemble's rendition of Stravinsky's Firebird Suite bounced off the high walls of the castle, invigorating the dancers and audience alike. The Slavic fairytale was brought to life and made all the more exciting and strange by the derelict gothic surroundings.

Even Vlada erupted at the conclusion of the piece, the triumph on her face matched by that of her troupe and the musicians. "Brava, brava!" she called over the applause. Duthie whistled through his fingers. It was a glorious moment. He looked for Abe, but couldn't find him at first. He wasn't standing where he had been.

He finally spotted him sitting on the grass with his back against the wall, looking downwards in despair. Cradled in his arms were the broken remains of his stringed instrument.

V.

"Sure you don't mind? Promise I won't be long, I just really need to do this on the way home," Duthie said.

"Of course," Abe replied. His voice was distant, as wide as the countryside they were driving through. He had been staring out the car window ever since leaving Cruden Bay. Morgan's Volvo filled the silence, rattling and squeaking with each corner, the engine seemingly powered by rocks rather than petrol.

"Let's have some music." Duthie turned the radio dial but nothing happened. "Maybe there's a cassette in the glove compartment?"

He opened the hatch above Abe's lap. It sprung open, revealing bundles of paper, bills, leaflets, something that looked like important legal documents, chocolate bar wrappers, but no cassettes.

"That's a 'no' too, then. I'm guessing you're all sung out?"

Abe made a small chuckle, obviously out of politeness. Duthie was determined to brighten his mood. The sight of him at Slains still stung: it was shocking to have seen him so distraught, holding the broken pieces of the *endongo* lyre as if they were a child. Nobody else had seen his tears, since they had been caught in the rapture of the performance.

The pieces of the stringed instrument were heaped in the footwell by Abe's bare feet.

"You'll be able to fix it, dude," Duthie said. "If not here, then when you get back home."

For the first time in twenty minutes, Abe turned to face him. His normally honey-amber gaze was pink-rimmed.

"I don't think so," he said.

Duthie patted his leg. "It's okay, you can get another," he said, then immediately chastised himself for sounding dismissive like his mother. He breathed out heavily. "But this one was important, wasn't it."

"It was my brother's."

"Shit, is he...?"

"He's alive."

"Phew! Well, you can't worry about that, Abe. Things get broken, accidents happen. He'll have known that when he gave it to you."

Abe's voice cracked. "He didn't give it to me."

"Oh. You nicked it?"

Abe's already knotted brow creased further.

"Stole it," Duthie clarified.

Abe nodded.

"Bad ass!" Duthie laughed. "Who knew Abel Okello was capable of thievery! I love it."

"Then you don't know me very well." The words were cold. They chilled – like Eddie's comments a few nights back when she berated Duthie for fixating on Abe's handsomeness rather than getting to know him.

"Maybe not," Duthie said. "I'm sorry about that."

Abe shook his head.

Duthie tapped the wheel. "I was a little preoccupied with, y'know..."

"What?"

"...I mean, come on, you must have noticed I was hitting on you?"

"Oh that," Abe said with the smallest of smiles.

"Oh fuck you!" Duthie grinned. "Look at that innocent face. Give me a goddamn break, mister."

"Don't worry about it," Abe smiled further.

"*Don't worry about it.* That's you all over, isn't it? So smooth and calm. You know it's infuriating, right? You never give anything away."

Abe held up a piece of the broken endongo and shrugged.

"Point taken," Duthie said. "I guess it took a broken family heirloom to get something out of you. It's a good thing though, Abe. You shouldn't be afraid to get emotional. Look at me, I'm all *'blah blah blah'* and messy half the time and I'm still standing."

"I'll try to be more messy."

"Good. Y'see? I'm a great courier: driving you around; giving you awesome advice; prying fawning old Scottish ladies off you so we can leave on time."

Abe chuckled more openly this time. "They do seem to like me."

Duthie pinched his cheek. "*Och Agnes, that wee African laddie is so polite and his funny wee stories are so charming. Here, Mr Uganda, eat anither mealie pudding. Aye that's right, and tak anither rock cake wi' ye. Canna hiv ye going hungry*'."

He pushed an imaginary cake into Abe's face which, to his delight, was now beaming.

The road wound through the foothills of Bennachie, past hamlets and farmhouses, and a few fancy new-builds. It all looked very pleasant.

"See that?" Duthie pointed to the highest point on the rolling landscape. "That's Mither Tap, the peak of Bennachie."

The hill's rocky nipple and peat-brown base stood out from the orderly greens of forest and farmland.

"The one from Morgan's story?" Abe said.

"The very one."

The car rounded a grassy corner and whooshed by a stone structure.

"Oh shit, that was it!" Duthie said. He made a u-turn and parked up in a slim space that hemmed the road. They got out the car and faced a rectangular monolith, three-metres tall by half a metre wide.

"There she is," Duthie said, hands on hips. Despite the Maiden Stone's size, she seemed delicate. Not frail, but whittled and elegant. The dipping sunlight cut across her, revealing the granite's pink hue and striating the carved surface with shadows. The markings were already worn from thirteen-hundred summers and winters, but the closer Duthie got, the more he could make out the shapes.

He opened Mary Seaton's book at the central page, which featured a black and white photograph of the standing stone. It was a washed-out rendition of the dramatic structure before them. He handed the book to Abe and pointed at the description.

Abe read aloud: "A centaur below three faded figures. A rectangle and Z-rod. A Pictish beast. A mirror and comb. And on the reverse, a single statement – a large Celtic cross." He looked up at the stone and smiled. "It's beautiful." He took a step closer and pointed to the right-hand shoulder where there was a large triangular notch. "That's where the Devil turned her to stone, isn't it?"

Duthie ran a hand along its edge. It felt smooth from years of exposure, but he could imagine its sharpness when the fracture had first occurred.

He tilted his head at the book. "There's a piece missing. A shard. Morgan's sister, Mary Seaton, found it."

"Morgan's sister?" Abe's eyes widened.

"Yup. Mysterious Morgan. Mary was her sister. Eddie's her niece. Professor Seaton's her, well, I guess her mortal enemy. Families, eh?"

Abe shook his head in disbelief. "This shard. Where is it kept?"

"Not a museum, that's for sure," Duthie tutted. "Mary's old fusty peers said she was wrong, that it was just a rock."

Abe considered his expression. "And this makes you angry."

"Hell yeah it does," Duthie flushed, all his frustration with the Professor – stoked by Morgan's story – rising to his cheeks. "It's bullshit."

"Why?"

"It just is. I mean look at it. The sculptor didn't make the stone like this with a great big gouge in it."

"Maybe they did."

"Whose side are you on?" Duthie said, trying to mask his annoyance with a laugh.

"Nobody's," he said, passive as the warm air drifting up the hill. "With something this old, it's hard to really know what is what."

Duthie sucked his teeth. "Some things are just right."

"If you say so," Abe said. He fingered through the book's pages. He reached the final section where Duthie's letter-cum-bookmark peeked out. He began to unfold the letter but Duthie reached out and snapped the book shut.

"If you make me lose my place, I'll have to kill you," he said.

He replaced the book in Abe's hands with the car keys. "Make yourself useful and fetch some paper and chalk from the boot. We're running out of light and I need to get rubbings of this entire Maiden."

VI.

You didn't need to be an expert for this, it was primary school-level stuff. Tape an A3 sheet of paper to a section of the standing stone and rub over it with chalk, pressing firmly enough to render a copy of the surface beneath, but lightly enough not to shade in the finer details. Once finished, lay a new sheet directly next to it and continue rubbing. To finish, fix it with hairspray found in the back of the Volvo.

Duthie and Abe took a side each – Duthie to the Pictish front which he rubbed in green chalk; Abe to the Celtic cross on the reverse, rubbing in red. They worked methodically as the sunlight slowly sank below Mither Tap. The humidity had been rising all afternoon and, despite being easy, it was sweaty, quiet work. The only sounds were grating scrapes of chalk on paper, punctured occasionally by the twittering of small birds and the crunch of asphalt beneath the wheels of passing cars.

Duthie occasionally looked round to check Abe's progress – not in his rubbing, but in his mood. The task seemed to have given him focus, but a mistiness still clung to him as closely as the humidity in the air.

After a while, Duthie bit the bullet. "Tell me the story."

"Which one?" Abe responded.

"The only one."

Abe stopped rubbing and shook his head in confusion.

"The one where Abe stole his brother's endongo."

"I don't think I want–"

"C'mon," Duthie coaxed. "I won't look at you as you tell it. See? I'm going back round to my side of the stone."

A long stretch of silence, broken only by chalk on paper.

Duthie sang softly. "*Olwatuuka ngambalabira...*"

There was a chuckle from the other side of the Maiden. "You're using my culture against me."

"That's how we Brits do things. C'mon, just treat it like one of your Hare stories. *Nobulabibwo!*"

"It isn't that kind of story, Rune."

Duthie had just finished rendering the Pictish beast carved on the Maiden's surface. It stared back with one wild green eye. Duthie peeled back the paper and ran his palm across the beast's rough surface. "Okay fine," he said, "here's how this will go: I begin the story, and you tell me if it's right. This is another British thing – telling other people's stories as if we know them. Colonial style."

A sigh from the other side.

"Your brother is called...Cain. Cain and Abel. You were brought up in the Garden of Eden, and competed for God's love."

"Very funny," Abe droned.

"You mean I'm wrong? Oh no, I guess you'll have to correct me."

Another sigh. "My brother's name is Kakuru."

"Is that Ugandan for 'Cain'?"

"It means 'firstborn of twins'."

"You're a twin?"

"I am. Twins are very special in Uganda, a big cause for celebration and superstition. It is a big responsibility for parents too, they must ensure our wellbeing or face bad luck."

Duthie laughed. "I like the sound of that: Your mum shouts at you and you're like: 'Uh uh, that's bad luck!'"

"Not exactly."

"Must be weird being an identical twin. Do you look exactly the same?"

"Very much."

"Wait, does that mean 'Abel' is 'second born of twins'?"

"No. Apparently my parents took one look at me and decided I was a very different baby."

"Interesting," Duthie said, tapping a finger on his chin, then remembered the green chalk all over his hands. "Okay great, this gives me something to work with. So here's the next bit of the story: Kakuru and Abe, identical twins but opposite in nature. Abe was musical and imaginative, his parents' favourite child. Kakuru, despite arriving first, was boring and bland."

A smile unfurled in Abe's voice. "You're very cruel. Kakuru is very…straightforward, very logical, very in control."

"You didn't say I was wrong," Duthie grinned.

"He's a smart guy. He was born only two minutes before me but he jokes that he got all the brains, leaving me what was left."

"I guess you got all the manners."

"He's not so bad. Those brains have been put to a lot of use. He is an engineer, a real problem-solver. He's also a devoted Christian, goes with my father to Church every week. They are big in that community."

"Ooh, interesting plot twist. Religion. Always a source of problems. What about your mum, she's religious too?"

"She goes to church, though she was not raised Christian like my father. It's not in her blood, but she does her duty to him each Sunday."

"Ah ha! Duty, tradition, but also difference. The mother and father – the source of all Kakuru and Abel's joy and strife. This is good shit. Names? Quick, I need them for my story."

"My father is Adroa, my mother Dembe."

"Meanings?"

"I have no idea."

"Fine okay, I'll embellish. Father Adroa, strong and silent, a God-fearing man. Mother Dembe, mild and sweet, a perfect wife and loving mother."

"No, no, you're too old fashioned in your storytelling, Rune," Abe said, with energy in his voice.

Duthie smiled at his success in coaxing Abe out of his funk.

Abe continued: "In many ways my parents are as different from each other as me and Kakuru, it's not about one being strong and the other gentle. Their differences come from where they get their sense of pride. Ask my father where he is from and he will tell you: 'Kampala, the fastest growing city in Uganda, the melting pot of politics, economics and God'. It's the same with my brother. My mother, though? She will have a very different answer: 'The Kingdom of Buganda, home of the Bantu, land of proud clans, ancient folktales and music of the earth'."

Abe's voice had morphed with each character, just as he did with his stories. These particular voices were thin and high for his father, lyrical and low for his mother.

"D'you get on with them?" Duthie asked.

"My parents? It has never been a question of 'getting on with them'. I respect them. They raised Kakuru and me to be strong, proud of our country, to contribute to society. I have always aimed to be worthy of their respect."

"Oh," Duthie said. It all sounded so formal to him. "And *do* they respect you? They've got to be proud of what you're doing, right?"

"My mother is proud that I am sharing the old stories and music with the world. My father, maybe, is less pleased."

"Ah yes. The Parents. The source of all trauma," Duthie hissed.

Abe carried on as if he hadn't heard, instead brightening at a recollection. "It's funny, my father was the one who first bought musical instruments for me and my brother. An endongo for Kakuru, a gourd drum for me. I think he hoped we would play Christian hymns with them, rather than traditional *Kiganda* songs. Kakuru knew the instruments were more a ceremonial gift than for playing."

"Ah Kakuru. Always his father's son. He didn't play it?"

"No, that was not his style," Abe laughed. "He hung it on the wall where my father could always see it. I could never see the sense in that. My mother always told me that music is for playing, just as stories are for telling. I tend to agree."

"Clever lady," Duthie smiled.

"Yes. Clever enough to tell me so in private, away from my father's ears."

"He wouldn't approve?"

"He hoped I would follow him into business. Imports and exports. I joked that I am doing that right now – with tales and songs rather than fish and cotton."

"Did he laugh?"

"What do you think?"

"Classic Adroa," Duthie continued in his pretend mocking. "No sense of humour."

"He was so pleased when I attended Makarere University. That's where he studied many years ago, where he met my mother. He presumed I had applied for the same course as him, a Bachelors in Business Studies. He didn't know until it was too late that I was actually studying a Bachelors in Music."

"What did he do?"

"Nothing really. Some elders from his church heard me

performing a recital, and told him I was good, that he should be very proud. He couldn't give up face, so just said it was his idea all along that I pursue my musical interests."

"Pretty brave of you," Duthie said.

"Not my bravery. It was all my mother's. She was the one who suggested I invite the elders to the recital."

"Okay, I'm liking Dembe more and more. I think I might make her the main character."

Abe laughed. "That would be a very good idea. She is the strongest, most clever of us all. Yes, she goes to church, does her duty, shakes hands and makes meals for neighbours – the perfect wife, as you say – but she knows exactly what she is doing. She can run rings around anyone in our community. My father and brother joke about it, that she always secretly gets her way."

The sound of Abe's smile made the words flitter round the stone.

"My hero," Duthie said.

"All mothers are heroes."

"If you say so," Duthie muttered.

"You don't get along with your mother?"

"I thought it wasn't a question of 'getting on' with parents."

"Touché, my friend. As long as there is respect."

Duthie huffed.

"A mother is someone whose example you must live up to, no? She gave you life."

"I don't *have* to do anything," Duthie bit, then tried to cover with a smile. "Tale for another time, babe. Anyway, this isn't my storytime, it's yours."

"Rune…"

"C'mon, tell me more about Dembe."

"Well, she was the one who first told me the old tales. Of clever Hare, of gentle Elephant and foolish Leopard. She told us the stories each night, even when my brother said they were just silly baby stories. I begged her to keep telling them. She knew how much I loved them, and the music too. It was she who encouraged me to pick up the instruments, to learn the stories, to perform them to anyone willing to listen."

"What did your dad have to say about it?

"He wasn't delighted. But my mother took the brunt of his disappointment."

"Disappointment?" Duthie said quietly. "He wasn't ever..?"

Abe came back firm. "No, never. That is not the kind of man he is, Rune. Do not make that part of your story."

"Sorry." Duthie felt chastened.

"His disappointment was as bad as it got, that was punishment enough. I have always known that I can never live up to his example, but he has rarely told me so. He only said it to my mother. You see, she is my champion, always has been. It's not an easy role to keep."

"I'm sure it's easier than you think," Duthie said.

"Drives my brother crazy. My father is more hard on him. Kakuru has always tried to meet my father's expectations. I've always known I wouldn't come close, but somehow my mother raised me to believe I would never have to. It has kept me immune, safe. So I can understand why Kakuru feels the way he does about me."

"And how's that?"

"The sun is setting, my friend. Maybe my story can wait for another day."

"What? But it's just getting good. Besides I'm not finished yet. I still have the top of the stone to get, and I can't reach it."

Abe stepped round to Duthie's side and looked up at the Maiden Stone, towards the centaur that galloped in the topmost section. Its stance was majestic despite missing a front hoof – the bottom of its leg having broken away with the notch in the side of the stone.

Abe sized up the stone, looked Duthie up and down, then patted his own shoulders. "Jump up. I can carry you while you do the rubbings."

"Don't be daft!" Duthie laughed.

Abe wore an expression he hadn't seen before. It promised a recklessness he wouldn't have expected on someone so consistently cool and collected. Duthie didn't let the moment pass. It took them a few attempts, and much hilarity, but soon enough he was balanced on Abe's shoulders. Their stacked height was more than enough to reach the centaur.

"So, your brother," Duthie said once balanced. "He's a bit of a dick cos he's got daddy issues."

"Really? I don't think now is the time–"

"Tell me or I'll topple us!"

"You are a very annoying person, you realise this?"

"I do," Duthie grinned and patted Abe's stubbly cheek. He was suddenly aware of the closeness of his crotch to the back of Abe's neck.

"Okay," Abe sighed. "You paraphrase quite bluntly, but yes, Kakuru has 'daddy issues'. If mother is my hero, father is Kakuru's. Personally, I think he could have chosen more wisely."

"And this has driven you two apart?"

"It's part of the story, yes. But you realise this is only my telling of the story? They always have at least two sides."

"Whatever," Duthie blew. "You're too nice to tell it like it is."

"Again, you presume. I promise, I am no angel."

Duthie paused a second, chalk mid-swipe. Half the centaur was now prancing on the page. "I'm glad to hear it," he said and nudged Abe's chest with his foot. Abe responded by rubbing his hand lightly up Duthie's bare shin, causing a ripple of excitement.

"But Kakuru is no angel either," Abe continued, voice darkening. "He can be very cruel."

"Like how?"

Abe sighed. "He outed me to our parents."

"Jesus. What happened?"

"I have a group of friends, my best friends really. Kind, funny, fabulous. We met at college and have stayed close since. You would love them, I just know it. They are cheeky just like you."

Duthie felt his cheeks redden. "Cheeky? Well that sorts it, I have to come to Kampala. We can go clubbing with your cheeky friends."

"That would be nice. But not wise. It's not…safe for us to meet in public, you understand?"

"Oh," Duthie said, embarrassed at his own ignorance.

"We usually meet at one of my friends' apartments. Kusemererwa and Mubiru have a place near the city centre. The boys have been a couple since college but still they must pretend they are housemates."

Duthie wanted to express outrage, but chose silence.

"We would come together, nearly ten of us, most weekends to talk, and laugh, and sing. To watch American TV shows, argue over who our favourite drag queens are and so on. We had our own little world."

Duthie smiled at the picture, he could see it so clearly.

"Until Kakuru followed me one day," Abe added quietly. "He had suspected for many years. I don't know why he chose action this particular night. He followed me all the way from home and watched from a street corner as one by one, my friends and I buzzed to get into Kuse and Mubiri's apartment. Hours later, when I was going home, I saw him. The look on his face. Disgust, that's what it was. It was as if my father was looking at me through those eyes."

Duthie had finished the rubbing halfway through, and was now still, held by the sound of Abe's voice thickening.

"How did they take it? Your parents."

"Not well," Abe said. He tapped Duthie's legs, indicating for him to dismount. Duthie pulled the pages off the stone and slid down Abe's back.

The pair locked eyes: Duthie's full of sympathy, Abe's an amber void.

"I'm sorry, Abe. That's horrendous. What did you do?"

A smirk formed on Abe's face. "I packed a bag and left."

"My God."

He shrugged. "I've been travelling from festival to festival ever since."

"How long?"

"Nearly five months."

Duthie struggled for words, for a happy end to the story he had drawn out. All he managed was: "Your mother..."

"She was the one who told me to go. Not in a bad way. To be free. To stay just out of reach." A look passed his eyes, something sweet and lost. "It wasn't me that stole the endongo from my brother's wall. It was her."

Duthie folded his arms around Abe and whispered how sorry he was. Abe stood stock still, not rejecting the embrace, but not moving into it either.

Duthie felt a droplet on his neck. Then another. Then another.

"Shh," he crooned into Abe's shoulder. "Shh."

And then he felt another on his arm, then on his leg. He looked up into Abe's dry amber gaze. High above, the skies were finally breaking, weeping after weeks of unrelenting heat.

They gathered up the paper and ran to the car. Safely inside, they wound down the window and breathed in the fresh scents being released by the rain. Duthie turned to Abe, expecting to see grief and pain, but found only exhaustion.

"Let's get you home," Duthie said.

He turned the key and the Volvo coughed. He tried again and it rattled. On a third attempt, nothing happened at all.

VII.

"And it definitely *disnae* start?"

"No. I mean yeah, it definitely doesn't."

"And yer nae insured on the car?"

"...no."

"And the owner disnae have breakdown cover?"

"I don't know, I can't get hold of her," Duthie said, though he knew the answer would be no.

Jock groaned down the phone line, ending on a chuckle. "Well, Runey. That's quite a pickle eh?"

"Aye. Could you maybe..." Duthie began, hoping Jock would complete the sentence as he usually would in these *pickles*.

"Could I maybe...?" the Big Man said.

"Please?" Duthie said, ashamed at the whine in his voice.

"All right. Hang tight, kiddo. Help is on the way."

"Thanks Pops. 'Preciate it."

The line went dead and Duthie threw back his head against the rest. "My stepdad says he'll be out as soon as he can. Sorry about this."

"Not your fault," Abe said. He looked like he could fall asleep in a single blink.

They sat in silence, listening to the *pitter patter* on the windshield. Night had fallen in earnest and the only lights belonged to the houses dotted across the landscape and the stars dotted above.

In time the sky cleared. Duthie climbed out of the car, careful not to disturb a now-dozing Abe. The ground had deep puddles across it, and the hillside had a glossy sheen. The Maiden Stone seemed to shine, her face washed clean and gleaming in the starlight. Duthie noticed her stance for the first time: she faced him directly. To her left was the roadside, to her right was the slow incline towards Mither Tap. He imagined wee Margaret from Morgan's tale, turning her head towards Bennachie, and the juniper tree where she would meet her father each day for lunch. The Devil himself had ended her story, clenching her shoulder in his stony grip, fixing her feet to the ground until they were part of it. If only Margaret had been quicker, or more resourceful like Abe's mother, or slippery and changeable like Morgan. Then she wouldn't be stuck to the spot for all time.

Duthie sighed and took out his phone. He created a new text message for Eddie, thumb pausing for a while.

Me: Hi. I'm showing Abe the sights. Be back late.

She came back quicker than expected.

    Eddie: Who's this?
    Me: It's Duthie.
    Eddie: Who?
    Me: Funny. Don't wait up.
    Eddie: Like I was going to.
    Me: ...

Duthie chuckled and shook his head. What a strange, spike person Eddie was. The Great Prophetess Fedelm. So disappointed with life's trajectory but never truly admitting it out loud.

The Maiden Stone's granite face lit up suddenly. Headlights behind Duthie threw his shadow on to her monolithic form. Gravel crunched beneath the tyres of an approaching vehicle. He turned and shielded his unpatched eye from the glare. The car ground to a halt and a door opened.

"Well, well, well," said a young voice, in imitation of a Southern belle. "I do believe, kind sir, that your help has arrived."

"Jock, you rat bastard," Duthie said under his breath. He forced a smile and replied: "Hey, Squirt."

A four-and-a-half foot silhouette with a halo of red hair ran at him, nearly knocking him over in the collision.

"I can't believe you came to visit!" Kelly said, arms gripping like a vice.

"I'm not sure it was on purpose," said a voice from the car. The window wound down, revealing another face, this one with red hair too, but long ringlets, with a few tendrils of silver sprouting from the fringe.

For the first time in days, Duthie craved a cigarette. "Hi Mum."

"Hi yourself," she said.

After a single look from Jacqueline Duthie's brown eyes, Duthie felt himself click into an old shape, a smaller, crooked one he had hoped to have left behind – the past week of adventure, and the strength it had built within him, erased like chalk off slate. He is Rune Duthie.

Rune was silent all the way up the treelined road. He and Kel were in the back of the Corsa. Jack was at the wheel, Abe beside her. The road meandered and inclined into the foothills of Bennachie.

Kel had nestled herself against Rune, her head lolling on his shoulder with the motion of the car. Rune noticed his mother stealing glances in the rear-view mirror. He recognised the look, saw questions forming behind those eyes.

The asphalt ceased, the road suddenly a knobbly dirt track. The trees on either side of the path reached for each other, forming a canopy of gnarled, steepled fingers.

The track opened out into a clearing. At its end glowed a single light. It belonged to a porch, and the porch belonged to a log cabin. The cabin looked like a sketch from a bedtime story – as much part *of* the woods, as something built *from* it – thick trunks stacked horizontally, a balcony on the second floor, a gabled roof.

Jack looked in the mirror once more. The questions in her gaze had gone, replaced with something quiet and new.

Part Six
Jack o' Bennachie

A dream, continued…

The Prophetess Fedelm approaches in her chariot, a weaver's beam in her fist.

She has followed the path through the wilds. The winding way is a golden thread to someone such as her.

It snakes and changes, branches and evades, but she always finds it. And follows it.

Ever the dutiful daughter.

She knows they wait for her on the other side of the valley.

The Crow and the Wizard.

The Prophetess Fedelm breathes, steadies herself for the encounter. She does not fear it. But what comes after the encounter fills her with cold dread.

She sees them on either side of the golden path. The thunder claps their presence, the lightning illuminates.

On the left of the path is The Morrigan. The Crow of Battle. Tendrils of smoke cough from her beak, carrying cries, carrion sighs:

"Come with me. You know this is the true way. It will lead you Ben-home. Be the Prophetess Benholm."

On the right of the path is The Wizard. Fearful sorcerer of Skene. Squat but fearsome, eyes alight. A voice strained and cracked, heavy with loss, laden with fatherhood:

"She lies. This is the true way. Come take your Seat-on my side. Be the Prophetess Seaton."

The Prophetess looks to her left and to her right, and then aloft to the lightning-split sky and cries:

"I am the Prophetess Fedelm. You pull at me, and I see where each path leads, but neither will claim me."

The Crow and The Wizard exchange a look. Opposing forces, but joined in mirth.

The Crow: "You cannot fight us..."

The Wizard: "...we are inevitable."

The Crow and The Wizard: "Choose, oh Daughter of Destiny."

The Prophetess Fedelm lowers her eyes to the golden path. It trails behind her like golden plaited hair.

She sings: "A warrior will come. He will slay you both. I see it crimson and I see it red; A sea of blood descends upon your head."

She sings the words, invokes the vision. But she is not placated.

The Crow and the Wizard are silenced, but they are not cowed.

They watch with beaded eyes as the Prophetess steps from her chariot and leaves behind her weaver's beam. Bare feet meet the path.

The golden way cuts between Crow and Wizard, and leads to the summit of a breast-shaped hill.

She knows what she will find there. Upon that hill is a plinth. And upon the plinth is one true choice.

The Prophetess Fedelm feels fear.

For this is where the golden path ends, and her vision fails.

I.

Crash!

Rune awoke with a start. An audience of wooden knots in the ceiling stared back at him in alarm.

"Oopsie," said a voice from the other side of the living room.

Rune sat up and wiped sleep from his unpatched eye. Morning light flooded the open plan room, catching the dance of dust in its shafts. He peered over the back of the couch and saw a crouched form next to the kitchen sink. His mother was picking up pieces of a broken cup. She looked up, a dismembered handle dangling from her finger.

"Did I wake you?"

"Mmm hmm," Rune murmured. He stretched his back which ached from the odd angles he'd slept in.

Broken shards tinkled into the bin. "That's what I get for trying to make you a morning cuppa," Jack said. "Should be another mug somewhere."

"What time is it?"

"Just gone eight."

Rune groaned. He untwisted the waistband of his boxer briefs, threw a rug over his shoulders and shuffled to the kitchen area where Jack was now considering a dusty cup. Rune took it and ran it under the tap. "Don't worry about it, I'll sort my own."

Jack leaned against the counter and watched him make tea, every step of the process, with the look of someone who actually enjoyed watching paint dry.

"What?" he said.

"Nothing," she smiled, and combed fingers through her long hair. "You know, you kind of look like a–"

"Pirate, yes," Rune said.

"How's it feeling?" Her hand floated towards his face.

He ducked out of its path. "It's fine."

"You should put some–"

"I've got some," he smirked. "Thank you."

She motioned to the kitchen table. It was a huge, marble-topped thing, totally out of kilter with the rest of the modest surroundings. Rune sat at one end on a stool that was so tiny by comparison he felt like a hobbit ordering a pint of ale. To make the point he lifted his elbows high and propped them on the edge.

"It's the 'inspiration piece' for the rest of the kitchen," Jack said with air quotes. "They've only started renovations."

"Are they very tall, your landlords?"

"Giant," Jack grinned. "So..."

Here we go. She had asked most of her questions when they arrived at the log cabin the previous night – the eye, the internship, the festival, the car. Rune had answered each as efficiently as possible, keen to get to bed and pretend this whole thing wasn't happening. But there were new questions in her gaze, Rune could see them glimmering.

He got in there first. "When's Jock coming to fix the car?"

"As soon as he can."

"Okay." Another beat, another sip.

This was all just a blip. The sooner the car was fixed, the

sooner he could get back on the road. If the Volvo was running again by afternoon, he'd be able to get Abe back to the city in time for his performance at St Mark's cathedral, and Eddie would be none the wiser of the screw up. He would give *Her Grouchiness* no reason to fire him. *'Goodbye festival? Goodbye internship'*.

"I'm surprised the Tasmanian Devil isn't out of bed yet," he said.

"She sleeps later here for some reason. She wasn't even kicking last night. I think it's the quietness here. The peace."

Rune stifled a retort. Jack ran fingers through her hair once more, teasing and ruffling. It irked him how untamed it was, and how loose her shoulders were, how untroubled her forehead was.

"Looks good," he said. She noticed him staring at her now. He attempted a smile.

"I'm trying something new," she made a little laugh and looked around the cabin.

He followed her gaze. The interior was stripped back, a shell bearing no trappings he associated with his family. No photographs of their holidays to France and Portugal, no magnets pinning 'To Do' lists and weekly planners on the fridge – Kelly's horse riding lessons, his turn to cook dinner. Not even one of Jack's famous potted plants filled an empty corner.

Jack cleared her throat. "Look, Rune, can we just…" But she didn't get to finish because Abe emerged from the ground floor bedroom.

"Good morning," he said.

"Good morning," Jack smiled. "Sleep okay, love?"

"The best," he said. "The bed is so comfortable. Much better than the thin mattresses in Hillhead."

"Tea?" she said. Abe thanked her.

"I'll make it," Rune jumped in.

Out of the corner of his eye he saw Abe looking around the living space then out the window to the unkempt lawn and the pine trees beyond.

"This is a beautiful place," Abe said. "How long have you had it?"

"Oh, no I'm just house-sitting for a colleague while she does it up. It's going to be one of those Airbnbs. I only moved in a few weeks ago."

"Just you?" Abe asked.

"Just me," Jack said.

Rune was surprised at the response. He'd expected evasiveness.

"Your husband..."

"We're recently separated." The simplest phrase in the world.

"Oh forgive me, I didn't know," Abe said, glancing at Rune.

"Not a problem," she shrugged. Rune squeezed the teabag.

Abe pointed upwards. "So Kelly is...?"

"Kelpie," Jack said.

A wry chuckle slipped out of Rune's mouth. "Finally gave in, did you?"

"It's what she wants to be called," Jack said. "Who am I to tell her differently?"

Rune ground his teeth.

"But yes," Jack continued. "During the summer Kelpie's staying one week on and off between here and the house in Aberdeen."

The *house* in Aberdeen. No longer the *home*.

Rune handed the steaming cup to Abe.

"Thank you," he said. "Are you helping with the renovation?"

"Me?" Rune snorted.

Jack laughed. "No, this is his first visit."

A crease formed on Abe's brow as he looked between them.

"To be fair," she continued, "I'm not helping with renovations either. Too busy with my job at the nearby library."

"Gave up a full-time job at the City Council," Rune smiled. "And now she works part-time in a library in the middle of nowhere."

Jack looked at him. The sanguine expression had tightened a little. "It's a secondment, actually. Kelpie loves it. Lots of books about horses."

"Because she doesn't have enough of those," Rune muttered.

Abe's frown deepened. "Tell me, Jack, was Rune this sarcastic as a child?"

She patted the table. "Oh ho, zinger! This one's got the measure of you, Runey."

Rune reformed a smile into a grimace and shot it at Abe, who raised his hands in the air.

"He's a keeper," Jack added.

"Do kindly shut up, Jack," Rune hissed.

Abe looked shocked. "Rune, you should respect your mother. She brought you into this world."

"It's fine," she touched Abe's hand. "This is just our patter. Rune's become the Mr Grumpy of the family. Haven't you, love?"

Rune felt his cheeks redden, his stomach twisted. If the table wasn't the size it was, he would have considered flipping it. But he wouldn't lose it, wouldn't react to the jibe.

Jack smiled at Abe. "Anyway, tell me about Uganda. Are you from Kampala?"

"I am," he beamed.

"And all your family are there?"

"Yes, that's right."

"Brothers or sisters?"

"Shine a bright light in his eyes, why don't you, Mum," Rune said.

"Sorry, I didn't mean to–"

"Not at all. I have a brother. A twin actually."

"Oh wow, really? And your parents, what do they do?" Jack nodded.

As Abe told his story Rune felt himself fading into the background. This *Jack 2.0* was a real piece of work. *"Oh wow! How fascinating. Tell me more!"* A performative upgrade. *Now with added maternal instincts!* He drew the rug around his shoulders and drifted to the couch. He searched his rucksack and found the trusty Zippo lighter and Eddie's packet of cigarettes. He tapped a fag out of the packet and popped it between his lips, in full view of his mother. Jack opened her mouth.

"Yes?" he smiled sweetly, the cigarette bobbing with the word.

"Nothing," she said just as sugary.

Rune opened the front door and stepped out to the grass. The thick smells of nature met him immediately. The final vestiges of rain gleamed on the grass and driveway. The Zippo flared to life and he drew on the cigarette. The hit flooded his senses – catching the back of his throat, stinging his nostrils, spinning his head. He persevered for the sake of the performance. After a few more drags he wandered away from his mother's sightline.

She was right, the place was unbelievably peaceful. Not even the sound of birds.

Birds don't like pine trees too much. Jock had told him that once on some walk through the woods. There had been so many family walks through the woods, his stepfather leading the way.

Something sharp pinged off Rune's head, then another off his neck. At his feet lay the heads of two Lego figures, fixed grins and shiny scalps. A third hit him square in the ear. He looked up and saw another head looking down on him from the balcony – the same grin, but a thatch of ginger hair.

"Smoking kills," Kel's head said.

"Not as much as strangling," Rune replied. "I'll give you points for the element of surprise, though."

"Ha!" Kel barked. Her disembodied head now had arms. The chin rested on them.

"Morning sunshine," she beamed.

Rune breathed out a plume and stifled a cough.

"I said 'Mooooorning sunshine'."

"I swear to God, Kelly, if you spit on me I'm gonna stub this fag out on your arm. Nobody will notice because of all the sodding freckles."

"Kelpie," she sang, a note of mischievous warning. She pursed her lips in preparation of a big old *loogie*.

"Fine. I will murder you, *Kelpie*."

"Thataboy!"

The floating head and arms disappeared. It was followed by the sound of bare feet slapping down wooden stairs.

II.

The first half of Kelpie's toast had fallen jam-side down on the floor. The second half was close to meeting the same fate, pinched as it was in her wildly-gesticulating hand.

"And I was like: 'No way, Jose'. And he was like: 'Yes way, Jose'. So that's why I pushed him down a well and he's never been seen again."

Rune caught Abe's questioning gaze and rolled his eyes.

"Great story, Kel," Rune said, cheek resting on fist. "Creative as ever."

"It's true," she said. "Tell them, Mum."

"It's mostly true," said Jack, looking at the jam smear on the ground. "Apart from the shoot-out at dawn, the failed rescue attempt from a tower, and the pushing-down-the-well bit."

"Yeah," Kel said through a mouthful, "maybe apart from those bits."

Abe looked wide-eyed, his mouth agape. The perfect audience. "My playtimes at school were never so exciting."

Kel shrugged. "It's just how we roll."

Rune mouthed 'I'm sorry' to Abe, who shook his head in response.

"It must be the red hair," he said, looking from Kel to Jack to Rune. "I am getting the sense that the Duthie family are very fiery and adventurous."

Jack was the first to laugh. She tossed a hand through her wild hair. "They get it from me."

"No shit," Rune grimaced. "A lifetime of bullying."

She made a 'boo-hoo' face. "Oh, my poor, wee angry boy."

"Ha! No shit, Mum. No shit!" Kel parroted.

"You see what a bad example you are, Rune?"

"Do my best," he squinted.

Kel leaned in to Abe and fixed him with a stare. "Rune is gay. And I couldn't be more proud."

"Oh," Abe replied, surprise turning to amusement.

Kel maintained her stare and stuffed the rest of the jammy toast in her mouth. "Are you gay?"

"Kelpie," Jack tittered, "that's rude."

Rune, who had been reeling on the edge of embarrassment, turned on his mother. "What? Are you saying she shouldn't talk about things like that?"

She blanched. "No, that's not what I was saying. You're putting words in my–"

"I *am* gay," Abe smiled at Kelpie. "Thank you for asking."

Kel's mouth formed a perfect circle. "Then I'm very proud of you too. I loooooove the gays."

"Jesus," Rune sighed.

Kel shuffled in her seat and tapped Abe's hand with a sticky finger. "Me and Mum are *suuuper* ginger. You see? But Rune is a little darker. That's because he's more like Daddy."

Rune exchanged a look with Jack, a momentary glance which she retreated from.

"Yes, Jock is not blessed with *super* red hair. Abe, you mentioned you'd met Rune and Kelpie's dad?"

"Briefly," Abe said. "He's a very tall man."

"He's huuuuuuuge," Kel guffawed, hands in the air. She brought them back down and leaned in to Abe again. "You know, a boy at school calls me 'Carrot'."

Abe patted her shoulder. "That's not very nice."

"S'all right. I call him 'Shitface'."

"You do not!" Jack said, alarmed.

"Maybe I do. Maybe I don't," Kel said, attempting a wink at Abe but only accomplishing a full blink.

"She's a compulsive liar, Jacqueline," Rune said. "I've never been called a 'Carrot' in my life. Kids are much more creative than that with insults."

"*You're* a compulsive liar!" Kel pointed.

Rune moaned into his hands. "Is the car fixed yet?"

Jack stepped back from the table and over the floor toast. "As much as I'm enjoying this morning's performance, I need to nip to Kemnay for some bits and pieces. You'll be okay to watch Little Miss for ten minutes?"

Rune looked up to see that the question had been aimed at Abe.

"Of course," he smiled.

"You're a lifesaver," she said, pulling on trainers. "And you, Kelpie, need to be ready in your riding gear, waiting for me by the door when I get back. Yes?"

"Maybe I will. Maybe I–"

"Yes, Kelpie?" Jack's tone shifted.

"Yessssss," Kel hissed.

The moment Jack drove away, Kel ran back to the table with fingers spread wide. "Let's. Play. A. Game!"

Rune splayed his fingers in imitation. "Let's. Not!"

"Aww come on," she said, dragging a stool along the floor. The noise was enough to set anyone's teeth on edge. "You're no fun any more."

"And you're too much fun. Go outside and run around."

She batted her eyelashes. "Pweeease?"

"Jesus Christ, Kel. You're eight years old."

"But I have nobody to play with. Not since..." she paused and stuck out her bottom lip.

"Don't you dare."

"Not since..."

"I'm warning you."

"Not since Annie died."

"Ugh," Rune crossed to the couch and flopped down. "How much mileage are you going to get out of this? It's been two months."

"Who's Annie?" Abe said.

"Oh God, he asked the question," Rune groaned to the Greek Chorus of ceiling knots.

Kel clapped her hands. "You mean, you don't know? Rune, he doesn't know. I simply must tell him. Here, come sit. Sit, sit, sit!"

She pulled Abe by the wrist to the couch and Rune begrudgingly retracted his feet. Abe settled down then placed a hand on Rune's ankle. Rune startled at the contact, then realised Abe was guiding him to lay his feet on his lap. He softly pinched Rune's big toe – which sent a thrum up Rune's leg.

Kel rearranged the floorspace, shifting the coffee table and chair to the sides. She walked calmly to the centre, swept fingers through her hair and cleared her throat.

"Presenting: The Very, VERY Sad Story of Annie the Dog. Written and performed by, and starring, Kelpie Duthie. (Moi!) *Ithankyou!*"

III.

THE VERY, VERY SAD STORY OF ANNIE THE DOG
Written and performed by Kelly 'Kelpie' Duthie (*Moi!*)

CHARACTERS

JACK – A beautiful lady with long, wavy hair and a very clever daughter. She likes new adventures and dark chocolate (the yucky kind). Hates doors being left as 'a jar'.

JOCK – A big, tall, huge man who gives the best hugs. Runs a car repair shop. Very mucky fingernails, but loves chicken wings (the spicy ones). Also has a very clever daughter. She's hilarious, seriously.

KELPIE – J&J's daughter. A brave little girl. Loves horses and dogs. Hates rainbows (can't touch them) and shampoo (the flowery one). Clever and funny.

RUNE – J&J's son. Smells like poo and looks like one too. Loves eye patches, hates happy things.

ANNIE – The sweetest wee doggie you ever did see. A *beeshon freeze*. White fur and a nose like a raisin. A big raisin. (Which is funny cos she's allergic to them).

OUTSIDE MY CITY HOME (I HAVE TWO HOMES, NO BIG DEAL, DON'T WANNA BRAG) – 14 NORTHFIELD PLACE, ABERDEEN, SCOTLAND, THE WORLD, THE UNIVERSE.

JACK and JOCK are shouting in the street. JACK is putting her suitcase into the car. JOCK is trying to take the suitcase out. RUNE is smoking a dirty cigarette cos he thinks it's cool. KELPIE is holding ANNIE the dog in her arms.

JACK
I told you, Jock. I want to live in the countryside. I'm tired of the city. It smells and it's very busy all of the time.

JOCK
But, my lovely wife, we all live in the city together, as a family. You can't leave.

JACK
I have to. It's the only way that our children can enjoy the fresh air, and to see the stars at night, and to ride on horses whenever they want. And also, I have an important new job – the little children in the library need me to read them stories.

RUNE
Well, I'm not coming. It's the *countryside* that smells, not the city. And anyway, I'm already grown up and an artist. I don't need any of you.

KELPIE (crying pretty tears)
Rune, don't say that!

ANNIE (wriggling)
Whine whine! Kelpie, what is happening? I am so terribly frightened.

KELPIE
Shhh, wee one. It will all be okay. Mummy and Daddy are just having one of their 'discussions'. It will all be okay.

JOCK
Are you seeing someone else, Jacqueline? Is that what this is about?

JACK gets the suitcase from JOCK, puts it in the boot and slams it closed (even though you are never supposed to slam doors, or leave them as 'a jar'!)

JACK
How many times, Jock? I do not *see* anyone else. I only see you and Rune, Kelpie and Annie right here in front of me. So, please stop asking. I am going now.

KELPIE
Mummy, please don't go.

JACK takes ANNIE from KELPIE, and strokes the doggie to make her quiet down.

JACK
You're coming too, Kelpie. You and Annie are going to stay with me in the countryside for a few days.

We have a beautiful new home for us in the forest. Daddy has some things to think about here in the city, so you will come and stay with me and ride horses and have adventures with Annie.

And then you can come back to the city for school and have fun with your friends. And then you can come back to the countryside again. It will be lots of fun.

KELPIE
Oh, I guess that does sound fun. How lucky I am to have two parents who love me so much, and to have two homes.

RUNE
You're such a *shitty* little girl, *Kelly*. You just believe whatever they tell you.

KELPIE
You're wrong! It's 'Kelpie', not Kelly.

RUNE
You're right, Kelpie. I'm sorry, I was wrong.

KELPIE *raspberries* at RUNE and gets into the back seat of the car with ANNIE. JACK is about to get into the car but JOCK stops her.

JOCK
Something something something. Please *something something.*

JACK (crying very pretty tears)
Something, something can't something. Something!

RUNE (rolls his eyes)
Something rude.

KELPIE
What are they saying, Annie? Can your little doggie ears hear?

ANNIE
No. My little doggie ears can't hear them, and neither can I.

KELPIE rolls down the car window.

JOCK (crying one big man tear)
I won't know what to do when you're away.

JACK
It's for the best.

JACK gets into the car and starts the engine.

KELPIE
Don't cry, Daddy. Come with us. Don't worry about the things you need to think about in the city. Come read books to the children in the library, and ride horses with me. Everything's better in the countryside.

JOCK (shaking his head)
I can't, Wee Girl. I'm sorry. (Looks at JACK) Can't you see what you're doing?

ANNIE (wriggling and wriggling)
Bark, bark, bark! Let me out!

KELPIE
Mummy, where is Annie's carrier? Shouldn't she be in it before we drive?

JACK
Stop it, Jock. Don't make this harder than it is.

JOCK
Fine, go! See if I care! Just do whatever the *<rude word>* you want, as always.

JACK
That's not fair!

ANNIE wriggles out the window and jumps on to the road.

JACK
I've always done what's best for our family. You know I have, how can you say that? But now it's time for a new adventure.

JOCK
I didn't mean it. Please don't go.

JACK (crying lots and lots)
Goodbye.

JACK revs the engine and presses the 'go' pedal with her foot.

ANNIE
Yelp!!!!

KELPIE
Annie! No!

JACK slams on the brakes. KELPIE rushes out of the car. ANNIE is under the front tyre. KELPIE kneels down and kisses the doggie on her raisin nose. Her little white body has red all over it.

ANNIE
Be…a…good…girl…Kelpie.

KELPIE
No, Annie! Please don't leave me. We were going to have adventures together in the countryside.

ANNIE
...

KELPIE (looking up at the sky)
NOOOOOOOOO!!! ANNIE!!!!!!!!!!

IV.

"Nooooooooo!... Oh hi, Mummy!" Kelpie flipped out of character the split second she spotted Jack in the doorway.

"What's...going on?" Jack asked. She looked as startled as Rune and Abe. "Are you okay, Kel?"

"I'm doing therapy," she chirped. Tears were still in her eyes, but she smeared them away as easily as a snotty nose. "Here Mama, let me help with your shopping."

Rune offered his mother an honest shrug. She responded with something harder. It was a subtle look, but enough to make Rune burn. As if this was his fault? She returned to the carrier bags and unpacked the contents while Kelpie bounced around the kitchen.

"Um, that was..." Abe began in a hushed tone.

Rune blew out his cheeks. "Yeah. I'm not sure what that was."

They began resetting the room, pulling the coffee table back to the centre, tidying the couch.

"She's very creative," Abe smiled weakly.

"Not this time," Rune said. "Pretty much every word of that was true."

"The dog? Annie was kil–?"

Rune jerked a thumb towards his mother. "It's still pretty fresh. But yeah, that happened. Horrendous."

In the kitchen area Jack cradled Kelpie's beaming face in her hands and wiped away the last traces of tears. "...if you say so. Now go get your riding gear on quick sharp. We're supposed to be at the stables in fifteen minutes, okay?"

Kelpie punched the air and cantered around the room. "Yahoo! I'll be ready in two shakes. Watch me go!" She ran to the couch, spotted Rune's backpack and flung it around her shoulders.

"That's mine, Kel. Bring it back." Rune hollered as she rushed up the stairs. He heard an 'Oops' from the upper floor, followed by the thunder of small feet all around the ceiling. The pounding was punctuated with excited phrases such as 'where are my jodhpurs...ooh there!' and 'oh boots boots boots, where are you?'

Rune brought the empty mugs to the sink. Jack opened her mouth but he got there first.

"I see she's working through things in a very healthy way."

Jack looked almost ready to bite, but breathed it out. "It's all a big adjustment. These things take time."

"How much time is enough time, would you say? When will you be over whatever this is?"

"Please don't..." she whispered.

"Fine," Rune crooned. "That's just fine. We'll carry on with saying nothing. That's worked well for us so far. I'll just look forward to Kel's next performance."

"Rune..." Jack began.

He turned sharply. "Hey Abe, while we wait for the car to

be fixed, do you want to go watch Kelpie riding horses? The countryside's just full of them apparently. And adventure, and fresh air, and libraries. It's so great."

"Sure," Abe said, eyes dotting between Rune and Jack.

"Fantastic," Rune said, thrusting a foot through his shorts which had been in a heap with the rest of his clothes. "It'll be a family outing. Well, apart from, y'know, the ol' stepfather."

He glared at Jack. Her face was red – a nice reminder of where he had inherited it from.

"Mum?" came Kel's voice from upstairs. "What's *suck-ess-ion*?"

"Eh?"

"*Suckession?*"

"Do you mean *succession*?" she threw a look of confusion at the ceiling.

"Probably? What's it mean?"

"It's usually to do with people inheriting things. What on earth are–?"

"Like kingdoms?"

"Yes," Jack replied, baffled.

Kel's booted feet clomped down the steps. "Then, did you know it was common in Pictish society for, uh, *over-king-ship succession* for an *hair* to the throne to have a Pictish mother but a non-Pictish father?"

Jack's reply was flat and dry. "Wow, I didn't know that Kel. Are you ready to go? We're going to be late."

Rune, who hadn't been listening to the inane chatter at first, suddenly felt the back of his neck prickle.

Kel continued: "Yeah. The foreign father would usually have nothing to do with the raising of the child. It says so in this book. It's been underlined a bunch of times!"

The prickle was replaced with a heavy thumping in Rune's chest. It was like slow motion. Kelpie descended the stairs with his gaping backpack slung over her shoulder and Mary Seaton's book open in her hands.

"And what does this letter mean? It's addressed to you and Rune." She was waving around the letter Rune had been using as a bookmark.

Horror and rage ripped through him.

"You little fucking shit!" he screamed and ran over to Kel. He tried to wrestle the bag and book from her. "You've been going through my fucking stuff? Fucking thief!"

It was all a blur. Kelpie's terrified eyes, the hardback book snapping on her fingers, Kel running to their mother, unheard words from Abe's mouth, fingers gripping Rune's shoulders. Abe pulled him free and held on tightly. The rage began to subside, replaced by a new impulse.

He turned and saw his mother reading the letter. Her expression was cold and distant at first, then morphed into something piteous. The questions, which had glimmered in her eyes, finally answered.

V.

Attn: Mr Rune Duthie, Mrs Jacqueline Duthie

This letter is to inform you of the death of Somchai Bunsong.

    My name is Sirikit Sainimnuan and I am a paralegal for Chantara & Partners. The firm represents the Bunsong family. I have been instructed to write to you on their behalf.

Khun Somchai died on 6 February of this year following a long illness, and his remains were scattered in Kanchanaburi at a family ceremony on 20 February.

The Bunsong family request you do not contact them directly. We at Chantara & Partners offer you our condolences.

Sincerely,

Sirikit Sainimnuan,

Legal Administrator

Chantara & Partners, 22 Sukhuvit Soi 15, Klongtoeynua Khet Watthana, Bangkok, 10110, Thailand

VI.

Pixie the horse wasn't budging. It was an enormous brute, a brown tank on tall, sinewy legs that ended in dirty great hooves. Sat astride it, Kelpie looked like a toy, a riding-helmeted, red-jacketed teddy bear perched on a gargantuan beast-horse.

Her half-hearted attempts to get Pixie trotting failed, heel nudges falling on deaf flanks. The wee girl kept glancing over at Rune at the edge of the paddock. Her face was ashen despite the late morning heat. He couldn't handle the confusion in her stare, so he tried to focus on other things: the musky scent of the stables, the grain of the paddock fence.

"That's a girl, Kelpie," Abe encouraged from the other end. "Show me what you can do."

Poor guy. Stranded on the foothills of Bennachie with a

dysfunctional family. A half-orphaned pirate with anger issues, a freewheeling mother going through some sort of mid-life crisis, and a wildcard of a sister who...who just found out she doesn't share the same father as the person she's called 'brother' her whole life.

"She'll be all right," said Jack. She too was picking splinters out of the fence. "She'll bounce back."

"Mmm hmm," Rune muttered. *She wouldn't need to 'bounce back' if she had been told years ago.*

"It's quite the shock, eh?" There was something thin and twittery in her voice that Rune had never heard before. "How long ago did the letter–?"

"Wee while back." *Three weeks to the day.*

A whispery laugh. "And when exactly were you going to let me read it?"

"Soon." *Never. You've always made it clear it has nothing to do with you.*

"I mean, my name is on the letter too, so..."

"Yep."

"You didn't think I had the right to read it?" It was a cautious approach, but definitely the first move. Definitely. *Game on.*

He laid out a simple smile. "I'm not going to apologise, if that's what you're fishing for." The delivery was perfect, just as it had sounded in his head. The words left a metallic taste.

She lobbed back a chuckle. "Oh no, I wouldn't ever expect that. From you."

"Meaning?" His heart quickened.

"Not our style, is it?"

"Inherited behaviour," he sniffed. "*Suck-ess-ion.*"

In the paddock, Kelpie had managed to coax Pixie into a plod.

Abe was congratulating her as if she had performed something medal-worthy. The horse made a slow but inexorable approach towards a huge puddle at the other end of the paddock. Kelpie noticed it too late, and before she knew it, Pixie was splashing his hammer-like hooves into the water, then walked into the centre of the puddle and began frolicking like a foal. Kelpie held on to the reins but slid off just in time for Pixie to roll in the muddy water. Kelpie stood in the splash zone, her red riding coat speckling brown. She clapped at the horse's playfulness. It momentarily brought a grin to her face, but it lessened with each glance towards Rune.

Jack continued. "I mean, it wasn't exactly the best way for me to find out, was it?"

"Aye well, y'know, *clearly* I thought it would be best to have Kel find it in my backpack and give it to you. Clearly." He couldn't look at her, this could only work if eye contact was avoided.

She tapped the fence. "All I'm saying is you could have told me sooner."

"Why? Does it make you sad?"

"Of course it makes me sad. Someone I knew long ago has died."

"'Someone you knew'."

She sighed. "Yes."

"Not 'the father of your child'?"

"What do you want me to say?" she suddenly exclaimed, arms spread wide. "Yes, someone I knew twenty-one years ago. A fling. Your mother was a promiscuous little whore! Is that what you want to hear?"

Bingo. His chin wobbled but he brought it under control. Why did success feel so fucking horrible?

"Rune," Jack breathed, her eyebrows steepled. "You have a father. And he loves you more than life. But he is *not* the man in that letter."

Tears immediately clouded his vision. An image bloomed in his mind, a gleeful child perched high on a giant's shoulders, the summer sun, the rolling waves. "That's not fair," he said through gritted teeth. "Don't you dare bring Jock into this when you're the one leaving him behind."

"Now who's being unfair?"

"Really?" he laughed and wiped his eye. He waved around at the stables. "What is all this, 'Mum'? The Adventures of Jack? Jack Buys a Farm? Or is it maybe, just maybe, a fucking breakdown."

Jack held out a single finger, a gesture of warning.

"You're breaking his heart, Mum. Is *that* fair?"

"Don't," she added, the quivering finger pointed at Rune's chest.

His words were coming now, free and poisonous. "It's just what you do, isn't it? You make choices for people. *You* decide. Not us. We're left behind picking up the pieces."

Tears were now flowing down his mother's face. She turned to him, accepting the arrows and bullets.

He carried on. "'*Oh Rune, you can't tell Kelly about your Thai daddy. It'll be our little secret, okay? It'll upset her too much. You don't want to upset your sister do you?*'"

Jack bit her lip.

"'*She already has enough to get her wee mind around what with you being...*"

"No!" she wailed.

"'*...a wee poofter!*'"

"I never said that!"

"You didn't need to, Mother," he spat. "You just..."

But the words caught, a sudden intake of breath, a sob wrenching him back. He held on to the fence for stability. "You just make these decisions for people. *You* decide our family is broken. *You* decide it's all coming to an end. *You* decide I can't have any relationship with my real father. *You*."

Her expression twisted. "You've never asked about him. Not really. Never showed any interest in Somchai."

"You never had anything to tell me," he said, gripping the fence.

"But why..." she cast around. "Why does it make a difference now that he's gone?"

"I don't know," Rune strained, new tears, a fresh lump in his throat. "I don't know!"

She reached a hand out but he stepped away.

"I don't know who I am," he shrugged.

"Show me a twenty-one year-old who does," she said, then looked up at the sky and chuckled. "Or a forty-one-year-old, for that matter. You want something from me that I can't give. An apology, an explanation, something. But I can't."

"Or won't," Rune said.

"Maybe," she said then raised her hands, gesturing towards the trees, the hills. "I'm being brave, Rune. I know I can't ask you to be happy for me. But I'm finally doing something just for me after years of putting others first. I'm trying to figure things out, for the first time in my life."

Rune sneered. "And in the meantime–"

"In the meantime, you're my son. That's it. End of. Mine, and not that man in the letter. I get that you're confused, but I really don't understand what you're reaching for. You've got everything here. That guy is nothing to you, Rune."

"Then why give me this stupid name?"

Jack finally placed a hand on his shoulder. "Because you didn't look like a Stephen. Or a Robert. Your wee face. It was mostly my face, but there was a little bit of him. A piece of something different among the freckles. Somchai held you in his arms. You were such a happy baby. He looked down at that sweet face. 'Rune,' he said. 'Happy'. That's what he gave you, your name. I couldn't take it away, could I?"

He had heard the story before, had coaxed it from her in secret moments, but it had never sounded so brittle.

"Why didn't he come find me? You said he was pulled back to Thailand against his will, to take up his family business or whatever. Fine. But if he couldn't visit, why didn't he at least invite me to go visit him?"

"He did," Jack said, almost a whisper. "He asked us both to go live with him."

"What?" Rune felt the air leave his chest in one sharp breath. He couldn't read his mother's expression. Was it sheepishness? Fear? Shame? Either way, it was quickly replaced by something stonier.

"He only asked once," she said. "Just after you were born. But I knew it wasn't out of love. Only obligation. I knew his family didn't approve of me. Of…us."

"He…he asked us to go live with him?" Rune stuttered.

"In Bangkok!" she scoffed. "A foreign city on the other side of the world, where I didn't speak the language, where I knew no-one. What kind of a proposition was that?"

Rune raked fingers through his hair. "Oh my God, Mum. We

could have been a family! But *you* decided that we couldn't."

"I was younger than you are now, Rune. Imagine what it's like to have to make that kind of choice at that age. Yes, I made it. But I made it for *us*, not *me*."

Rune clapped three times, slow and spaced apart. "Wow. So selfless. Your 'Parent of the Decade' award is in the mail."

She opened her mouth to continue her rebuttal but nothing came.

He reached into his pocket and took out the Zippo lighter. The sunlight caught every scratch and score on its surface.

"*This* is all I really have of him, Mum," he said, fighting back rage. "No experiences, no memories. *This* is the only thing that's real. That lawyer's letter and this. That's my real inheritance."

He held up the lighter and watched it glint. He looked at Jack. Something was there in her expression, a flicker of the eyelid, a purse of the lips. His heart sank.

"Not even this?" he said. A little laugh rose from his chest. "Oh God, not even this. You made it up, didn't you? How he was pulled back to Thailand against his will. How he left this lighter with you so you'd always be reminded. Fucking hell, Mum, was he even a smoker?"

She held his gaze. The next thing she said was the cruellest yet. There was no malice in it, just a terrible weight. "The truth is...he never wanted anything to do with you, Rune. Or me. He was only trying to do the *honourable* thing, inviting us. So, hate me if you want. But I made the right choice."

He let the Zippo fall. It landed on the grass without a sound.

VII.

Ngoma...endingidi...endongo...endere...
Drum...string...lyre...flute...

Ngoma...
The stone's filed edge looked sharp enough now
Endingidi...
He stared at the boulder's face, smeared with lichen, surrounded by heather
Endongo...
And began to carve, stone against stone
Endere...
With no sense of design or direction.

Ngoma...endingidi...endongo...endere...
Drum...string...lyre...flute...
Ngoma...endingidi...endongo...endere...
Carve...chisel...scrape...file...
Ngoma...endingidi...endongo...endere...
Mother...father...liar...son...

Halfway up Mither Tap the trees had suddenly ceased; the pine forest which blanketed the foothills gave way to a new terrain of heather, moss and boulder. This brown and purple land parted for a pathway, a snaking trail which steepened towards the rocky summit.

The sun beat down on Rune's neck. He could feel the beginnings of burning, could imagine the new freckles which would appear in its aftermath. He carried on carving, scraping and digging with the filed stone in his hand against the canvas of the flat boulder. He barely made an indentation, but the lines were clear. Maybe they were just the stone crumbling with each stroke, like chalk on a board. The design was abstract, curving and interlocking. He had no idea what he was creating but the longer he worked at it the more elements began to rise up at him: this could be a Pictish bow here, and that could be a drum there, and that, was that the profile of a face? Was it his own, one-eyed and lost? Or Kelpie's, confused and sad? His mother's, wild and changing. Perhaps it was his father's, unknowable and dead...

Mother...father...liar...son...

It was so unfair. He had come so far this past week but, in one morning, he'd fallen back into old habits and mind-emptying mantras.

Drum...string...lyre...flute...

Abe was approaching. Rune saw him long before he arrived – a solo traveller emerging from the pine trees, wandering into the midday sun, following the path that would, in time, lead him directly to the boulder. Rune could have sobbed at the certainty of Abe's arrival.

Ngoma...endingidi...endongo...endere...

"I like it," Abe said. He knelt down and felt along the lines, gently as if tracking a centuries-old hieroglyph.

Rune leaned back and considered his creation afresh. Already the lines were looking more crude, the details more amateur. He lobbed the stone into the heather and breathed out heavily. "Where's Kelpie?"

"She's okay," Abe replied, understanding the real question. "Before I came up here, she was telling me about what she'd like more than anything."

"What's that?"

"To ride all over Bennachie on Pixie's back, all the way to the river, where they would swim together and follow its flow out to sea. It's a dream she's had many times, she said. I said it sounded nice, but perhaps she should first focus on trying to get Pixie walking."

Rune smiled, but it soon died at the memory of his sister's despondent eyes, staring at him from across the paddock.

Abe seemed to catch it. "Your father...stepfather arrived at the stables. He's working on the Volvo."

Rune's stomach curdled: first with unease at the idea of his mother, stepfather and sister all in one place; then with guilty relief at the idea he might soon be back on the road away from them all. He tried to perk up. "We're going to make it in time for your performance, I promise."

Abe ran a finger across the back of Rune's hand. "It really doesn't matter if we do."

"It's my job. I'm not giving Eddie any excuse to fire me. Besides," he motioned towards the etchings on the boulder, "I've got a meeting with the Professor first thing tomorrow. I guess I've finally got something to show him. Such as it is."

He took out his phone and snapped a variety of shots. The design looked even more pedestrian on screen, but it was all he had. His stomach clenched. He breathed the tension away. Screw it, he could make it work. He'd got this far with bluster, what was one more day?

Abe settled directly opposite him and waited quietly, watching Rune go about his work, amber eyes never leaving him. Only when Rune finally sat back down did he speak.

"So," he smiled. "Your father?"

Rune chuckled and combed his hair with stone-roughened fingers.

Abe continued: "You're half Thai."

"You didn't know?"

"I wondered if there was something," he said, a hand gliding in the air between him and Rune's face. "But no."

"It's the eyepatch. Confuses people," Rune joked. "Most people don't see it. *I* barely see it, let alone feel it. Kit told me there's a Thai word for people like me. *Luk khrueng*, or something like that."

Abe's eyebrows pinched.

"It's something to do with people being part Thai, part something else. Apparently, it's a nice word, a cute one. Just sounds like a foreign word to me. I've never really felt what I am, if that makes sense."

"Your red hair," Abe said, a non sequitur and yet somehow a natural response.

"He wasn't fully Thai himself, my father. His grandad or great-grandad was also *luk khrueng*. Half Scottish, in fact. It's why my father was visiting here twenty-one years ago, some kind of pilgrimage to find out where his paler skin and green eyes came from. Must have already been some ginger hidden in his genes because when his met my mother's...bang!"

He ruffled his hair once more. Abe looked like he was about to reach over to do the same, but his hand drifted back to his lap.

"I'd love to see a photo of him."

Rune shrugged. "Me too. I've never seen one. A handful of stories are all I know about him."

"Your mother couldn't tell you more?" Abe said.

Rune shook his head. "Bits and pieces. Apparently he said Scotland was beautiful but cold. He thought Aberdeen granite was ugly. But he liked eating strawberry ice cream in a *slider*."

Abe looked mystified once more.

"It's a, what do you call it, wafer sandwich with ice cream in the middle. They sell it at the beach. He and Mum used to go there for walks. He liked to see the sea."

"They were together for a while? Your mother and Somchai?"

It was strange to hear his father's name in the mouth of another. A stranger's name, lifted from the death notice letter and given warmth in Abe's voice. "I don't think so. A summer romance, then he had to go back to Bangkok to work for his family business. Made it back once for my birth. And then, well I guess that was it."

"What do you mean?"

"I've been told different stories. Turns out he asked her, and me, to move to Thailand to stay with him. But she wouldn't leave. Imagine that? She'd rather stay in Aberdeen, dealing with my bitch grandma always calling her a 'hussy' for getting pregnant so young, than go on a big adventure."

"*Embiro tezimala musango*," Abe said. "Running away does not resolve disputes."

"A phrase for every occasion," Rune mumbled.

Abe was silent for a beat. "Sorry, storyteller's habit. I don't know if I even believe them any more."

Before Rune could ask what he meant, Abe came back in. "I think I can understand why she didn't go with him. Is it not better to lay down roots where you know what is what? Find someone kind to build a family with?"

Jock's bearded face swam through Rune's mind. It seemed to find a home on the stone-etched design. Was that Jock's eye, his chin?

"Doesn't matter anyway," he said, scraping at a patch of lichen. "She's right, it's pretty clear Somchai never really wanted anything to do with me or her. Suppose I've always known it. If he really wanted me in his life, he wouldn't have given up so easily."

"Are you sad about that?" Abe asked.

"I don't know. Maybe not. I mean, how can I? He's not even a real person to me. I don't know what he looked like, what he sounded like. All I have of him is my name. The only thing I feel is...angry. At Mum. Maybe that's unfair, but she's the only part of the equation who's left for me to feel anything towards. My father's just some abstract thing, but Mum? She chose this. Chose not to go with him, to get pregnant, to stay in Scotland, to not even to have a fucking photograph of the guy."

"I'm not sure she necessarily chose all those things, Rune."

"But chose to let him name me? Chose to tell me about him, but in the same breath beg me never to tell Kelly. Kelpie, whatever. Why do that? Fuck!" He slapped the boulder with an open palm. The impact stung. "You know what the worst thing is? She's right. I never really gave him much thought. Not really. I was too busy being a stupid kid, and now it's too late. Not that I'd necessarily want to meet him. But it would've been nice to have the choice. If she'd just told me more about him. If I'd just been more curious."

Abe got up and walked around Rune. His long shadow stretched over him and the boulder, blocking out the burning sun, turning the warm breeze cool. Rune sensed Abe settle on the ground.

"Here," he whispered, hands pulling at Rune's shoulders.

After a moment's hesitation, he leant back into Abe's arms.

It should have felt strange, sexy, or at least awkward, but it wasn't any of those things. A few rays of sunlight met his face like a kiss. The patch blocked most of them out, but he closed both his eyes and breathed slowly, in and out, falling in synch with Abe.

"Tell me a story," Rune said. "Any story."

Abe's chest jerked a little with laughter. "One has come to mind, actually. But you won't like it."

"Then I'll do my best to pretend."

"Okay, well there was–"

"No, no. Properly."

Another chuckle. He whispered: "*Olwatuuka ngambalabira.*"

"*Nobulabibwo,*" Rune smiled.

"There was a woman who wanted very badly to have children, but try as she and her husband might, they could not bring their dream to reality. They were out of ideas, except one. They travelled to the very bottom of a valley to find the diviner who lived by Lake Kyoga. The old diviner took pity on the couple and gave them four berries. He told the woman to swallow them whole as soon as she got home, and in nine months' time, she would have children."

"I don't think that's how kids are made," Rune said, eyes still closed.

"The woman was not convinced either, but she saw such sympathy and wisdom in the old diviner's eyes. 'There is just one condition,' the diviner said to her. 'You must never tell the berry babies where they came from. They can never know'. 'Is that the only rule?' the woman asked. And it was. So, as soon as she got home, she did as the old diviner said and swallowed the berries whole. Nine months to the day the woman gave birth to four beautiful babies. Forty fingers and forty toes. Healthy and happy, four little miracles, two boys, two girls."

"Were they purple?"

"No. Beautifully black, of course.

"Phew, I was worried."

"The woman and her husband could not be more pleased. The berry babies grew up strong and with great curiosity about the world around them, but their parents were always afraid for them."

"Why?"

"There are many reasons to be afraid for your children. They might fall and hurt their knees, they might choose their friends poorly at school, and they might crumble when they learned the world's many scary truths. But mostly, they were afraid of their children finding out how they came into being. They had done well never to tell the children they were berries, just as the diviner had told them, but the children's curiosity and wilfulness made it very difficult sometimes.

"One day, when the children were ten years old, they were playing with their friends and having lunch. They stayed in the shade, just as their parents told them. They ate carefully so they didn't accidentally choke, just as their parents told them. But now they were thirsty and they had run out of water. 'No problem,' said one of their friends, 'let us go to the spring and fetch some fresh water'. Now, the berry children knew they were never to step foot outside of the village, as many dangers were there."

"Lions and tigers and bears. Oh my!" Rune grinned.

Abe pinched his shoulder. "But the children were also very curious, and if they really thought of it, wouldn't their mother be proud of them showing such bravery and initiative? 'I know just what we should use to collect the water,' said one of the berry children. She went to collect one of her mother's precious clay pots. She wasn't supposed to use these, but what harm could come if the children were careful?

"They managed to get down to the spring, collect a full pot of water and bring it back without a single problem. They drank the water and congratulated each other on their cleverness. But on their way home, the berry child holding the pot tripped on a rock, and down came the pot, splitting into many pieces. 'Don't worry, we shall stick it back together. Mother and father will never know!' They sneaked into the house but, as ever, their mother was waiting for them.

"She couldn't believe her eyes, that her children would disobey so many things at once – to use her precious pots, to step outside of the village, and to break something so important. 'How could you?' she shouted at her daughter with the broken pot in her hands. Seeing his sister crying, one of the brothers reached out to a pot on the shelf and tipped it onto the ground, where it too smashed into pieces. 'You are disgraceful!' the mother raged. The third and fourth children did the same, and broke two more pots – they were in this together, if one was to be scolded then all were to be scolded. The mother screamed at the top of her lungs, 'You drive me mad, you ungrateful little brats. After everything we have done for you. I shouldn't be surprised. After all, you are berries, not children!'

"She wished she could have taken it back as soon as she said it. She apologised and grovelled but the damage was done. She had broken her promise to the old diviner. The children had heard the truth. One by one, they turned from her and walked out of the house, out of the village and out into the dangerous, wide world, all the while saying:

"*'Maama agambye nti sitwali baana twali ntula.*' (Mother has said that we were not children, but berries.) *'Agambye atya?'* (What did she say?) *'Nti sitwali baana twali ntula.'* (That we were not children but berries)."

"Are you calling me a berry?" Rune said, peeking up at Abe's upside-down face.

He smiled an upside-down smile. "Maybe."

"Charming."

"I said you wouldn't like it."

"Go on, then, hit me with it: what's the moral?"

Abe looked across the hill. "You could look at it many ways, I suppose. That parents should be careful about what they tell children. Or maybe children shouldn't be sheltered from the truth. Either way, it's just people trying to do what they think is right in difficult circumstances."

"Oh," Rune breathed. He considered both interpretations. He sought the one that was most detrimental to him, the most sympathetic to his mother. But he stopped this train of thought, choked it tightly and let it die.

A whisper of warm air washed over the Rune and Abe. Their breath once again fell in synch.

"I did like it," Abe said.

"Hm?"

"Your flirting."

Electricity. There it was. "I thought…" Rune started.

"I know."

"…it seemed like you…"

"I know."

"The way you looked at me when...*Whatshisname* spoke to me at the party. And then when I kissed Kit."

"I know."

"I felt a little judged by you, Abe."

"That wasn't my intention. But maybe I did judge. A little."

"I'll never apologise for being who I am," Rune said.

Abe's smile was wide and warm. He brushed a tendril from Rune's forehead. "I'm glad."

Rune twisted out of Abe's arms and turned to face him. There was so much in the Storyteller's expression, and yet nothing at all. He was learning to read it, understanding that the meanings lay in the finer details. It felt like a word on the tip of Rune's tongue.

"I liked your flirting very much," Abe said.

Rune considered moving in, but held himself in place, understanding this wasn't the end of the tale.

"But I can't," Abe said. "It's...complicated for me."

"Tell me," Rune replied, searching Abe, seeking the word. "Because of your family? What your brother did?"

"In a way," he said and then, with a hand ever so slightly trembling, cupped Rune's face. "You have a beautiful family, Rune. They are learning to be something new, which can be painful. But they want to learn. That's a very special thing."

VIII.

He watched his parents for a time from a safe distance. They were unified in the task, as they had been so many times before. Jack selected a wrench from the toolbox, Jock took it without a word and disappeared under the bonnet of the car. His hand reached out behind and she replaced the tool with another.

Rune couldn't hear their words at this distance, but their tone carried on the breeze: it bore neither tension nor weariness, it was straight, simple. Where were the fireworks? The slamming doors and gritted teeth?

Free for a moment from her duties, Jack raked fingers through her long hair and felt her wrist, but it was bare. There was always a hair tie on her wrist, it was one of her little magics. As a child Rune had marvelled at the whole business of it, the hair, the scrunchie, the simple eyeliner-and-lipstick preparation. He had asked to do it for her. Even now he could recall the softness of her wavy locks, and the way they became greasy after hours of playing with them, brushing, plaiting, clasping. She would read or doze while he played, or watch her daytime shows. The day she caught him with the lipstick and eyeliner was less tranquil. She was never the high heel type of person, so he had to make do on tiptoes. But 'makeup and dresses were for mummies, not little boys'. A simple statement, a kindly one even, but enough to plant a seed.

It was protection, of course he understood that now. Protection comes in many shapes. A lesson. A telling off. A *bosie* hug. A secret. Many secrets *'Just between you and me, Runey. Okay? No need to tell Kelly about the Thai man.'*

Jock reversed from under the hood. He pressed a hand against the small of his back as he unfurled to full height. Jack reached out to massage, but retracted her hand. And there it was, in one tiny moment: the new normal. The distance despite the nearness.

Jock turned and caught her expression. He offered a joke to break the mood before it could even land. He was good at that.

A giant as big as the sky, but with a keen sight on the ground. He left no sadness unconsoled, no argument unmediated, even when it meant putting his own needs aside. Those big arms were made for hugging.

Yet, from up so high everything looks small and manageable, but even small things fester and grow if you're not looking properly. Small things, like a truth which lurks at the heart of a marriage.

'I can't do this any more. You're my best friend, but I want more from life'.

Her small truth. The closer you looked at it, the bigger it became until it was too big for Jock to wrap his arms around and hug back down to size.

He closed the hood of the car and raised a hand up. She high-fived it without hesitation. From this distance, the new normal almost looked like the old one. The Big Man leaned into the driver-side window and the engine thrummed to life.

IX.

Unseen, Rune bypassed his parents. A check of his watch told him there was still time to drive Abe to his evening performance in the city if they left in the next twenty minutes. This was his job, and he would do it.

The log cabin was quiet. He crossed to the sink and filled a glass with water, it was lukewarm from the summer heat but tasted clean and crisp. *'Everything's better in the countryside'*. A line from Kelpie's play. 'Play' might be a strong word. Performance therapy? A cry *for* therapy? Or just attention. Even in the privacy of his own mind he could hear the snark, the cruel edge of his sarcasm rasping like chisel on stone. Poor wee girl. She had exploded a bomb in her own face. The death notice letter waved in his memory, pinched between Kelpie's little fingers. *'What does this thing mean?'*

He placed the glass down, preparing to call out her name, but stopped short at seeing her bare feet poking out of the sofa. He crossed the room and peered over the back of the sofa. Kelpie was asleep, freckled arms bundled together, red curls splayed across a cushion. She was wrapped in an invisible cocoon – the sweet, musky smell of horse. Her red riding jacket, still muddy from the puddle spray, lay on the ground. Her forehead was a sun-kissed pink, but there were no longer the signs of worry and confusion that had been there in the paddock. Maybe it was fine. No need for 'the talk'.

A cigarette was held in her fist, its unlit end cradled against her chin. The packet lay next to her shoulder, all the other cigarettes accounted for, bar the one in her grasp. *Baby's first fag.* She held it to her chest like a dear old teddy bear. It was an image that would haunt Rune for years to come. This his baby sister would find comfort in her older brother's vice. A vice born of a false image of his father. He reached over and slipped the cigarette from her hand, and lifted the packet away. He crushed the whole thing in his fist, and dropped it into the bin.

He heard a voice coming from elsewhere in the house, a mumble through the wall. He followed it round the corner, past the vestibule to Abe's bedroom door.

"Yes, yes I know but...". Abe's voice was low, but there was a formality that carried the words clearly beyond the door. "...I understand, but if I could just get five minutes, that is all...yes...

yes ma'am, I understand. Hm? Well, as I say, it is a personal matter so I would rather not…mm hmm…eh heh…yes…yes…no of course, I wouldn't want to…but perhaps he would have time in the next few days…right, no I am sure you are correct, he is a very busy man and I don't mean to pester…yes of course. But forgive me, ma'am, maybe if I called again tomo– Hello? Hello?"

Rune opened the door gently. Abe was sat on the edge of the bed, his back stooped as he looked down at a smartphone.

"Hey," Rune said.

Abe turned, panic in his eyes hurriedly covered over. "Hi."

"What you up to?" Rune nodded at the phone. It was his own phone.

"I just…uh," Abe waved it in the air as if he had just found it on the ground. "Sorry, I was…"

Rune sat next to him. "It's fine, you can use it. What's wrong?"

Abe handed the phone over and gave his best smile, but it didn't stretch as far as his eyes. He got up and packed a shirt in his bag. "How's the car?"

"Fixed," Rune said. As soon as Abe's back was turned, he looked at his most recent calls list. He recognised the top number. "You called the university switchboard?"

"I said I was sorry, I just needed to…" Abe flustered, indignation rising. "You know, it's quite rude to…"

"Abe," Rune said more firmly. "It's me. Chill. Who were you trying to get hold of?"

Abe chewed his lip. "The Professor."

"The Professor?" Rune said. "Why on earth would you want to talk to him? Wait, is it something about me?"

Abe's shoulders sagged. "It's nothing to do with you. Let's get going, my friend."

"C'mon, stop being so bloody cagey and tell me."

"I need his help, okay?" Abe spat, his breath quickening.

"Why would you…" Rune began, realisation dawning. "You've been trying to speak to him for a while. After the parade you asked to speak in private with him."

Abe nodded, his expression suddenly deflated. "I need his help. He has helped people in my situation before. Well, his wife did at least."

"Situation?"

"Please don't make me say it."

"Abe, I don't have a clue what you're talking about."

"Asylum."

The word was foreign to Rune's ears, almost meaningless. He chuckled at its sound. "Why would you need that? Abe? Why would you need asylum?"

Abe didn't reply for a long moment. "I can't go home," he said.

Rune shook his head, imagination drawing a blank at any possible reason Abe would be seeking something so drastic. And then. "Your brother."

Abe picked at a Ugandan badge that was sewn into his bag. "I told you Kakuru waited for me at my friends' apartment one night. He suspected I was gay, but he needed proof. Seeing us all together was what he needed."

"Kakuru told your parents," Rune recalled. "Such an asshole."

"Yes, he is an asshole," Abe said. His eyes were becoming pink around the edges. "But, unfortunately, he didn't stop there. After he told my parents, he returned to Kusemererwa and Mubiru's apartment. He saw them kissing through their window."

"What a perv," Rune said.

Abe shook his head. "You don't understand. It's not safe to be like you and me in my country."

"But it was just a kiss."

"Kakuru told the police, Rune. He said Kuse and Mubi were engaging in a 'sex act' outdoors, said he saw them from across the street."

"But that's a lie…"

"It was all they needed to search the apartment. To turn it upside down, to look through their computers, their books, everything."

"But…" Rune stammered.

"They are in prison, Rune," Abe said, eyes now red-raw. "My friends."

Rune made to embrace him but Abe held out a hand.

"Kakuru said I would be next."

"Oh my God," Rune breathed.

"My mother helped me pack. Gave me all the money she had spare, and told me to run."

"'*To stay just out of reach*'," Rune whispered. Abe's words from the previous night. "I'm so sorry, Abe. I can't imagine…"

Abe sniffed. A steeliness had come to rest on him. Now that he saw it, Rune realised that Abe's coolness, his apparent ease with the world around him had always been part steel.

"I need asylum," he said.

"And the Professor…?"

"His wife helped people like me. People unable to go home."

"Mary Seaton helped people get asylum?"

"She knew a lawyer who knew people in the Home Office. Celia told me about it."

"Celia?"

"Mary and the lawyer helped her many years ago."

"Wow," Rune blinked. "So, if you can speak to the Professor, you think he might help like his wife did?"

Abe looked pained. "But he won't see me. Won't answer my calls."

Rune took Abe's bag and slung it round his shoulder. A new sense of purpose buzzed in his fingertips. "Well then, it's a good thing I've got a meeting with him tomorrow morning."

Part Seven
The Wizard of Skene

A dream, concluded.

The Prophetess Fedelm approaches the plinth on the summit.

Atop the breast-shaped hill, high above the winding ways of the world.

She stands among the stars. They watch with shining eyes, too enraptured to blink.

Everything has led to this point. Every thread, path and step.

The Prophetess Fedelm feels afraid. For this is where the golden path ends.

Where her foresight fails, where the visions cease.

She looks back at the golden path.

She remembers the Shard. The Mother's voice. The glass turned to stone.

She remembers The Crow and The Wizard. Their mocking chants and grasping words.

And now she is lost.

She whispers a ghostly tune: "A warrior will come…a warrior will come"

Tears fill her eyes, reflecting the stars all around. She is but a twinkle in a universe of suns.

On the plinth are two objects.

A looking glass. *Imbas forosnai*, all-seeing knowledge, given form.

And a sword. Its bejewelled hilt promising action.

She doesn't know which to choose.

Is it better to know, or better to do? The comfort of knowledge, or the uncertainty of action?

She cannot decide.

And so she waits at the summit, at the end of destiny's golden path, and whispers:

"A warrior will come...a warrior will come..."

A dream, looped...

The Prophetess Fedelm approaches the castle.

Her visions have led her here, through forest and misty lake, bracken and briar.

Back to the tower of her childhood

The Shard. It waits for her at its top, singing its mournful song...

I.

Jack: You made it back into the city okay? xx
Me: Yup.
Jack: I think we should talk more. I'd like to. x
Me: Sure
Jack is typing...

Jack is typing...
Me: Got to go. Working.

Celia had been looking backwards and forwards between Rune's chest and her own huge bosom for a good few minutes. She went through cycles of narrowing her eyes, tilting her head this way, then that, and making small noises under her breath. She would end the circuit with a contemplative look at her breasts then nod in approval. The world below the Cromwell Tower would occupy her attention for a few seconds, then she would start the whole thing again.

"Stop," Rune eventually broke, laughing despite the anticipation that gnawed at his guts. Abe had been in the Professor's office for ten minutes, but neither he nor Celia could hear a peep through the wooden door. They were stuck in the corridor with nothing to do but wait for the verdict.

"Sorry. Just gimme a wee *lookie*. Promise I'll stop," Celia said in her gloriously mixed Venezuelan-Scottish accent.

"I know you're just trying to distract me," Rune sighed. He undid two shirt buttons slowly then halted. Celia mouthed 'ooh baby' and licked her lips, which made Rune chuckle more. He snaked his hips from side to side and circled his shoulders. He popped a third button, a fourth and then thrust his chest out, letting the shirt gape wide. Sunlight poured in from the stained-glass window and glinted off his nipple. "Bang!"

Celia fluttered her fingertips together in applause. She peered in and reached out with thumb and forefinger. "Can I?"

"If you must."

She approached the piercing cautiously, as if inspecting a rare gem. It didn't last – in seconds she was tugging the ball bearings from side to side as if it was lodged in her own nipple. "*Asombrosa!*," she said then clutched her left breast. "I think I could get away with it, you know? I really do."

"Go for it. Just be prepared for the bleeding and the itching and the catching-it-on-every-bit-of-clothing. And also the ogling from weird women."

She flicked his nipple with a shellacked nail and returned to the stone windowsill. Rune rubbed the sting away, did a few buttons back up and stared at the Professor's door. He checked his phone and groaned. *Eleven minutes...* "Is this a good sign?" he said.

"Maybe," Celia said, her gleeful expression trickling into concern.

"I feel like there should be white smoke coming out of the chimney by now. Was it like this with you?"

Her curly hair swung left and right. "Not so formal. I was pretty drunk when I asked Mary to help me get asylum."

"Why am I not surprised," Rune laughed. "What was she like?"

"She was very kind, in a straightforward way. But much warmer than him," she nodded at the door. "She wanted to get to know us. Always coming round for chats, watching the performances, speaking to us in the bar. So, no, the process was a lot more 'organic', I guess you would call it? *Nae* like this."

Rune recognised the suspense rising in her eyes, he felt it too. "Must have been hard for you to leave home."

Celia shrugged. "Not at first. I was too focused on trying not to go back home. I see the same thing in Abe, that's why I know he's serious."

"Yeah," Rune exhaled. Abe flashed in his mind, his excitement at the possibility of a face-to-face with the Professor. Was Rune giving him false hope?

As if reading the struggle, Celia smiled sweetly at him. "He'll be okay. He has people who care about him."

Rune leaned back against the wall. "'*A man finds friends wherever he goes.*'"

"Just friends?"

He felt his neck begin to redden just as the Professor's door handle *crunked* and the door swung open. Rune and Celia immediately stood to attention.

Abe emerged from the office. The Professor followed, patting Abe's back.

"...really am looking forward to tomorrow's Closing Gala," the Professor said, his tone bright. "I'm sure it's going to be wonderful. I've got my ticket ready."

"I will look out for you in the audience," Abe said.

"Look no further than the front row, my boy. I'm guest of honour."

"Ah, of course. Wonderful."

Abe's face was unreadable, his voice level. Both Rune and Celia tried to catch his eye, to find any sign that could indicate the Professor's verdict. When Rune finally connected, he found nothing but a cool reflection, the amber in Abe's eyes muted by the stone corridor.

"Excellent. Ta-ta for now," the Professor clapped.

Rune and Celia each placed a hand on Abe's shoulders, guiding him down the corridor.

The Professor cleared his throat. "Mr Duthie? Shall we?" he waved a hand into his office.

"Oh, uh yeah, of course." Rune sent an apologetic glance to the other two then walked towards the office.

Once they were both inside, the Professor closed the door behind him with great care, as if placing the final ace on top of a playing card pyramid. "And so we meet again," he said, still facing the door. "How goes it?"

"Uh, fine thanks," Rune said to the man's tweed-covered back. "Did everything go okay with Ab–"

"How is my Fedelm doing?"

"Good. A force to be reckoned with."

The Professor's shoulders jiggled, but still he didn't turn. "She is that. And the couriering? Tell me, how has that been?"

"Well, I think. It's been interesting. Meeting people from all over the world."

"Mmm," the Professor bobbed his head. Daylight found the scalp beneath his thinning hair. "I'm sure you've met all kinds of interesting people."

"Yes," Rune replied, unsure of the Professor's enigmatic mood. He began to rabbit. "But the internship has been going very well. I'm really making progress." He reached into his bag and pulled out the sketchpad and a few sheets of paper with the Maiden Stone rubbings on them.

The Professor muttered something under his breath and drummed the door with his fingertips.

Rune stopped rustling the paper. "Professor, is there something wr–"

He suddenly swung round, hands on hips. "Do you know what?" he said, eyes wide, teeth bared in a grin. "Wouldn't you believe it, my blooming television is back on the fritz. The aerial has been knocked off kilter once again. But my knee is giving me heck this morning. You couldn't possibly help an old mannie out, could you?"

Rune tracked the gesture towards the open window, and snapped back in confusion.

"Just a wee waggle?" the Professor's lips pursed.

"You mean...out on the sill?" Rune said.

"And then we shall have a look through your, um," he said, looking at the Maiden Stone rubbings, "progress."

Rune searched his expression for any possibility of escape – a joke hiding between the crinkles, the smallest indication of insincerity – but found nothing. He approached the open windowsill and peered down five storeys to the concrete slabs below, and the playing fields beyond. He clambered up on the sill and gripped the frame. He looked back at the Professor, who raised his eyebrows in encouragement.

"It's just up there on the right. Shimmy out and you'll see it."

Still holding tight, Rune shifted both feet to the outer-side of the sill. He felt exposed in the hot rays of sunshine; the humid air offered no cushion, nothing between him and the wide outdoors. A cold trickle ran down his spine.

Five storeys suddenly looked like one hundred. The view seemed to bulge from up here. The vertigo was exacerbated by only having monocular vision, but Rune didn't dare release a hand from the frame to remove the patch. "Jesus," he gasped. He blinked and looked to the right, where a flat expanse of bricks met him.

No aerial.

Suddenly, the window behind him slid shut and closed with a *thunk*. The sound was followed by the rattle and click of a clasp.

Rune howled. "Professor! What's going on?" He twisted his neck as far as it would go, but could only catch the whites of the man's eyes in his periphery. Rune's ankles felt immediately wobbly, his grip on the window frame suddenly weak. He pressed his back against the window pane. Only half a foot of stone separated him from a five-storey plummet. "Professor!"

The single pane of glass muffled the Professor's voice, but the words were clear. They were sharp, laced with malice. "What does she want?"

"What? Who?" Rune said, heart thumping.

"You know who. What does she want? What's this whole charade about, eh?"

"I have no fucking idea what you're on about!"

The Professor slammed an open palm against the glass. Rune yelped like a dog.

"Don't give me that. Her!" the Professor screeched. He was pressing something large and green against the window. In his periphery, Rune recognised the wild eye of the Pictish beast from his rubbings.

"M-M-Mary?" Rune fumbled. Sweat was now pouring from his brow – he felt the sting in his uncovered eye.

"Don't be so bloody stupid," the Professor bit. "Why has she sent you to me? What does she want?"

"Who?" Rune wailed.

"Margaret!" the Professor screamed, rattling the window frame.

Margaret? Who the hell is..? "Morgan?"

A raspy laugh issued from beyond the glass. "Aye. Still going by that, eh? She did so enjoy my Celtic tales, didn't she. *The Morrigan* flying high over the battlefields, manipulating dim-witted warriors to do her bidding. Did she even try to tell you her family's from Ireland? Fiction upon fiction!"

"I don't know what you mean. Morgan didn't send me anywhere. Let me back in! For Christ's sake, I'm going to fall!" He twisted a foot, the stone scraped beneath it. It felt like gravity was pulling him forward.

"Don't act the fool, Mr Duthie," the Professor crooned, his voice light and dripping with venom. "She's paid you off."

"No she hasn't!"

"The Mary Seaton scholarship, ring a bell? Who do you think is funding your internship, eh?"

Rune's mind raced, a hundred thoughts flitting and dying, all battering against a single instinct. "Let me in! Please!"

Silence. All Rune could see were the mad, unblinking eyes of Professor Alasdair Seaton.

Rune pleaded. "I'll...I'll tell you everything, I promise."

There was a click and the window swooshed open. Rune tumbled in, hands splayed. He rapped a wrist against the corner of a chair and tumbled to the floor, instinctively curving his neck so his shoulder took the brunt of the impact.

Rune heaved, gasping for air. "Are...you...fucking...crazy?!"

The Professor towered above him, face jutting like rock. And then suddenly bright, his tone silvery. "So, laddie? You have something to tell me?"

Rune clambered to his feet. "Morgan has paid for the internship?"

The Professor considered the response, amusement spread across his brow. "I see Margaret remains as tricky as ever. Fine, you're ignorant of her manipulations, that's not much of a surprise. What tasks has she set you?"

"Tasks? She's not told me to do anything. I mean, yeah, I've met Morgan. Or, I happened to have met her, and I've seen her once or twice since. But I barely know anything about her. I thought it was a big coincidence."

"There's no such thing. What has she told you?"

Once again, Rune grasped at his thoughts which were still fizzing in all directions. "I dunno, she told me a bit about you and her being in some kind of fight for years. That Mary was her sister, Eddie's her niece. But that's it. I only said I'd tell you 'everything' because I was scared for my life out there. I could have died."

"Oh don't be so melodramatic. It's perfectly safe. Why, I do some of my best thinking on that ledge."

Rune searched the Professor for any trace of humour, but found only a glazed, beatific sincerity. "Have you got a death wish? What the hell is wrong with you?"

"Oh a great many things, dear boy. And each one very likely beyond your meagre ken." The Professor paced the office: one step then a pondering pose, another step then a pause to reposition a pile of books, a third then a glance Rune's way. "One, I don't take kindly to that crone in the castle's pointless chess moves and machinations. Two, I don't enjoy discovering my charges are covert agents for said crone in *yon* tower. And three, I especially don't like said agents trying to take advantage of the current situation."

Rune exhaled loudly. "I swear I have no idea–"

"It's the last festival, you stupid boy!" The Professor bellowed. "How do you think it looks for the festival to end with yet another performer filing for asylum? No, no, no. Not on my watch. Just because my wife is gone...I..." He flushed, the words were leaking out. He reset and spoke through his teeth. "Does it look like I have a target on my face? A weak spot to aim for?"

Rune shook his head, bewildered.

The Professor continued, his voice scratchy, his expression pinched. "It is a cheap trick to send some African stray to me when I'm in the very depths of... The cheapest of all tricks."

"You think this is some game? That Morgan and I are setting you up?" Rune felt fire kindle in his chest. "You think it's some trick for Abe to ask you for help? Are you really that blind?"

"Oh I see perfectly well," the Professor said, swiping the spectacles from his face and casting them on the table. His eyes were small and mean without their magnification. "Unlike you, you one-eyed pirate, smuggling some asylum-seeking wretch in here, playing on my better nature."

"What better nature?" Rune scoffed. "Abe needs help! It's not safe for him to go back to Uganda. His friends are in jail just for living their true lives, and Abe could be next. What about any of that is a cheap trick?"

The Professor smiled. "Oh deary me, he has convinced you, hasn't he? Trust me, lad, they all come with their sad tales, their big eyes and quivering bottom lips. I've seen it more times than I care to tell. Well, it never washed with me. Not once, that was never *my* weakness. You forget, I founded this festival long before you were born. Don't think I'm not aware of every trick in the–"

"You didn't found it alone. Your wife helped people like Abe. *Mary* did everything possible to–"

"Do not dare!" The Professor slapped the pile of books to one side. They crashed against the wall. "Do not dare tell me about my own wife, you red-headed mongrel faggot! Do not begin to pretend you know a single thing about my..." His voice twisted, mouth contorted. He turned and faced the book shelves, shoulders heaving. He continued in a hushed tone, like waves on a winter day. "Mary was mine. And mine alone."

Rune's entire body crackled. His covered eye prickled as he screwed it up. He longed to leap into battle, but something the Professor had said in the midst of his tirade swam up to meet him. "You said the festival–"

"Is over. On my recommendation."

"But–"

"It's done and dusted," he waved. "Tomorrow's closing ceremony will be the end of the whole sorry thing."

"Eddie–"

"I have *Fedelm's* interests at heart. She knows this festival is nothing without her mother."

Rune steeled himself. "This isn't what Mary would have... you're putting her memory, her legacy in a box just like you did with her. Just like you locked her away from her career."

A soft chuckle rose on the dusty air. "Ah there it is. Margaret's seed that's been planted in your tiny skull and left to bloom in the fertile soil of your *artist* brain. It's not even worth my breath to offer a rebuttal. Get out. We're quite finished here. Consider your internship most definitively severed."

"I couldn't give two tiny shits about your internship," Rune said, numbness spreading through his limbs. More words came to mind but they fell to the floor. "Please. You have to help Abe. This has nothing to do with him. Please."

The Professor opened the door, concealing himself behind it. A feeling of impotence chilled Rune. He glanced around the office, with its towers of dusty books, its musty scent, its lofty ceiling. He collected the Maiden Stone rubbings from the desk and left.

II.

The Brig o' Balgownie used to play a vital role in the north east. For hundreds of years, it connected Aberdeen to the northern coast, and the north to the south, providing safe passage over the Don just as the river ended its course into the great North Sea. Now, the bridge is more of an end point than a passage. People come to photograph it, to paint it, to gaze at it. Its sharp gothic arch has captured imaginations as much as the folk legend suggesting it was Robert the Bruce himself who completed it in the fourteenth century.

At least this is what the university pamphlet said. The inside scoop from Hillhead was the Brig was a perfect spot for sundown drinks, given as it's only a few minutes' crawl back to the halls of residence.

Abe and Celia stood on the centre of the Brig beneath the Victorian street lamp, their hands clasped, heads bowed like lovers. Rune stood at the edge where Don Street met the cobbled surface of the bridge. His forehead felt each breeze, the sheen of sweat on his brow was a damp cloth against the heat. In the far distance, past the little houses and the River Don's ending, the North Sea glinted. Gulls circled above calm waters, but didn't come any nearer.

Celia was speaking to Abe, her expression sweet and reassuring. She nodded, encouraging him to do the same but his responses came slowly. In time, they broke formation, Celia guiding him in Rune's direction. Abe's eyes were half suns, hidden beneath shaded lids. When their light reached Rune, they were accompanied by a lopsided smile.

"Abe," Rune said, his palms held skywards. "We'll find another way."

The Ugandan patted Rune's arm. "Thank you for trying, my friend. I'm tired. I'm going to have a sleep at Esslemont."

"But I–"

Celia gave Rune a conciliatory wink. "Eddie's called a rehearsal this afternoon for tomorrow's closing ceremony. He needs some rest."

"I'll see you later," Abe smiled and headed towards Hillhead.

Rune stood for some time at the edge of the Brig, imagining all the work and sweat that must have gone into its construction, only for it to become a place where someone would walk halfway along it then turn back. The thought burned him. His knuckles began to strain, his knees tensed, his nails grasped at the thick air. Red energy thrummed in his feet, sending pokers up through the sinews of his muscles and crackled between his teeth. He felt the urge to run across the bridge, to pound up the north, along the ancient coastal road and beyond – to race around the whole of Scotland in a single day, to thrash and scream and burn his enemies, to release the indignation that had been living within him for all this time. Finally, to use the fire.

But his feet didn't move forward. They turned back. Back along Don Street, and into Hillhead, along the driveway, past the turning circle, through the tall grey buildings, across the grass to its edge, into the woods, past trunk and branch, under canopy, over root, and through thicket to emerge at...

The castle loomed above his head. Despite the tornado in his chest, the building's presence seemed solid, unshakeable, like a stake driven into the flesh of the earth. The iron-studded door was open. He strode into the coolness of Benholm's Lodge, his steps echoing on the stone floor. He waited at the bottom of the spiral staircase and breathed in the ancient air. An army of costumes looked down at him, their headless mannequins awaiting instruction.

He lifted his head and called: "Morgan."

The question climbed up and up and up.

The reply boomed like thunder. It was a simple answer. The oldest answer.

"Aye."

III.

They waited until nightfall then drove the old Volvo out west to Skene. Neither spoke for most of the journey, the silence only broken by Morgan's raspy humming. Rune didn't recognise the tune, but the occasional words that punctuated it, and the cyclical melody, suggested something traditional and Celtic.

Rune pulled at the black turtle neck she had given him. It felt claustrophobic in the evening heat, and the dark joggers bunched and clung in places too, requiring regular readjustment. *Cat burglars must get terrible wedgies.* In the driver's seat, Morgan looked very different. Her tweed jacket and brown trousers must have been stifling, but there wasn't a single droplet of sweat on her furrowed brow.

"We're close," she said then pointed at the dashboard. "Hand me that."

Rune looked at the furry thing and groaned. "Really? He doesn't even have a moustache."

"Hmm, well he used tae."

"Seriously, Morgan, this is overkill. You really think dressing up as him will stop onlookers thinking it's strange 'the Professor' is breaking into his own house?"

Morgan tutted. "Gimme it and grab the flat cap from the back seat while you're at it."

Rune muttered at the ridiculousness of the situation, but even he had to admire the final effect: mossy-green cap covering the silver hair, hunched shoulders, grey stubble stippled across the chin and cheeks, a hint of shadow applied beneath the lids – her transformation from lofty, angular Morgan Benholm to squat, dishevelled Professor Alasdair Seaton was pretty convincing. From afar. Which she said was all they needed.

"And here we are," *Professor Benholm* grinned. She turned the car off the road and into a dark driveway.

Moonlight shone from a cloudless sky and hit an awesome sight: two symmetrical stone towers, four storeys high at least, complete with turrets and battlements. The towers were connected by an iron gate. At either end of the gate were fifteen-foot-high plinths. A griffin was perched upon each, their hind legs rearing, wings splayed out, beaks gaping and fierce.

Rune gaped too. The grand towers, the turrets, the griffins – he'd driven past the Loch of Skene countless times, and had seen these grand stone structures, but he'd never looked properly.

"The Professor lives in there?" Rune said, looking up at the windows which studded each level of the towers.

Morgan laughed. "He wishes."

The gates were open enough to allow the Volvo passage to the single-track road beyond. Morgan pulled in to a gap in the trees and switched the engine off, plunging them into moonlit blue.

Her tweed jacket rustled as she turned in the seat. Her blue eyes were like jewels. "Just as we planned, okay?"

Rune clenched his jaw and got out of the car. They crept across the pathway towards the southern tower. The air was still and warm, carrying a mulchy smell from the loch. From this angle the water looked like a black mirror, stretching one-mile wide in each direction. A thin mist covered its entire glassy surface, the uncanny stillness broken only by occasional flitting in the darkness. Rune cast his eye across the loch and saw bats twitching and skittering around.

Connecting the second tower to the loch edge was a long boathouse, constructed from the same granite but only two storeys high. Wooden doors, wide and rounded at their tops, lined the rectangular building. Morgan approached the second door from the right and turned the metal handle. It didn't budge. She muttered something then tried again. When that didn't work, she moved to the other doors, trying each in succession to no avail. Her blue eyes searched Rune. Panic rose in his chest, he raised his arms in question. She crept over. In the dim light, it was almost as if the Professor himself was loping towards him out of the mist. "We do this the old-fashioned way," Morgan said, a devilish smile forming beneath the stuck-on moustache.

The boathouse jutted out into the loch by a few metres. Morgan took off brogues and socks and rolled up trousers to knee-level, indicating for Rune to do the same.

"We're going in?" he hissed.

"Och *wheesht*, it's only a few feet deep at the edge. And *onywye*, it's only six feet deep in the middle."

"Eh?"

She flung an arm towards the water. "It's man-made, *ye feel gype*! It's not a real loch. Just a bloody great puddle for fishing in. Yer nae going tae drown."

Rune rolled up his joggers just as Morgan began wading into the water. Her steps sent out ripples across the surface, causing wisps of mist to drift and swirl with a ghostly butterfly effect. Ripples reached the stripe of moonlight that cut clean across the centre of the loch, highlighting blooms of algae on the water's surface.

"For God's sake," Rune said, entering the loch. It was warmer than he thought it would be, slimier too. Morgan was up ahead, following the edge of the boat house. She disappeared for a moment, whispered something triumphant, then her flat-capped head peeped back round the corner. She scooped a hand towards Rune. He joined her at the edge and looked up at the huge entrance to the boathouse.

"The portcullis is up! We're in!" Morgan exclaimed.

"What's a portcul...whoa!" Rune breathed. Suspended high above his head was a metal grille that ended in a row of pointed teeth – a dragon's mouth open wide to tempt prey into its hungry belly.

Morgan sloshed through the opening, beckoning for Rune to come. In the darkness, he could make out a series of shapes bobbing on the water at each wall. As his eye adjusted, he could make out dinghies. The floor was deeper here, just enough to keep the boats afloat.

"Grab those oars," Morgan's voice boomed around the cavernous interior. She was unhooking one of the small boats, grunting as she undid a thick rope. Rune waded through the water, the ground slippery between his toes, pulled two wooden oars from their housings in the wall and laid them in the dinghy. With a nod, the pair guided the boat out of the entrance. They paused to collect their shoes and socks, then climbed into the dinghy and rowed out on the black surface of the Loch of Skene, disturbing its veil of mist.

Morgan rowed well, her shoulders rolling with smooth, powerful strokes. The oars slid in and out of the water with only the slightest of splashes. Her eyes seemed to fizz with glee. It was an infectious stare.

Rune chuckled. "You look like you've done this before."

"Rowed or done a heist?"

"Rowed. But now that you mention it..." he raised an eyebrow.

"Aye well," she smiled, "I'm just doing my bit for your pirate training."

For a split second he considered asking more. About the internship. Why she secretly funded it. Why she had been lurking in the woods all those days ago. The Maiden Stone tale. Was it all part of her grand design? But he decided adventures aren't a time for questions.

With a few rolls of the shoulder, she began steering them across the loch's central stripe of moonlight in the direction of something on the far bank. As they approached, the structure became clearer, though Rune couldn't quite believe it. A Roman temple, comprising eight towering columns, stood on the edge of the water. Their feet were covered in mossy ground, as if the pillars were pushing through from the soil itself, or being devoured by it.

"What's that?" Rune asked, aghast.

Morgan made a dismissive sound. "Just a folly. It was built at the gates of Dunecht House down the road. When they made a new entrance, they stuck this one over here. It's ridiculous."

"No, it's not," Rune whispered. The water lapped against the edge of the temple, its ghostly white fingers stretching to the sky as if about to pluck down the moon. "It's incredible."

"If you say so," Morgan grunted as she stepped onto the bank. "Pick your jaw up and help me pull this thing onto land. And be quiet – the house is just on the other side of those trees."

She thumbed backwards, beyond the temple towards a line of trees. Through the shadowy gaps, Rune thought he could see the outline of a large property, but nothing definitive. He helped Morgan drag the dinghy far enough onto the marshy land, so that it wouldn't drift back out to the water, then followed her up to the temple. They each sat on a plinth and pulled on socks and shoes.

Morgan clopped her brogue heel against the column. "And now for the hard part. Ready?"

Rune felt butterflies in his stomach. "Sure."

"Follow me," she whispered and set off for the trees. Rune followed behind, adopting her half-stoop creep. The wood, if you could call it that, was only a few trees deep. They crouched together at its inner reaches.

"Jesus Christ," Rune gasped. A house…no, a mini castle…met his eye from across a wide lawn. It had all the trappings of Scots baronial construction, just like the ones he'd studied during an architecture elective in his first year – conical roofs, tall windows, a tourelle tower, even a square battlement, jutting up like a chess piece. It should have been breath-taking, should have looked like an indelible part of the land. But it didn't. It looked…

"Grotesque," Morgan whispered.

Rune looked between her and the mansion. His confusion must have been apparent because a knowing smirk blossomed beneath the moustache.

"Welcome to *Château Seaton*. Circa 1985."

"What?"

"Our good friend, the Professor Alasdair Seaton, came into a windfall when his daddy died. Spent the lot on building this monstrosity. Talk about a folly." She nodded back at the temple.

"Must have cost an absolute fortune."

"Well," Morgan shrugged. "He couldn't have my castle, so he built his own."

Rune could see it now, the artifice lurking in every element of the building: the double-glazed windows, the breeze block stonework, the harling. And a family crest stamped above the wooden entrance.

"There," Morgan pointed towards the battlement tower. It must have been three storeys high. "That's how you get in."

Rune's throat constricted. "But you said you had a key to the house?"

"No, no, no," she held out her hands. "I said, 'the *key* will be getting in without setting off the security lights'."

"But how the hell am I...what do you expect me to..." Rune stammered.

"There's a trellis up one side. Strong as anything. It'll be an absolute *caker* to climb," she waved.

"Morgan, this is–"

"Now, as we planned, I'll be on lookout down here. Stick in your wee wireless earphone thingies and I'll talk you through the whole thing."

"But what if–"

"It's very unlikely Wee Ali is in, and if anyone spots us from afar..." She wafted the lapels of her tweed coat.

"Then it's just the Professor walking about the grounds of his own house," Rune groaned, finishing the sentence. "At twilight."

"Exactly. What could possibly go wrong?"

IV.

"Well," Rune said looking upwards. "I am *so* gonna die."

There was indeed a trellis that scaled the full height of the battlement tower, a sturdy one at that. But what Morgan hadn't mentioned was that it was currently occupied by a flourishing array of roses. Thorny roses. The gardener's gloves she had given him suddenly made sense.

"Dinna be so dramatic," Morgan's voice hissed in his ear. "Now get climbing."

He caught a glimpse of her by the trees and hoped she could see him grimacing. He found a bare spot on the wooden lattice and tugged. It didn't budge an inch, courtesy of the hundreds of nails which he now saw had been driven into the concrete at intervals all the way up.

"Okay," he exhaled and began the climb. Finding gaps in the roses was difficult, but his unpatched eye began to find them. His mind plotted a pathway, but only ever a few feet ahead at a time. At first, he was surprised by his strength. He'd always been proud of the outline of his biceps, had been complimented by many an admirer, but he'd secretly presumed they were more a product of his slimness than any actual muscle being there. Maybe the carving had helped tone him up? However, thirty seconds into the climb, joggers already beginning to snag and rip on thorns, the first red-hot nicks on his bare shins and arms, this theory began to give out. "My legs are feeling wobbly. Am I nearly there?"

"Depends what we mean by 'destination'," Morgan lilted.

"Oh God. I don't know if I can do this. The thorns are everywhere, it's nearly impossible to–"

"You're fine. You just need some adrenaline."

"Fine. Send me up a double espresso and a fucking Mars bar!"

"I've got something much better."

"Oh?"

"The trellis is starting to come awa' frae the wall."

"What?" Rune wailed. He looked down. This far up, the ground was too dark to properly make out. He could be halfway up or a thousand miles high, the ground bulged and stretched. Why did he keep finding himself on the edge of buildings today? He instinctively clung to the wall, but flinched a centimetre away from poking his remaining eye on a thorn.

"Go go go!" Morgan said, urgency fizzing in her voice.

"Ohmygodohmygodohmygod!" Rune cried. With a surge, he grasped at anything resembling a gap and pulled himself up the trellis, yanking himself free of anything that snagged. The final hurdle drew nearer – the lip of the battlement. It stuck out from the tower hall by about half a foot. In a series of moves he couldn't quite believe, he managed to get a foothold on a tiny keyhole-shaped window and hoisted himself up enough to be able to grab the top of the parapet. But this was as far as his newfound strength could take him.

He could hear Morgan in his ear as well as her true voice on the ground. "Quick! The whole trellis is falling away!"

"Fuuuuuuuuuuuuuck," he yelled. With a final, desperate heave, he dug his fingers in and pulled himself up. He kicked at open air, but the momentum was just enough to get him over the parapet, where he promptly thudded onto the flat roof of the tower. He could barely breathe, could hardly feel his poor limbs at first, but the sensations returned with each gasp. He was sure the nail had come clean off his middle finger beneath the glove, his muscles felt rent and white hot, and he could track the tickling trickle of blood on his shin. He looked down and saw the right leg of his joggers was hanging by a thread below the knee. But the blood was less than he thought. "That. Was. A. Stupid. Idea."

"It got you up though," Morgan replied. There was something self-satisfied about the way she said it.

Rune got to his feet with a series of grunts and peered over the edge of the tower. A wall of roses looked back at him pleasantly. The trellis was completely intact.

"You absolute cow!" Rune roared, not caring if the whole of Skene heard him. "You goddam liar! I thought I was going to die".

"Focus," Morgan sang in his ear. "What can you see from up there?"

Rune could make out the full outline of the loch from the battlement. It was like a huge oval puddle. The grounds about it were segmented into woodland, farmland and roadways. He spotted the main road to the far right where it splintered into a small track which brought him full 360 degrees to Castle Seaton.

"Morgan," he said through gritted teeth, "there's a road that leads directly here."

"Yes. And?"

He laughed, pulling himself back from the edge of hysteria. "Why did we take a fucking row boat if there's a road that takes us right here?"

"Oh, for goodness sake. Adventure. Leaving no trace. Doing the unexpected. Pick one and tell me what you see behind you."

"I see a bloody road–"

"On the ground behind you!"

"Oh." A few feet away from Rune was a trapdoor with a metal latch.

"Yes 'oh'. Now get down there, we're already behind schedule."

The latch was unlocked, which shouldn't have surprised Rune but by now he had very few expectations of certainties on this heist. He pulled it up and laid the trapdoor flat. A slim ladder led down into the dark interior of the tower.

"Morgan, if I lose signal let's–"

"You *winna*. Those walls are as thin as a new build. Not real stone like *my* castle."

Rune tutted and crept down the ladder, the numerous thorn nicks on his legs prickling with each step.

"Now," came Morgan's voice, "at the bottom of the ladder you'll find yourself in the top room of the tower. There's a stairwell at the opposite end. See it?"

"It's pretty dark. Hold on." He pulled out his phone and flipped on the torch function. Its beam cut a path directly to a bannister, catching motes of dust in the beam. "Jesus. This place needs a clean. Okay, yeah, I see the stairs."

"And are you going down them?"

"No?"

"Why not?"

"Because you didn't tell me to," Rune hissed.

"Go down the blimmin' stairs!"

At the bottom of the first flight was a room much like the top floor, the same dancing dust but a few more pieces of furniture for it to settle on.

Morgan's whispering voice sounded suddenly serious. "Take the door into the main body of the house. You'll find a corridor with all the bedrooms off it."

The door creaked at first touch, which made Rune wince. "Are you sure there's nobody in the house?"

"Positive. Nobody's been in for weeks."

"Then why are you whispering? Why am I creeping around?"

There was silence down the line. "Drama?"

"Sod this," Rune huffed, throwing the door open. He cast the torch down the hallway. Most of the doors were ajar, which made it easy to peek in as he passed by. The first two bedrooms looked like guest rooms, each with four-poster beds, pretty side tables but not much else. "If nobody's staying here the Prof should rent it out," he said. "He'd make a fortune."

"Aye he could probably do with a bob or two. He put every penny into building this monstrosity," Morgan said.

The third bedroom looked much more lived in – a standard IKEA bed, some clothes slung across its rumpled duvet, a side table with books and notepads similarly strewn over it. On the wall opposite the door Rune could make out a landscape painting. He stepped in for a closer look. It was impressionistic, but realistic enough that he could recognise the place straight away. The nipple-like peak of Bennachie was the biggest clue, and a meandering River Don the second. A third, located at its base, was the Maiden Stone, its shape unmistakable from the bite into its shoulder. It was an original painting; he could see the brushstrokes in oil. The colours were muted, the sky above the landscape's greens and browns was a swirl of stormy greys and blues. The lines were lyrical, flowing, naturally leading the eye to a juniper tree at the far left of the scene. In its branches, preparing for flight, was a crow. A cold light sparked off its open beak. By its taloned foot was a name, scratched in black.

"M. Seaton," Rune muttered.

"Eh?" Exclaimed the voice in his ear.

"Mary was a painter?"

There was a beat of silence. Morgan's voice came through softer than before. "Aye, she wisnae bad wi' a brush, my sister. Where are you?"

Rune took in more of his surroundings. Its sparse decoration, and neglected state told him immediately. In life, its owner was all about order, but he knew that people who bark orders often have messy private lives. "I'm in Eddie's bedroom."

"Ah, the Bennachie painting," Morgan's voice drifted into his ear. "That's an old one."

"It's stunning. She was a talented artist. Is that…is that why you funded the internship? An artist residency in Mary's honour?"

Yet more silence.

"Is that why, Margaret?"

A little raspy laugh. "You know, then, do you? He told you?"

"He did," Rune smiled. "He wasn't happy to find out you were behind it. Shut it down there and then."

A heavy breath came down the phone line. "Thought he might. Are you angry?"

Rune became captivated by the painted crow. Its beady eyes, full of devilish intent. "Depends on why you did it," he said to the crow.

Its voice came back, quieter than its fearsome expression. "You know, I've thought about that. I keep coming back to it."

"And?"

"And, I don't rightly know. Why does anyone do anything like that? Maybe a bit of nostalgia, a bit of 'why not?' Drop a pebble into the water and see what the ripples touch. All of that."

"Margaret?"

"Aye?"

"What am I to you?"

"Ah, now *that* I've never doubted," she said, her voice as wide and full as the open sky in Mary's painting. "I called into the wind and look who heard me: my champion."

Rune's throat tightened. He wasn't sure why her words made him want to cry. It felt partly like relief, partly like something else. Maybe it was knowing that he was needed, feeling an adult's approval, having purpose. He wavered on the edge of tears but swallowed it down. "Well then," he whispered, "let's do this, eh?"

"Let's. The bedroom opposite is where you'll find it. That's my bet."

He strode across the corridor into the master bedroom, the door was already wide open as if welcoming him in. It was all as he imagined it would be: four-poster bed, heavy curtains with pelmet, grand oak wardrobe and dresser, faux beams on the ceiling. It may as well have been Robert the Bruce's bedroom.

"I'm in," he said.

"Good. Try the dresser."

Much of the Professor's office desk was clogged with books. Rune shifted a stack of them, memorising their orientation to replace them later. Behind the stack were two framed photographs. On the first was a photo of Eddie, dressed in ceremonial robes, a mortar board and scroll. Her face, shiny with perspiration, looked almost happy, were it not the ever-so-slightly pinched expression around the eyes. He smiled in recognition. It was the same look she'd worn when shaking hands with the festival's steering group at the opening ceremony. A thinly veiled '*fuck you*' look.

The other photograph was of a couple, somewhere Mediterranean possibly, the bright sunlight and azure sea as welcoming and warm as the expressions on the couple's faces. The woman exuded joy, her mouth wide with laughter, silver hair shining, eyes crinkled at the sides. Rune could nearly hear her. The man was in profile, his nose and forehead pressed into the side of the woman's face. His expression, too, breathed contentment. It almost didn't look like the Professor at all. Rune lifted his eye patch to chance a better look. At first his vision doubled but the twin happy couples came together, joined in happy union. He could make out the blue in the woman's eyes. Like sapphires in a lake.

"Mary looked like you," he said quietly.

There was a crackle down the phone, then a voice both mournful and wistful. "She was more delicate though."

It was true. Mary Seaton's features were finer than Morgan's, her shoulders slighter. Even her height was less – her eyebrows level with the Professor's thinning hair. Rune felt himself drifting, his anger towards the Professor waning, as if the vision of the cruel, petulant man was blurring. The photograph, this captured moment of marital bliss, didn't fit with the image Rune had etched in the stone of his mind. He placed the patch back over his eye.

"It's not on the dresser," he said.

"It must be," Morgan said.

"I'm telling you it's...wait."

"What?"

Rune turned towards the four-poster bed. The sheets were pulled tight, the cover neatly tucked, as if nobody had slept in it. He crossed to the head of the bed and steeled himself: if it was here, then there was no way he could bring himself to steal it. If the Professor kept it below his head, then obviously it was dearer to him than Rune or Morgan thought. Rune lifted one pillow, and then the other, but there was nothing underneath either. He sighed, whether out of disappointment or relief he couldn't tell.

"Never mind," he said. "Morgan, I have no idea where else to look."

"Just try everywhere. In the wardrobe, in the drawers. Inside that Ottoman at the foot of the bed."

"Ottoman?" Rune muttered. Right enough, on the floor at the end of the bed was a large footstool-looking thing with a velvet cover. "Good memory."

He looked inside but only found more books.

"Shite!" Morgan said, her tone turned to ice. "Rune. You need to get out of there now."

His stomach flipped. "What?"

"A car is coming into the driveway. Quick, get out of there."

"Get out how? Where?"

"Figure it out. Dinna worry, I'll stall them. Just stick to the shadows and I'll see you back on the other side of the loch."

"Morgan this is…Morgan?" The line was dead. "Shite!"

He looked out the window and could see headlights drawing near. He crouched and paced about the room, numbness setting in, yet somehow his mind was still trained on completing the mission. Where could it be? It wasn't on the dresser or under the pillow. Think!

He could hear gravel underneath tyres coming up the driveway. No time. He needed to get out that door and…the door. The bedroom door had already been open when he came in, propped open by something. He scrambled to the floor. Right enough, something slim was holding it open. He prised it free. From the feel of its rough surface, he knew this was it. It was smaller than he thought it would be, but the shape was unmistakeable – a

– 270 –

simple wedge, a sliver of stone no longer than his hand, only three or four centimetres at its widest part. He held it up enough to be illuminated in the edge of the light from outside. Pink granite. A triumphant sound wheezed in his chest. He turned the shard in his hand and imagined placing it onto the shoulder of the Maiden Stone, bringing it home.

The sound of a car door opening and slamming broke his reverie.

V.

Rune rushed to the ground floor, the shard of the Maiden Stone safely in his pocket. He didn't even consider the options, he refused to go out of the castle the way he came in, didn't want to tempt fate and die at the bottom of the battlement tower. Down was the only way. Every door he tried was locked, the front door, side door, back door. In a final ditch effort, hope giving way to blind panic, he found a walk-in pantry next to the kitchen. At its far end was a decent-sized window. He tried the handle and, mercifully, it opened outwards. He clambered over packets and tins of food, praying to whichever gods were listening he wouldn't topple them, and climbed out the window and pushed it closed behind him.

The fresh air was sweet. He edged around the side of Castle Seaton, all the while listening for voices. He could hear two, faint but enough to know their tone was serious. One was Morgan's, low and mocking, and the other, without question was the Professor's, higher pitched and sharp.

The car's headlights were now off, so Rune only had

moonlight to go by, but through the silver glow he could make out a route across the grounds and into the trees that didn't involve cutting across the driveway. He braced himself and crept towards the trees, suddenly grateful for the dark clothes Morgan had made him wear. He reached cover without incident – no noises, no accidental tripping of security lights. He was home free, now all he needed was to find a way across the loch unnoticed.

He knew this should be his priority, to get away, but the voices drew him back. This close, he was able to make out some of the words. If he just got a little closer, hid in the trees to his right, he would be able to hear them both clearly. The impulse was too strong. He crawled into the darkness and propped himself up against the rear of the nearest tree, confident of being hidden from view.

He couldn't see them, but their words were clear and true. The conversation sounded cold and strained, but not furious. Transactional almost. Of the pair, the Professor sounded closest to anger, Morgan as ever maintained a knowing amusement.

Unable as Rune was to see their faces, he instead cast his vision across the loch, beyond the columns of the Roman temple, over the water with its veil of mist, to the boathouse – and settled on the twin towers at the iron gate. The granite behemoths faced each other, as they had for a hundred years in a permanent impasse. The voices behind Rune seemed to meld with the granite obelisks.

Professor: ...happen to have come for a visit at this late hour? You really expect me to believe that?

Morgan: Yes. Why is that so strange?

Professor: Oh, I don't know. Perhaps the tweed coat? The cap. The moustache?

Morgan: Ye ken I love a disguise, Wee Al. Stops your neighbours getting curious.

Professor: You look ridiculous.

Morgan: Like looking in a mirror?

Professor: Take it off. Take it all off!

Morgan: Fine, here you go. You'll forgive me if I leave the shirt and trousers on?

Professor: Yes well...of course. Look here, uh, what the hell is all this?

Morgan: Well now, as I say, I just happened to be in the area–

Professor: Stop it. Just stop it. I don't have the energy nor the inclination to hear one of your concoctions.

Morgan: You buried her here, Alasdair. I have a right to visit my own sister.

Professor: ...Oh. Right. Well...

Morgan: And I didn't expect you to visit. Looks like you've hardly been staying in the place since Mary died.

Professor: You broke into the house? That's the absolute limit!

Morgan: Oh calm yer wee red face doon, Al. I can tell fine from here. The weeds are taking over the flower beds.

Professor: That was Mary's pastime, not mine.

Morgan: Tending to the garden? Helping the flowers grow? Making things flourish. You're not wrong there.

Professor: Save your poetry, Margaret. You've completed your visit, I trust? Spoken some nonsense at Mary's graveside?

Morgan: Well, I didn't get a chance to say it at the funeral, did I?

Professor: You really expected an invite?

Morgan: I guess not, no.

Professor: I saw you there. In the back row. Another ridiculous disguise. Think I wouldn't spot you?

Morgan: I had a right to be there! To say goodbye.

Professor: *Tut tut tut.* So indignant, even when it's your own fault she wouldn't have wanted you there.

Morgan: Don't you dare! That's the story you tell yourself, is it?

Professor: Now who's red-faced, eh?

Morgan: You never saw the damage you did her. Every day, chip, chip, chipping away at her until all that was left was the perfect image of your little wifey. Nothing left of the free-spirited girl. She must have barely recognised herself in the mirror.

Professor: Oh, do stop with this tired diatribe. The same for decades. You're exhausting yourself, Margaret.

Morgan: Stop calling me that name.

Professor: Ah yes. What did the boy call you? Morgan? Very clever, I'm sure. It took me all of two seconds to recognise the word play. *The Morrigan*, battle goddess of Irish mythology. The Maiden, Mother and Crone all rolled into one bitter package. Appearing on the hero's journey, a disguised figure ready to manipulate the footsteps of adventurers who pass by. I can see how the boy lapped it up. And I suppose I should feel honoured that you have taken the name of a legendary figure I have studied so closely?

Morgan: I thought you'd like it.

Professor: When really, it's just another of your costumes. One more layer of fakery. A distraction from the lonely spinster who rattles beneath. Pacing the floors of her castle, muttering empty words into night.

Morgan: Now who's the poet. As I remember it, you quite enjoyed those night time mutterings.

Professor: ...

Morgan: What's the matter? Crow got your tongue?

Professor: You stand there gloating. But look at where your manipulations have got you. Absolutely nowhere. I would think someone as experienced as you would know when you don't have a case. The jury's in, my dear. You've lost. *Morgan*.

Morgan: This was never a competition. Nae for me.

Professor: So, what was this whole sham with the boy, eh? The charade of the internship? The Mary Seaton scholarship.

Morgan: *Dr* Mary Seaton scholarship, *ya wee turd*!

Professor: Of course, please forgive me. That makes the whole thing much more legitimate. What was your plan? Fund a scholarship to take me down? Send some dim-witted, one-eyed assassin to come twist the knife in my moment of bereavement?

Morgan: Ha! Poor old Alasdair, still making the same old mistake. Thinking this was all about you.

Professor: Naturally, it was about me. I am the golden thread connecting all your machinations. For all these years, everything you do is in some way about me.

Morgan: Oh please! The Great Wizard of Skene. Here let me kiss your feet.

Professor: What are you–? Get off! You ridiculous woman, get off!

Morgan: Oh sir, please I am not worthy. Please let me take your coat, let me see these powerful, bony shoulders. These strong, stubby fingers. Let me kiss that glorious, piggy nose.

Professor: Margaret stop!

Morgan: You think I funded the scholarship to get at you?

You stupid, conceited little fuck. I did it for her. So there was some legacy of Mary, beyond motherhood and servitude. You stole her spark, so I lit a candle.

Professor: Oh, don't be so–

Morgan: What? Melodramatic?

Professor: You did it for one reason and one reason only: guilt.

Morgan: Guilt?

Professor: Yes, guilt. Guilt for...for what we...what you and I...

Morgan: Don't flatter yourself. You know very well what that was. I admit it was misguided, a failed plan, but I don't feel guilty. I feel angry! That little dalliance between you and me was nothing more than an unsuccessful trick to try and open Mary's eyes to what a no-good piece of *dog shit* you truly are.

Professor: It was more than that, and you know it.

Morgan: Maybe for you. I didn't feel a–

Professor: It was more, Margaret. And it very nearly destroyed everything. You say you feel no guilt? Good for you. Well, I did. Still do. To this day I feel ripped apart by it, the lying, the sneaking around, the illicit trips in the middle of the night. When she found out, I thought she would never forgive me. But she did. And do you know why?

Morgan: ...

Professor: Because she knew that I loved her. Simple as that. And do you know why she never forgave you?

Morgan: ...Don't....

Professor: Because she never truly knew that *you* loved her.

Morgan: I loved her with everything I had!

Professor: Which isn't very much.

Morgan: You stole her from me, from my family. I don't need you to tell me how much I loved my own sister. Everything I did was to try to bring her back.

Professor: And everything I did was to give her a life she deserved.

Morgan: A life as your slave? As your simpering sidekick?

Professor: As my wife. As my beautiful...my one and only...my....

Morgan: What are...no, stop that now, Alasdair. That's not fair, it's not how this works. Don't you dare cry on me.

Professor: I don't know what to do...now that she's...gone.

Morgan: Stop it.

Professor: I don't think I can...

Morgan: You can and you will.

Professor: I can't.

Morgan: ...

Professor: ...

Morgan: Look, you silly man. You can't simply close every door the way you've done with the festival.

Professor: I just couldn't keep it running. Everything reminds me of her. Everything. It's like a noose around my neck. Around Fedelm's. I just couldn't...

Morgan: Oh for heaven's sake, come here you blubbering fool.

Professor: I...I...

Morgan: Shhhh shhhh.

Professor: I...miss...her so much.

Morgan: I know. I do too. Now just quiet down. Breathe, breathe. That's it.

Professor: Margaret?

Morgan: Shhh.

Professor: Does this mean…are you coming back?
Morgan: …
Professor: Coming back to me?
Morgan: I…I don't…
Professor: Please.
Morgan: …

It was the sound of the kiss that finally broke the spell. As if a candle was snuffed out in his mind, Rune was free. And it felt wretched. He crawled into the darkness as quickly as he could without making a sound, leaving no trace, all the while ghastly images ran through his mind, revealing things as they truly were.

He reached the waterside. The boat would be too conspicuous, the Professor would spot him. But he needed to cross the loch, to put as much distance between himself and what he had just heard. The water was warm on the surface, the mist a blanket of humidity, carrying the scent of algae. He entered the loch, and began a careful breaststroke. The green blooms were slimy to the touch, they parted with each stroke, revealing dark water beneath. Rune slid through it.

How could Morgan have done it? An affair with her sister's husband. Lies upon lies upon lies. Were all adults just liars and manipulators? Lying to those closest to them, perhaps even themselves, telling stories, spinning tales, simply to make life a little more palatable. He felt utterly cheated. Betrayed.

The water was cooler below the surface, almost chilling towards his feet. It wasn't a natural loch; he could sense it now. Unnatural stillness, pitch blackness, suggesting despair rather than life. A tear drop deep enough and wide enough to drown in.

Rune added a few of his own to its depths, a fare for safe passage across an undying surface.

VI.

He waited by the Volvo, sopping wet, thoughts slowly becoming clearer. A solitary figure in a row boat cut across the strip of moonlight on the Loch of Skene. He tracked its serene journey along the surface. Morgan parked the boat at the loch edge then ambled up the grass towards the car in long, relaxed strides, tweed coat slung over her shoulder, shirt collar gaping, silver hair scooped back. For good measure the moustache was still on, but at a jaunty angle.

She looked him up and down with a hazy expression. "You're absolutely *drookit*," she said with a dopey smile. "Soaked to the skin."

"I am," Rune said, wishing for a cigarette for the first time in days, not for the craving but for the air of nonchalance it would have afforded. "The loch's slimier than you'd think."

Morgan jutted her chin to the driver's side of the car that Rune was leaning against. He moved out of the way, walked with squelching feet to the passenger side and got in. The car purred to life at first turn of the key.

"Doesn't she run well?" Morgan said, patting the dashboard.

The way back to the city was quiet, the country roads dark and winding. Morgan occasionally snatched looks at Rune, but didn't actively invite conversation.

He took his time, chose his words carefully. "She was buried at the castle?"

Morgan considered the question. She peeled the moustache off and stuck it to the dashboard next to a plastic tortoise air-freshener. Its long neck bobbed up and down with the motion of the car. "How did you know?"

He looked out at gnarled trees lining the road, their knuckled roots outlined in the moonlight. "I overheard," he said.

In the window's reflection he could see what he'd hoped for: a crack in Morgan's veneer. It was in her eyes, a flicker. He watched her cover it up, like grout over tile, but it was too late, he had seen behind the disguise.

He turned to her. "I lost the shard. It fell out of my pocket into the loch."

She snapped her face towards him. A kaleidoscope of emotions played across her face, small tells, tiny, but he caught every one. There was shock first, as he expected, then anger, then disbelief, then a coldness as she searched Rune's face. He didn't blink. The whole time he had waited by the car he promised himself he wouldn't blink.

A softness settled on her brow. Was it disappointment, acceptance? Had there even been a flash of approval, the split second before she turned back to face the road? Her profile gave little away, but Rune could see the power in it waning. It pulsed softly with each passing suburban streetlight.

She smiled. It wasn't a happy thing, but finally an honest thing. "Let's get you home."

Part Eight
The Kelpie

V.

"Kelpie!" Rune shrieked at the banks of the Don. "Kelpie!"

The horse thrashed in the river. Whether playing or struggling, he couldn't tell. Its brown sinewy neck tossed up and down, its teeth were grinding, the whites of its eyes flashed against the dark night sky. There was no sign of its little rider.

Rune ran into the water. The cold shocked his senses, breath seizing in his chest. He pushed the sensation down and waded in up to his midsection, arms held wide to keep him upright. All the while he scanned frantically up and down the river. The water was swift but not so fast that he couldn't find purchase on the pebbled riverbed.

The horse was just out of reach. Its huge body was half covered by the river, only when it stamped could its knees be seen. It whinnied at the sight of Rune.

"Pixie, whoa! Calm, calm," Rune held out his hands.

The horse's ears pricked alert, twisting at the sound of its name. Its nostrils flared, snorting as if in warning, but Rune waded closer.

"Kelpie?" he wailed again, desperately searching the rushing water for any sign of his sister. It was too dark to see anything, he couldn't even see his own feet this deep in.

And then he saw it: a red hooded riding coat drifting down the centre of the river.

Time slowed. He lost all sensation in his body. "Oh my God," he whispered then drew in a long, ragged breath. With a click, time regained its flow and energy poured back into his frame.

"Kelpie!!" he bellowed.

Startled by the sound, the horse reared and split the air with a cry of its own. Powerful legs flung an arc of water high into the night sky. Its hooves were backlit by moonlight, hammers against a silver disc, just as they came crashing down upon Rune.

I.

It must have been nearly half-eleven by the time they arrived back at Hillhead, but from the bustle it could have been midday. Festival participants were coming and going from the main building, carrying boxes and instruments, huddling in small *bourachs* to rehearse dances and musical riffs. The turning circle was occupied by three enormous white vans which were being filled with equipment by rosy-cheeked youth team, tech crew and office staff.

Morgan pulled up the Volvo as close as she could get. She looked as confused as Rune. He got out of the car and grabbed his backpack, then looked again at the hive-like activity all around the campus grounds. He recognised the faces, he had drawn many of them at one point, but these expressions would have been more exciting to sketch – they all had the same brightness in their eyes, energy practically sparking off them.

Rune spotted Kit and some of his angklung orchestra members on a patch of grass a few paces from the main building's entrance. They were busy explaining something to a couple from the Algerian folk group, the main drummer from the Botswana group and the Chilean breakdancer. Kit was placing the bamboo instrument in the breakdancer's hand, teaching him how to make it trill, as he had with Rune. Meanwhile, one of the Algerians was cross-legged on the floor next to an angklung player, teaching her how to play a stringed instrument that looked halfway between a violin and a guitar. The Thai girl's face lit up as it produced a crisp twanging sound.

Rune waved to the Thai musicians but none of them saw.

Abe emerged from the main building, carrying a bundle of flagpoles to the nearest van. Rune jogged over.

"Abe!" he called. He was nearly speared on a pole when the Ugandan swung round to greet him.

"Sorry, these things are very cumbersome," he grinned and fed the poles into the van. He had the same light in his eyes. It was as if his melancholy from the Brig o' Balgownie had been burned away.

"What's going on?" Rune said, waving at the motion around them.

"The closing gala," Abe said.

"But rehearsals were down at the theatre this afternoon, weren't they?"

His eyebrows raised conspiratorially. "Oh, this is something different."

"What do you–"

"Eddie," Abe said, nodding to the main building. "I've never seen her like this."

"Eddie?" Rune echoed, feeling like he'd walked into a parallel universe. He tried to snap himself out of it, to get to the matter which had grown in his mind the whole journey back to the city. "I need to speak with her. She's down there?"

"In the sports hall," Abe said, then looked down at Rune's tattered leg and the dried patches of blood where the thorns had pricked him.

"Are you okay?" Abe said.

"It's nothing." Rune scratched his head. His hair still felt damp from sweat and loch water. "Abe. I'm sorry I disappeared earlier. There was something I really had to do, but I should have been there at rehearsals."

Abe placed a hand on Rune's forearm and smiled. "It's okay."

Rune stammered: "What happened at the Professor's office, the way he treated you, it made me so angry."

He expected to see at least a hint of the loss that had so defined Abe's features after the Professor's rejection. But all he saw was unshakeable confidence.

"We tried," Abe said. "We couldn't have done more. And Eddie was right."

"You spoke to her?"

He nodded. "It seems the Professor was correct. The festival hasn't been able to help people gain asylum in a while. The Home Office became suspicious long ago, seeing the festival as a pipeline for seekers 'abusing the system'. They began rejecting applications. Eddie said I would need to find another way, outside of the festival's shadow."

Rune cast around for inspiration. "Then we'll just think of another way, maybe if we..."

"Rune," Abe said, his voice low. "My flight is tomorrow."

"But...Abe, why aren't you looking worried? What am I missing?"

"My friend," he chuckled. There wasn't just amusement in the sound. Was that also a hint of pity? "I think you prefer me a little sad and hopeless."

Rune flushed. "That's not true. I just mean–"

Abe then did something he had never seen him do. He winked. It was a cheeky expression, spry and clandestine. "I'm okay, really. There's always a way."

"Do you mean you've got a plan? I can help..."

"You've already done so much for me," Abe said, his grip pulsing when Rune tried to press further. "You said you needed to speak with Eddie? What about?"

"About all this," Rune said, catching the exasperation in his own tone. "The festival, it's all for nothing. It's going to end no matter how good tomorrow's performance is going to be. The decision's been made."

Again, Abe's response was not what he expected. No surprise, no outrage. Just a close-lipped smile. "Go tell her," he said and winked again.

Rune balled his fists, grasping at his sense of purpose before it could wane any further. "I will. I'll do it. She needs to hear this."

Abe's gaze moved over Rune's shoulder to the driveway. Excitement flared. "Is that Morgan? Fantastic!"

Through the Volvo's windscreen, he could make out Morgan's pale fingers wrapped around the steering wheel. She lifted a finger and waved it.

Abe immediately started walking towards the car, entranced, pace strong and sure.

"She's not what we think she is," Rune called, but the words were lost in the crowd.

Abe glanced back and smiled. "Go to Eddie."

The sports hall was a din of voices and music, the thudding of heavy objects, the squeaking of feet on linoleum, all of it echoing up walls to high ceiling. Instructions were being hollered from one end to another by people with clipboards; tech crew in black t-shirts were shifting mega-decking slabs onto castors and AV systems into boxes. In one corner, Fraser was conferring with members of Ceòl Mòr, their bagpipes and fiddles and whistles blurting out riffs. Rune cast his good eye around the brightly-lit scene, searching for Eddie among the sea of people and boxes and buzz. When he finally found her, he realised why she had been invisible: she was wearing a pink t-shirt like the youth team. It was her voice that drew him, the gravel and authority, so similar to Morgan's voice. Eddie was standing by a tower of boxes, a clipboard in her hand, a lanyard of keys and cards around her neck. She was issuing directions to people around her, some queuing up for instructions, readily awaiting orders, then going off as soon as she gave them. Her face was a fierce thing, alight with concentration and purpose.

"Eddie," he called. When there was no response, he strode over and said her name again. It was only on the third attempt that she looked up. She blinked twice, once as if coming to, and then as if instantaneously bored of waiting for Rune to say something.

"Can I help you?" she said. "Kinda in the middle of something, Red."

"I need to talk to you. It's important."

"Oh," she said in hushed reverence. "Oh well, if it's important, then...hey!" She yelled at a pink t-shirted girl lugging an amplifier to the corner of the hall. "I said take it out to the van, not 'just dump it anywhere and walk away'!"

"Eddie–" Rune tried again but was cut off by a tech crew member. The guy must have been at least six-foot-five. He had taut, tattooed arms and reeked of strenuous work. When he spoke, he rolled his r's in a broad 'Toonser' Aberdeen city accent.

"Right, that's the flags a' in, the lighting rig's packed awa', and the marquee roof's ready tae roll."

"Cheers Shorty," Eddie said, patting the lanky juggernaut's arm. She ticked three things off on her clipboard. "That should be you and the team all done. Grab some sleep. Early start, yeah?"

"Aye," he said. There was exhaustion in the big guy's smile, but also something electrified and awestruck. "Ye realise this is mad, aye?"

"Good mad or bad mad?" Eddie asked.

"Nae idea," he shrugged then backed away. "Defin*ately* memorable though."

Eddie let out a whoop of laughter then returned to the checklist.

Rune grew desperate. "I have to tell you something, Eddie."

"Then tell me," she muttered without looking up.

"Not here," he whispered.

"Then don't."

"For God's sake!" he snapped. "The festival's been cancelled!"

His voice echoed around the sports hall, silencing all other chatter. Eddie slowly lifted her gaze, did a full sweep of the crowd, and landed on Rune's hot cheeks. Her voice was flat and droll.

"Oh my God," she intoned. "I can't believe it. What ever shall we do? All my life's work and that of my beloved parents...ending. How unceremonious. How cruel."

The onlookers tittered and returned to their tasks.

Rune stammered. "What...but it's your dad who's ended it. He's agreed with the council that tomorrow's the last closing gala. Ever."

Eddie sighed, her lids heavy with disinterest. "My own father, you say? Oh the betrayal. Like a stab in my heart."

"You knew?" Rune said, unsure whether to be relieved or furious.

Eddie tutted. "I told you I saw doom on the horizon."

She wandered over to a box, flicked through its contents then ticked another square on the clipboard. When she glanced back up her expression crinkled in amusement then drooped into something piteous. "Oh your wee face, Rune. Did you come running all this way to tell me? To be my hero? I'm sorry, I'm being cruel, come here." She closed the gap and put her arms around Rune and patted his back. "Thank you, you brave boy. There you go. Is that better? If I can find a medal somewhere in all these crates I'll give it to you, okay?"

Rune shook her off and grabbed her shoulders. "What the hell's wrong with you? How can you be so cold? Don't you care about this?"

"All right, that's enough," Eddie said, peeling his hands away.

"You've got to stop your dad. Where's your fight?"

Something twinged in her expression. She pointed a pen at his chest. "First it was cute, now it's annoying. Back off."

"This was your mother's legacy."

"I said that's enough!" she hissed through gritted teeth.

Rune's fingers tingled. He reached into the deep pocket of his tattered jogging bottoms and took out the shard of the Maiden Stone. He held it before Eddie, as if brandishing a cross before a vampire. "She would be so disappointed."

Eddie's face slackened, the whites of her eyes withdrew. She scrutinised the shard. Its rough, pockmarked granite surface was bleached of its pinkish hue in the hall's strip light, but he saw the recognition on her face. For a moment she seemed to struggle against it.

Bingo.

She put down the clipboard and pen, tapped her chin. She spoke barely above a whisper, but power crackled in it. "Put that away."

He stowed the shard in his backpack.

She continued. "You think I don't care?"

He pursed his lips, but didn't respond.

"That I'm just rolling over and dying?"

He crossed his arms. "Looks like it."

She mirrored his stance. "Tell me then, *Mr Saviour Complex*. What's all this?"

Rune followed her eye line around the hall. The people were back to full industriousness. Having pulled their attention away from the scene between Eddie and Rune, they were now carrying the final boxes and pieces of equipment outside.

Rune shrugged. "It looks like you're setting things up for tomorrow's closing gala."

Eddie smirked. "That's what it *looks* like."

Rune's brow furrowed. "But it's not?"

She waggled her head from side to side, indicating his answer was both correct and incorrect. "Follow me. But not too close, you stink like...pond water?"

"Good nose," he muttered as she led him towards a fire escape at the top of the hall, giving winks and thanks to each worker she passed, telling them to get some rest. They wore the exact same expression as the tech crew guy: tired but satisfied, full of intention.

The warm night air greeted Rune and Eddie. She gestured to the three vans in the turning circle. The festival workers queued up to deposit their boxes inside, like the procession of animals towards the ark.

Eddie stared at the cavalcade, her face drawn. "This was never my fight, you know? I didn't want any part of it, not really. So, I guess you're right in some ways: I'm not fighting it. But I'm not rolling over either."

Rune breathed out, long and deep. "Look, I just said that because..."

Eddie raised her chin. "I'm ending things my way."

"What is all this?" Rune asked, the pieces still not clicking.

She lifted an eyebrow. "Let's say the people of Aberdeen are going to get their closing gala. Just not as they imagined it."

Her smile was infectious. "What are you up to?"

She suddenly lit up like a firework. "We're staging a coup, Red. A musical, theatrical, noisy, bangy-drummy, shouty-singy coup right on the streets of Aberdeen."

"Oh my God," he laughed at her enthusiasm.

"It's good, right?"

"It's something."

"It's going to say exactly what I want it to say."

"Let me see. Is the message 'Fuck you?' by any chance?"

She grinned and leaned against the concrete wall. "Ah it's going to be so sweet."

Silence fell between them. The wall felt uneven against Rune's back. He became mesmerised by the final bits of business at the vans. Eddie nudged his ribs. "You got a cigarette?"

"'Fraid not."

"What a time to quit."

"I'm not actually sure I ever started. It just felt like something I should do."

She squinted into the dark sky. "You're a weird kid, Pirate Red. Knew it the first time I looked at you."

Rune pushed a stream of air through his lips. "Whatever."

"What?" Eddie said. "You are. You march into my office all *'Your dad says to give me a job'*, then act all sour when I ever-so-slightly push back."

"Ever-so-slightly? You told me to sod off."

She smiled. "Yeah, I did, didn't I? But then, when I finally agree, you get all weird and start asking me all about my arsehole father and dead mother, as if my family's your favourite soap opera. What's up with that?"

Rune pointed past the vans, along the driveway to the Volvo. It was almost lost in the darkness, but he could just make out Abe leaning into the driver side window, and the driver herself, silver hair nodding.

"Morgan." He didn't turn immediately to witness Eddie's response, but when he did he was surprised to be met with something so vulnerable. Her guard seemed to have blown away on the breeze.

"Of course, she would involve herself. Did she show you round her castle? Trick you with clever words and costumes?"

Rune smirked. "I first met her in the woods."

She groaned and massaged her eyebrows. "Do I want to know how you came by that stone in your pocket?"

"Probably not," Rune said.

"Fair enough."

"Your dad was using it as a doorstop."

"Jesus," she laughed ruefully. "What a guy, eh? I mean, it's only a rock, but still. That's dark."

Rune propped himself up. "You really think that? It's just a rock?"

Eddie pondered then nodded.

"Why?" Rune said. "Is it so unbelievable that your mum found a piece of the Maiden Stone?"

Eddie leaned her head back against the wall. Her eyes were glassy. "See, this is exactly what I'm talking about, Rune. Why do you care so much?"

"I..." he began, but the words wouldn't come. He felt the answer, but had no idea how to bring it into the world. It was beyond his ability to tell. Eddie seemed to recognise the struggle and gave a look of genuine sympathy that surprised him.

"I just don't understand why you *don't* care," Rune finally said. "I mean...your dad's clearly in a bad way, making terrible decisions that affect everyone here – the festival, you, poor Abe. I mean he's forgetting who started all this. He should be honouring your mum's legacy, not having an aff..."

He cut himself off.

"Not what?" Eddie said.

"Never mind."

"Oh God, don't tell me he's restarted his affair with her," she flicked a finger towards the Volvo. She spotted Rune's pained look and chuckled.

"How can you laugh?" Rune whimpered. "Doesn't it hurt? Don't you hate him for it? And Morgan too?"

"You expect too much, Rune. Of them, of me, of yourself. I can see it, clear as day. It's messing you up. Believe it or not I used to be the same. You expect adults to be these pure, heroic figures. Selfless, noble, or whatever, totally sure of who and what they are, one-hundred-percent living for their kids. But they're not, and they never have been. They're as stupid as you or me. You just didn't see it until now. I get it, really. It's a shitty lesson to learn. But trust me, give it a few years and you'll be standing where I am."

He studied her face. The stoniness had returned, but moisture lingered at the edges of her eyes, darkness remained in pools on her face. "Eddie, I think we're standing closer than you think."

She yawned and rubbed her eyes. "Maybe. Everyone's a work in progress."

"How are your *dreams of doom* these days?"

She studied his expression, perhaps looking for mockery. She smiled. "My dreams? They've stopped."

"What did the trick?"

"This," she said, gesturing between the hall and the vans. "The moment I finally got tired of waiting and made a choice. And now, I've got to get some rest. Tomorrow's *my* day. Not my dad's, not my mum's. I'm taking it for myself."

He brought the shard back out and offered it to her.

She stared at it blankly. "Do you know what her last words to me were? 'Look after him'. Not 'look after yourself'. *Him*. The man who cheated on her with her own sister. I'll never understand that. A few nights ago you asked me what she was like. That's what she was like."

Rune kept his hand out. Eddie groaned and scuffed the ground. She grimaced, but there was a smile in there too. "Actually, I was wrong, I was never like you. I was never this big a pain in the arse."

He thought she was going to take the shard, but at the last moment she pushed it back to him. She loped towards Esslemont house, twisting briefly to point in the direction of the Volvo. "Tell that *crabbit* auld witch I said 'hi'. And that she better come see my show tomorrow."

II.

But Morgan wasn't at the Volvo any more, and neither was Abe. Rune stood by the empty car. Stillness had finally settled across Hillhead halls. It was like when he had first arrived for his internship – an empty village of residential towers, with only the Ghosts of Students Past for company. How long ago had that been? It felt like a lifetime, and yet for all he had to show for his adventures and misadventures, it might have been seconds ago.

He immediately wished the bustle would return, any hint that indicated the adventure wasn't over: a vague, knowing comment from Morgan, a perplexing instruction from the Professor, a snarky glance from Eddie, a quiet whisper from Abe. Even a wink from *Whatshisname*. Nathan. That's what his name was. Even Nathan's window was dark.

Rune walked through the empty campus, feeling more insubstantial with each step, despite the weight of the shard in his backpack. He couldn't quite understand it – he had battled all this way, for what? The realisation leached him of energy.

He could feel the old thoughts returning. He felt lighter than he should, it wasn't a carefree sensation but a dizzying one. He tried the mantras – *seat of learning*, *endingidi endongo endere* – but they didn't work, his heart was no longer in them. He felt exposed, thin-skinned against his own thoughts, unmoored without the security of anger or wilful blindness. There was no defence against Jock's sadness, Jack's defiance, Kelpie's confusion, Abe's mysteriousness. He was too tired to push them away any longer.

Esslemont House loomed above him, an obelisk of crumbling concrete, chipped sills and thin-pane glass.

He felt it before he saw it: a fresh whisper of adventure. That particular air of strangeness had become a familiar sensation, one he had welcomed so openly in recent days. He stepped to the side of Esslemont and caught a glimpse at the edge of the forest. The silver hair was the surest sign that his eye wasn't deceiving him, a lynchpin in the darkness. In time, other shapes became clearer, Morgan's height, her angular frame, sharp shoulders. But there was more, someone else. Abe.

The pair were only a few trees deep, just enough that Rune could perceive the nature of their conversation. It was like the first time they had met in the gay bar, their body language in synch, storytellers from different continents, sharing the same role, the same energy.

This was their story. How had he not properly appreciated that before? Just as inheritance was Eddie's story, and grief the Professor's, and freedom his mother's.

Nobody needed Rune to tell their stories.

A clever breeze whispered through the trees and found its

way over to him at the edge of Esslemont. It licked over the scabs on his shin, lifting the scent of loch algae from his clothes to his nose, snaking up and over his patched eye.

With the little strength he had left, he turned away from the forest and walked back to Esslemont's front steps, and into Flat 3, down the long dark corridor and into the shower room. He shed his bag and tattered clothes and stepped into the cubicle, under the lukewarm stream. The water stung his shins. He stared at his feet as the droplets fell upon him. He saw everything leave: a murkiness sliding off his hair and body down the drain.

He stepped out of the cubicle and approached the mirror. A naked ghost looked back at him through a single eye. *So much for supernatural insight.* He pulled at the patch, finding that the action no longer caused a prickle. The ghost now looked back with two eyes. They attempted a smile, the eyes, and almost achieved it too, but they weren't convincing enough for the rest of the face to follow.

He gathered his clothes in a bundle, held them over his crotch and walked down the dark corridor, drip, drip, dripping as he crept.

Halfway down the thought occurred, he had left his keys in the shower room. He was about to turn back when he noticed a sliver of moonlight coming from his room. The door was already open. His heart fluttered. He pressed a toe against the door and it slowly creaked wide.

Something was already inside, on the bed. Someone.

"You didn't go into the woods," Rune whispered.

Abe blinked, his eyes defiantly amber against the moon's silver glare. "Not yet," he smiled.

III.

They hardly spoke. There wasn't need. It wasn't that enough words had been said between them, or that this was a purely instinctual act, it was simply that words weren't the right fit.

Instead it was all about what wasn't said. The initial timidity, the tentativeness, giving way to adrenaline, to need. The new facial expressions and sounds, the tastes and deeper sensations, the laughter mixed with moments of total sincerity, the joy and burning hunger for more. And more. And more.

Even the silence spoke more than words ever could have. A finger travelling the ridge of an ear, hot breath against cold nipple, scratch of stubble against stubble against stubble – all of these things were novels, sprawling and epic. A moan was an entire poem spoken to the air.

There was experience on both sides. That surprised Rune. It carried them through the stages, true and strong to a wonderful conclusion. But there was also something new there that Rune had never experienced with other men. Sweeter maybe, was that it? Or softer? He couldn't quite explain, and when he tried it brought a smile to Abe's lips. The words, so clumsy, but the intent behind them understood.

They lay together at the end of their tale, exploring each other in whisper and touch, gathering whatever they could, committing it to memory. The lines on a palm. The shape of a navel.

Rune joked that he prided himself on his timing, but he had to admit this time he was off. This didn't feel like a beginning, but he could not accept it was the end. He considered bringing up the topic once more, but the set of Abe's jaw told him all he needed to know. The end.

So they held to the moment and to each other, hand in hand, falling into sleep and dream, to the place beyond time where their story remains alive to this day.

IV.

It could have been anything – a mosquito, a crow, a party in a neighbouring room. But it wasn't. It was a phone. It rang somewhere in Rune's consciousness for seconds, maybe hours, then rose up through his mind until finally it roused him free of sleep.

The bedroom was lit by the screen. His eyes were slow to focus, even more so, now they were reunited.

He reached to the floor and swiped along the phone's surface. A voice, distant but fervent, erupted from it. He sprang up and held it to his ear.

"…ind her! I can't find her!"

"Wha– What do you mean? Mum? Slow down, I'm still half asleep," he rasped. The adrenaline was helping, the panic in her voice was causing a surge of it, sharpening his attention.

Jack cried down the line. "Kelly. She's gone! She was in bed with me but now she's gone and I can't find her anywhere in the house and the front door was open and I've looked absolutely everywhere! I…I didn't want to call Jock, I can't handle his disappointment, I…"

Rune held the phone away from him. It was nearly three in the morning. The sky was still dark outside. Jack's voice continued its ramble.

"Okay, okay Mum, breathe," Rune said. "We'll figure this out, she won't have gone far. She's probably just playing in the–"

"You don't understand. She had a meltdown last night. We had a big argument. I...I..."

"About what?" he said, grabbing shorts and a t-shirt from a pile on a chair and jamming them on.

"It was about lots of things. Me and Jock. You."

"Me?"

"I'd never seen her like this. I managed to calm her down and off to sleep but now..."

"Okay hang on I'm coming. Think about where she might have gone. I'll be there as soon as I can. Shit!" He glanced at his phone again, where his battery had a thin red line on it. "Mum, my battery's about to die but I'll be there."

"Hurry," Jack said. His mother sounded small, defeated, totally unlike her. It terrified him.

He only had a split second to gather his thoughts, to look around the empty room, at the two pillow marks on the empty bed, and out to the corridor.

"Bag," he said to himself and ran to the shower room, but his backpack wasn't there. He ransacked the room and stopped when he spotted it across the corridor. It was opened out on the kitchen floor. He ran in and, to his shock, found Eddie propped up on the counter top, reading Mary Seaton's book, the shard of the Maiden Stone in her other hand. She looked up a little alarmed.

Rune searched his bag, hoping Morgan had somehow slipped the Volvo's keys in there.

"It's three in the morning," Eddie said.

He didn't respond, just kept searching. "Sister's gone missing. Mum's just called. Need to get out there now."

Eddie hopped down and placed a hand on his shoulder. "What are you doing?"

"I don't know!" He said, trembling.

In a single flip, her expression switched to business. He had seen it before, but never had it been so welcome. "Where do you need to go?"

The van crunched and roared into fifth gear as soon as they cleared the city limit. Eddie was hunched over the wheel. At every bump and corner, rumbling sounded in the back of the van, as equipment and boxes shifted.

Eddie seemed oblivious, instead glancing regularly at Rune beside her, as if she was waiting for something to happen. "Tell me about her," she finally said.

"What?" Rune took his fingernail out from between his teeth.

"Your sister. What's she like?"

"I don't know," he said, mind still leaping from one horrible conclusion to another, all the while calculating how this was in some way his fault.

"Come on, you're all about the personal questions. It's long past my turn."

"She's eight years old," he said, fiddling with the direction button on the air vent. "Red hair, about four-foot–"

"For God's sake not a police profile. What's she like?"

Rune cast his eyes across the vista, looking for the right words. They had broken out over the crest of the Tyrebagger Hill and were careening down the dual carriageway. Soft hilltops rolled all around, the city fully behind. The many peaks of Bennachie were smooth as mounds of grass. Only one feature stood out. Mither Tap. Bennachie's most rocky tip was a rupture on an otherwise velvety landscape.

"Kelly...*Kelpie* is..."

"Kelpie?" Eddie mouthed.

"Don't ask. She is a massive pain in the arse."

"Run in the family, does it?"

"I guess. She's been having a tough time of it recently. We all have. So much change in the family. She's trying to figure out who she is in all this."

Eddie cocked an eyebrow. "We still talking about your sister?"

"Very funny. This is different, she's always making shit up. More than just an overactive imagination, it's like she's looking for any kind of distraction, anything that will make life seem more interesting or…okay stop looking at me like that. Fine, yes, I heard it that time too."

Eddie chuckled, momentarily victorious, but brushed it aside with the wave of a hand. "So anyway, you think that's why she's run away?"

"She won't have run away," he said, nibbling a patch of rough skin on his thumb. "She'll just have woken up in the middle of the night and decided she's a fairy queen of the woods or some shit like that. Mum'll find her playing in a tree. She'll be fine. She'll be fine." He muttered the end of the sentence, the words trailing. He winced when he bit too far.

Eddie slapped his thigh. "You're right. She'll be fine."

They rushed past a way sign. Rune scanned the dark road, seeking any familiar landscape. Before he could give directions, Eddie took the correct branch that would lead them towards the foothills of Bennachie. He was relieved to have someone so capable at the wheel. He leaned his head against the window.

"Abe's gone." He wasn't sure why he said it, but it was out before he knew.

"Aye," Eddie sighed.

"You knew?"

"Said goodbye not long before you woke up."

"How was he?"

"Quiet. But okay, I think."

"He's not catching his flight."

"I know that too. But if anyone asks me, I'll swear it's news to me."

Rune smiled. He knew Eddie wouldn't have reported Abe for absconding the festival, but it was good to hear it nonetheless. She was giving him the head start he needed.

"Sounded like you said bye to him too. A pretty fucking great goodbye at that." She waggled her eyebrows up and down.

"Shut up," he replied into his fist. "Perv."

The sounds of the country road filled the silence.

"*She'll* look after Abe," she said. "Think what you like of her, trickster witch that she is, but she'll help him."

Morgan's angular face swam before him. He grimaced. "How do you know?"

A smile curled at the edge of her mouth. "She wasn't always a wardrobe mistress, y'know. Some of those costumes are real."

"What do you..?" He thought back to his midnight conversation with Morgan in her castle, the costumes hanging on iron hooks the whole way up the spiral staircase and draped over headless mannequins in her bedroom. The pinstripe suit. The black feathered gown. The black robe and barrister's wig. Rune's heart skipped. "Morgan's a lawyer?"

"A good one too, if a little unconventional," Eddie nodded. "Did you really think I was just going to let Abe flee without at least pointing him in the right direction?"

"Jesus," Rune exhaled, rested his head back against the

window, catching the beginnings of a smile in his reflection. "Just when I think I have her figured out."

The headlights hit the winding road and the trees on either side, but were engulfed by the darkness directly ahead and above. Rune's mind drifted into that empty space. It took him back to Mither Tap, not to the hill they were nearing with each second, but back to the recent past.

Ngoma...endingidi...endongo...endere...

He saw Abe approaching from the trees.

Drum...string...lyre...flute...

A solo traveller emerging from the pine trees, wandering into the midday sun, following the path that would, in time, lead him directly to the boulder.

Carve...chisel...scrape...file...

He could have sobbed at the certainty of Abe's arrival.

"Where's Kelpie?"

"She's okay," Abe had replied. *"Before I came up here, she was telling me about what she'd like more than anything."*

Rune lurched forward and slapped the van's dashboard. "I know where she's gone! Let me out here."

*

Rune's breath was ragged as he pounded along the dirt track that led around the base of Bennachie.

Abe's voice sang in his mind.

"Before I came up here, she was telling me about what she'd like more than anything."

He made it through the trees, using up the last of his phone's battery to light the way, breaking free of the forest just as it died.

"What was that?"

He found the path that skirted the foothills of Bennachie; it branched away from the one that climbed to Mither Tap's summit. He sprinted along it, sweat beginning to roll off him.

"To ride all over Bennachie on Pixie's back..."

*

Eddie hunched over the steering wheel, rounded a few corners and then pulled into a long lay-by. The headlights stretched ahead, settling on a tall, slim shape on a grassy knoll at the far end of the parking bay.

"Is that...?" She said under her breath. She peered ahead and took in the sight of the standing stone, its pink granite face stark in the headlights.

"Well, hello there," she smiled and slid out of the car.

She was transfixed by the Maiden Stone, almost glided up to it, one long stride after another until she reached it.

She ran a hand over its surface, exploring the carvings she knew so well.

*

Rune felt like he could throw up, but pushed onwards, past the gates of the stables and down into the valley below.

"...all the way to the river where they would swim together and follow its flow out to sea."

The River Don glinted like an eel at the bottom of the valley.

"Please let me be wrong, please let me be wrong," he chanted, with what little breath was still in him. But then he saw fresh hoofmarks bitten into the steep decline towards the water's edge.

"Kelpie!" he shrieked as he reached the banks of the Don. "Kelpie!"

*

Eddie tore her eyes from the Maiden Stone and looked up to the top of the hill, its fortress-like nipple outlined against the night sky.

A new idea came to her, carried like a voice on the wind.

"Okay Mum," she replied. "I hear you."

She reached into her pocket and took out the shard of the Maiden stone.

Her gaze drifted back to the Pictish monument, across its engraved markings, and up, up, up to the cleft in its right shoulder.

VI.

The horse reared and split the air with a cry of its own. Powerful legs flung an arc of water high into the night sky. Its hooves were backlit by moonlight, hammers against a silver disc, just as they came crashing down upon Rune.

Something grabbed the neck of his t-shirt, pulling him backwards and under. He was engulfed by the river, the world twisted upside down. A hoof cut through the water mere inches from his face. Whatever force had yanked him out of harm's way let go, leaving him adrift and disorientated. He lived hours in this moment, with no sense of direction or purpose. The panic in his breast was fleeting, what remained was a true silence that he had never felt before. If it hadn't been for the pressure on his lungs he might have stayed longer. But the world above the water won.

He broke through the surface. The noises were pin-sharp, keener than they had before he was pulled under – the descant of the water rushing by, the whinnying of the horse, and now another noise: the spluttering cough of a child. He twisted each way, seeking the sound, flailing against the direction of the Don.

There she was. Red curls, pale face, a wild stare.

"Kelpie!" Rune croaked. His sister was just about holding her head above water, but her expression was strained, her colour ashen. She was losing the fight.

He kicked towards her. No current, no matter how persistent, could hold him back. Upon reaching her he hooked an arm around her torso and dragged towards the bank, gulping in air with each stroke, closer and closer until his feet found purchase on the rocky riverbed. He began to feel the full weight of his sister, her body supported less and less by the water. He gritted and took her completely into his arms, holding his cheek against hers.

For a terrifying second, she was dead weight. But then he felt her grip. He reached the bank, took two huge strides, then fell in a controlled collapse onto grass. He breathed, deep and ragged, moaning with each exhale, eventually forming words. "Oh God. Oh God. You're okay. That's it. You're okay." He could hear the water in her lungs. He thumped the centre of her back, her ribs expanded then constricted violently as she hacked it all up.

She clung to him long after the coughing stopped, her voice eventually coming through in soft mewls. "Rune," she said. "I didn't mean to. I'm so–"

"Shhh," he interrupted. On the road here, all he had wanted to hear was Kelpie's apology – for running away in the middle of the night, for creating drama for the sake of it, for being such a brat. But with her first syllable of apology, he wanted to stop it, to make it go away, to say it had no right claiming her. Because she had nothing to say sorry for. None of this was her fault, he saw that now. He held her tighter, hoping his embrace would say it all, and if that didn't work, maybe the hot tears which were now running down his face into her hair would say it better.

She pulled herself away and looked down on him. He felt exposed under her gaze, there was no hiding his trembling chin, his crumpling face. He looked up, ashamed then surprised, for she wore the exact same expression. Her eyes were bloodshot, ringlets were plastered across her forehead, but a rosy sheen had returned to her cheeks. He had seen that rosiness every day of her life, from the moment he first saw her at the maternity ward, to every time she had run into a room to regale him with some far-fetched story. It was a rosiness which he saw in the mirror every day too.

Her eyebrows steepled. He felt a new tear leave his now-unpatched eye. She caught it on her thumb, lifted it to her mouth, blew on it then placed it back on his cheek.

"There," she said, voice hoarse. "It's now a happy one."

A high-pitched neigh came from the river. Pixie was playing at the edge of the water, casting sprays from each hoof.

"I think Pixie likes the water," Kelpie said with a little cough.

"*I* think Pixie should be turned into glue," Rune said. She made a half-laughing, half-pleading 'No!' then huddled next to him for warmth. Neither of the pair moved from the spot, they simply watched the horse frolic, becoming transfixed by his untamed joy.

"I made a mess of running away," Kelpie said.

"I dunno, looks like a nice place to run away to. Maybe we should stay here forever."

"Okay," she said. After a while she looked at him, pushed the hair from her forehead. "I don't think Mummy and Daddy are getting back together, are they?"

He looked into her eyes expecting to see a glimmer of hope, a childish twinkle, but only saw truth. He shook his head.

"Are we a broken family?" she said, thickness rising in her voice.

"Where did you hear that?"

"A boy at school said it."

"What's his name?"

"Michael."

"Well next time you see Michael tell him your big brother is going to find him and break his nose."

Her gap-toothed grin bloomed. She laughed and burrowed back into his side. A few feet away, Pixie snorted, tossed back his mane then jumped into the water.

"We're not broken, Kelpie," Rune said, once more recalling Abe's words. "Just learning to be something new."

"Like a horse?"

"Sure. Like a horse."

"If we're changing, does that mean I can be called Kelly again?"

"I thought you didn't want to be called that anymore?"

"I've been liking *Kelpie* less since Pixie tried to drown me."

"That's fair enough. Kelly." He rubbed her shoulder. She was warm, like a hot water bottle. Pixie was now on dry land once more, nibbling at the grass.

"But you still have to be called Rune, okay?"

"Don't have much choice, Squirt. It's my name."

"Good. This way I can pretend you're still my brother."

Rune propped up on his elbows. "Hey. What do you mean?"

She looked up, expression small. "Well, I guess we're not really proper brother and sister. We have different daddies."

"Kel," he whispered, the word catching in his throat.

A tremble rose in her voice. "I know it must make you feel different from us. But I think it should still count for a lot that we've got the same mummy, and that we've eaten breakfast together hundreds and thousands of times, and that you find me annoying like big brothers find little sisters annoying. It's good to have an annoying little sister, even if she's a pretend one. Because even if it's for pretend I'd like to have a big brother–"

He buried his face in her damp hair and nuzzled his way down to her ear. "You'll always be my annoying little sister. You have to make me crazy every day, always." He pulled away and held her gaze. "Promise?"

She nodded. He managed to catch a tear before it fell from her chin. He blew on it and put it back on her cheek. She made a long, rattly sniff and wiped a wrist across her nose.

"I'm sorry about your other daddy. What was he like?"

"I don't know, Kel. I never met him," Rune said, looking across the river to the quiet bank on the other side.

He followed the land up to the foothills where a tree stood alone. Its trunk was gnarled and sinewy, bent in the direction of a wind that wasn't there, the bush-like canopy of needles telling a story of movement, of defiance against harsh winters and wet summers.

"Do you think your daddy was tall?"

"Maybe. I never–"

"I think he had good eyebrows."

"Okay," Rune chuckled.

"And when he laughed, it sounded like a cute little goat." There was no hint of mocking on Kelly's face, just the spark of imagination written across her eyes and freckles. She reached for a piece of driftwood and placed a pebble and a leaf on it, then looked up at him expectantly. He shook his head.

"One foot was a teensy bit bigger than the other. Don't you think?" She placed a twig on the driftwood.

Rune looked at the little collection. He reached into his pocket and took out a perfectly folded, but perfectly soaking tissue and placed it on the wood. "He loved ice-cream."

Kelly's face lit up. "And his favourite day was Monday, which is strange because nobody likes Mondays, but he did. He said 'every week is a new adventure'. And his favourite colour was green." She added more twigs.

Rune added a new leaf. "Actually, it was green *and* red. He could never decide between them."

Kelly grinned. "He loved action movies, didn't he?"

Rune smiled. "He did. He would even go to the cinema on his own if nobody else wanted to come. He didn't mind. More popcorn for him."

She added a handful more twigs and pebbles. "And do you remember that time he broke his finger and they put that giant bandage on it?"

A fresh tear ran down Rune's cheek. He let it run and fall. "I do. I do remember."

Kelly held out her fist above Rune's palm. She dropped something warm and metallic into it. The moon glinted off the surface of the Zippo lighter. Countless tiny scratches criss-crossed but didn't dull its smoothness to the touch. To his surprise, the wet lighter sparked at first go. A flame sputtered and coughed, then settled. The flickering light made Kelly's face glow. She stared at the pile of twigs and leaves and pebbles on the driftwood. He leaned over and held the flame to the dry twigs. They smoked a little at first, but in time were aflame. He got to his feet, carried the burning wood to the water's edge and let it drift free.

He sat back next to his sister, pulled her close, and watched Somchai Bunsong's pyre float away and out of sight.

"Look," Kelly pointed across the river, up to the foothills of Mither Tap where Rune's gaze had been moments before. A figure was silhouetted in the moonlight, with long hair flowing in the breeze, the wavy locks wild, untamed. Their mother looked terrifying and beautiful. A giantess of Bennachie, fierce and free, standing beneath the Juniper tree.

At that precise moment, on the other side of the hill, under the same moon, a daughter returned a missing piece of her mother's story to its rightful place. It fit perfectly. Or perhaps it didn't. Either way, the story was now hers to tell.

Epilogue
The Battle of Bennachie

Olwatuuka ngambalabira!

Have you ever heard the tale of the Battle of Bennachie? When the great warriors gathered at the very top of Mither Tap to make their final stand? It was an unforgettable sight, a very special feeling, a glorious sound.

You haven't heard it? Well then, my friends, let me share it with you.

It began, as many battles do, with the banging of drums. This was a hollow *dum, dum, dum!* that echoed over the hillside and across the land.

'*Come*', it sang, '*we begin*'.

And they did come, in three white chariots and a cavalcade of wagons, all the way from the Granite City to the foothills of Bennachie. They were artists. Musicians, dancers, drummers, singers, folk tellers. Warriors of the world, but not the kind you may think of. Not like the fearsome Picts who stood against the Romans more than a thousand years ago at this very same hillside for the Battle of Mons Graupius. No, no, they were not warriors like that ancient people, but they were inspired by them. Like the Picts, they came painted blue, their bodies and faces alive with swirls and stripes, ancient symbols and modern markings.

The paint said: '*We are one, united in battle, a common cause against our oppressors. See us and know fear!*'

They marched up Mither Tap, the proudest peak of the Bennachie hills.

(Ah yes, I too struggled to pronounce the word at first. I learned it was not *Benna-chee* as it looks, but neither was it *Benna-hee* as some say it. It was somewhere in between, half soft, half hard. Ha! Yes, it took me a while. But I have had many new words and customs to learn on my travels throughout your green and rocky land. And now that I am proudly one of you, I can say the word as if it was my own.)

Like the Picts, the artist-warriors made the hilltop their home. They created a civilisation-for-a-day, a fortress-for-an-afternoon: over here was the place for eating and drinking; over there was the place for sharing and singing; here for painting and making; there for watching and resting. As protests go, it was one of the most gentle, but make no mistake it was a protest! They were supposed to be in the Granite City, inside the great stone pillars, framed by a proscenium arch, performing nicely for their patrons. A final performance, a formal ending in a cold hall. But this was not the warriors' fate. Instead, they were here, on the sun-scorched hillside, living for each other, performing for their own kind.

In time, the word spread, louder and farther than any drum, across the Shire, down the valleys, over farmlands until it reached the city. The great insects were the first to come, with their *thuppa-thuppa-thuppa* wings rotating in the sky, on their backs were crews of onlookers, documenting the sight, reporting back to the people of Aberdeen that here was something different to see, an uncanny sight, a civilisation-for-a-day!

And then the audience came, at first a trickle, then a crowd. The artist-warriors welcomed them.

'*Come*,' they sang, '*share our culture, learn our songs and tell us your own*'.

At the very tip of the hill stood The Prophetess, her hair plaited high upon her head, face blue with swirls and symbols. It was just as she had imagined. She had banged the drum, and they had come. There had been a time when The Prophetess dreamt only of doom. She had waited for a warrior to come, to ride in and save the future with sword in hand. But one had never come. So, she picked up the sword herself, and swung it, feeling its weight, hearing it slice through the air – *swoosh, swish* – and became her own hero.

Now she looked down the hill, past crowds and *bourrachs* (another nice word) of artist-warriors and audiences – the distinction between the two blurred blue – down past the forest until she saw The Mother. A stone-pink woman, once held in place, now taking her first steps in millennia. The Mother waved to The Prophetess, who waved back.

Halfway up the hill, in the middle of the *bourrach* sat The One-Eyed Scribe. He was busy building a cairn, one that would tell the story of the Battle of Bennachie long after it was done. He gathered rocks, some wide and flat, others small and round, and arranged them in a pyramid. He looked up every now and then to see the blue faces, to listen to their songs, but never long enough to remember either fully. Just as he was about to lay the smallest stone on the top of the cairn, he realised: art is not just about looking and listening, but living.

The One-Eyed Scribe left the rocks and walked through the crowds, speaking with artist-warriors and audiences, learning their names, letting their stories into his heart, allowing their tales to mark his skin, becoming a rune of Aberdeen, of the city and the shire, of the twin rivers that cut through the rolling land.

All was well and harmonious on the hillside until The Wizard came. He arrived on a stiff west wind from his castle on the unnatural Loch of Skene. In his wake flew a line of patrons with grey faces and cloaks. They formed a perimeter at the bottom of the hill and rattled tickets in their hands, like daggers against shields. The Wizard of Skene wore a scowl that made the sky thunder. *Boom! Ba-boom!*

'What is the meaning of this?' he sang.

The Prophetess pointed her sword down the hill straight at The Wizard's heart, but didn't sing a word – she knew her people would understand. And they did. With arms linked, teeth bared, and blue faces held up against the dark clouds, they formed a ring around the fortress-like-tip of Mither Tap. They drummed their feet and raised their voices. It was a fearsome war song, one of many voices and tongues and melodies, but all singing the same message:

'We are here! We are here!'

The sky split with lightning. *Skra-ka-kooooom!* And out of the crashing blaze came The Morrigan, Great Crow of Battle, her raggedy wings carrying her to the summit against The Wizard's gale. She reached the top and her feathers twisted until she had taken the shape of a person, neither man or woman, and held Their hand to The Prophetess. The young woman hesitated, then put down the sword and took The Morrigan's hand.

She held her open palm to the crowd. Slowly, slowly, the

people parted, and so did the heather and the bracken, revealing a golden path that snaked down the hillside. A single person walked up it, a woman whose stony feet were now human once more. The Mother took The Prophetess's hand and stood atop the nipple of Mither Tap. She looked to The Morrigan and smiled full of forgiveness. For they were reunited once more: The Maiden, The Mother and The Crow.

The Morrigan wept. First a *drip, drip, drip* then a *drop, drop, drop*, then a crashing *woosh!* as the sky broke. The rains had finally come. They washed down the hill, a sweeping, warm wave that took the blue paint from the faces and bodies of the artists, revealing their many colours beneath. The blue was carried down, down, down to The Wizard of Skene and his grey patrons, and it smashed against them. *Kwashhhhhh*! The grey regiment could not withstand the wave, and their line was broken.

Only The Wizard remained, but he was on his knees, hands touching the land, fingers stained blue. He looked up and for the first time saw things as they were.

Do you know what he saw?

A rainbow of people. Beautiful as the sun after rain. It shone from faces, thrummed in songs and in heartbeats. The Wizard realised that a rainbow does not last, but it is made all the more special because it is fleeting.

It sings, '*I am here. For now. See me. Join me. Then remember me. And smile.*'

Did you enjoy the tale of the Battle of Bennachie? Where I am originally from, we would call it an *enfumo*. A tale. If you liked my enfumo, I have many more like it.

Tales of trickery. Tales of greed. Tales of love. Tales of need.

The Giants of Bennachie. The Girl Who Longed for Water Horses. The Scribe Who Found Truth Beneath a Juniper Tree. And many more which I have collected on my travels.

Yes, my friend, you are right, they are tales, but that does not mean they are false. I know them to be true, in all the ways that matter, because I have seen them *olwatuuka ngambalabira, nobulabibwo*.

Once upon a time, with my very own eyes.

Acknowledgements

The stories in this novel are real. In a way. Folktales, fairy tales, real tales. They all have a way of blending and merging in our minds and histories.

For instance, the strange and wonderful years I spent working at the Aberdeen International Youth Festival are just as real as they are fairytale in my mind. I'll always dream of those humid summers in Hillhead Halls where I trudged with a hangover through the woods to cross Seaton Park into Old Aberdeen to open up the Festival office. I can still hear the opening ceremonies in the Music Hall, where people from all around the world gathered to drum their feet and sing and clap. It feels unreal what we accomplished. We invited artists from around the planet to our city and they rsvp'ed 'yes'. For a short, chaotic, beautiful moment we formed a rowdy civilisation.

No character in Rune of Aberdeen is inspired by a single real life person, but pieces have been borrowed from all directions, including from myself. People I love, people I've been taught by, people I knew for a tiny amount of time, and others I'll know for a lifetime. Whether we put it down on paper or not, I think we all write stories about the people we've known.

Of all elements, the settings in the book are the most real. The handsome spires of Old Aberdeen, the quiet rustling of Bennachie's foothills, the strange beauty of the Pictish stones. They're all there in North East Scotland, just waiting to be experienced and remembered for a lifetime. Such as the Wallace Tower, completely out of place in its surroundings, but undeniably there on the edge of Seaton Park. And hopefully one day soon to be opened to the public and given new life. In the meantime, I wanted to open it up in our imaginations. My story is fiction, but the building is real.

The folktales were the best bit of preparing for this. I adored reading, and re-reading, the works of storytellers such as Fenton Wyness ('Legends of Northeast Scotland'), Sheena Blackhall and Grace Banks ('Aberdeenshire Folktales'), Immaculate N. Kizza ('The Oral Tradition of the Baganda of Uganda'), as well as history books such as Tim Clarkson's 'The Picts' – rediscovering that lost civilisation was a reminder of how much I loved them as a child.

I've always been fascinated by folktales, legends and ancient mysteries, and couldn't help but weave as many as possible into my book. Tales from Aberdeen City and Shire such as Jock o' Bennachie, where two giants are locked in battle, and poor lady Annie caught in the crossfire; or the Maiden stone, the tragic tale of a young woman forced into an impossible deal with the devil. Irish mythology also plays a big part in the novel – a nod to my time in Celtic Studies class at the University of Aberdeen, and also to my Irish heritage. Tales of the battle goddess Morrigan, the prophetess Fedelm, and the Táin Bó Cúailnge – The Cattle Raid of Cooley – are epic Irish legends and figures which have long captured my imagination. And, of course, the Ugandan folktales were an absolute joy to discover, from vibrant stories of trickster Hare and gentle Elephant. It was so much fun reimagining all of these folktales for my novel, and finding how surprisingly easily they slotted together.

A huge thank you to everyone who helped me on this journey through the woods. Sculptor James Winnet (who created the magical Kemnay Steens), for sharing the joys and tribulations of carving stone. My old boss Luke Blair, and my international school friends Pailin Wedel and Dionne Biddie for sharing what it's like growing up mixed heritage. To performance-maker Ira Brand for sharing her adventures in drag king land. To Duncan Lockerbie at Lumphanan Press for making my fairy tale book real. To all the incredible, and patient people who listened to me as I blabbed on about my story ideas, who read my many drafts and who gave crucial feedback: Alex, Mum, Dad, Neil, Stu, Wendy, Tish, Margaret and Hayley, I can't thank you enough.

And finally, to my AIYF friends and family. The Festival may be gone for good, but we were there. Those fairy tale moments are locked in time forever. x

Printed in Great Britain
by Amazon